THE EXORCIST'S HOUSE

NICK ROBERTS

Crystal Lake Publishing
www.CrystalLakePub.com

WELCOME
TO ANOTHER

CRYSTAL LAKE PUBLISHING
CREATION

Join today at www.crystallakepub.com & www.patreon.com/CLP

Based on the untrue writings of the Satanic Panic.

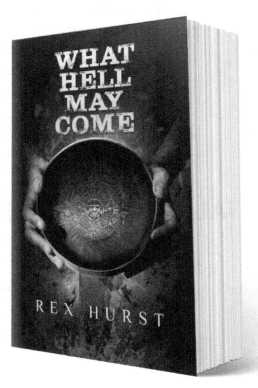

WHAT HELL MAY COME

REX HURST

"The mix of true horror, dark humor and poetic descriptions of utter depravity make Hurst a true standout among modern horror writers."
- Brian Young, author ECW Press & Host of Transatlantic History Ramblings podcast

For Amy

Pandemonium (noun)

pan·de·mo·ni·um | \ ˌpan-də-ˈmō-nē-əm \

Definition
1. a wild uproar (as because of anger or excitement in a crowd of people): a chaotic situation
2. *capitalized* : the capital of Hell in Milton's *Paradise Lost*
3. *capitalized* : the infernal regions : HELL

Merriam-Webster Dictionary

PROLOGUE

March 1993, Southwestern West Virginia

THE OLD MAN struck a match against the large rock on which he rested. He brought the flame to his pipe and puffed the tobacco alive. The amber glow illuminated his aged face in the darkness.

Stillness in the night.

Stars burned bright in the clear sky above him. This was still God's country, no matter how much evil he'd seen in his day. He looked at his sprawling farm that stretched out into the abyss. He was grateful that he couldn't see much. He had let his land go to shit as of late.

Puff, puff, puff on the pipe. Plumes of smoke twirled to the heavens. The house where he'd spent the last forty years stood about fifty yards to his back. He did his best to ignore the sounds coming from it. He chose to focus on the constellations. He recognized the usual celestial suspects: Orion with that damn belt; that little red thing they called "Betelgeuse"; the Big and Little Dippers. They'd been up there his whole life, and he'd just now taken the time to marvel at them.

A rhythmic trot approached him from behind. Buck, his bloodhound. The large dog stopped at the old man and began pushing him with his snout. The old man took a break from the stars and embraced his worried dog.

"It's OK, Buck," he said as he wrapped his arm around the loyal companion and gave a few pats.

The dog whined regardless.

"I'd give you a puff to steady your nerves if you'd have it," the old man said as he angled the pipe toward Buck.

The dog sneezed and backed away.

"It's not for everyone. I'll give you that."

Buck shook it off and lay on the grass beside his master's rock.

A door slammed within the house behind them. Buck looked up at the old man and let out a muffled cry.

"Just look up at those pictures in the sky, Buck."

He pointed with his pipe to Orion.

"That one right there is said to be one of the fiercest hunters the world has ever known. You should respect that, old buddy. If he'd had you and that nose of yours on his side, he'd likely to have not left any game for the rest of us."

Buck's eyes darted from the old man to the pipe to the stars. His floppy ears perked up at the sound of glass breaking behind him. He let out a whimper as he shuffled his body on the earth.

"I hear it, Buck. I do."

The old man refused to turn around. He thought about the knife tucked away in his overalls and wondered if it'd be better to put Buck down now, or let him run the farmland free, fending for himself. He concluded that the old bloodhound was wily enough to get by without him by now, and ruled the case closed right then and there.

The old man stood up and felt that his ass had gone numb. Buck followed suit, snapping to attention. The old man stretched his aching body as best he could. He took a final puff and then sat the smoldering pipe on the rock.

"Reckon it's time to put an end to all this," he said, looking down at Buck. "I want you to stay right here, old boy."

Buck cocked his head sideways.

"Now, listen to me, you stubborn son-of-a-bitch. No matter what racket you hear from that house, you stay your ass right here. I know you're itchin' to chase whatever it is that's in there, but it wouldn't do any good. It'd just get ya killed."

Buck stood motionless.

"Lie down!"

Buck did. The old man turned and faced his home. One of his eyes twitched, and his palms began to clam up. He couldn't count how many times he'd faced similar situations, but this one was different. This was his home.

"Say, Buck," he said to the dog lying beside the rock. "If I don't call for you by sunrise, go ahead and eat one of the chickens. Drink from the glen up yonder. You know what to do."

Buck tucked his head between his paws and closed his eyes. The old man began taking steps toward the house. He spoke as he walked.

"Dear Heavenly Father, I pray that you be with me in this time of darkness. I pray that you remove this fear from me and replace it with your love and your warmth."

A shadow moved in the window of an upstairs bedroom. The old man felt a shudder, but kept trudging.

"I pray that you give me the strength to combat the wickedness that I'm about to face. You've always been with me, and I know you won't abandon me now. I put my faith in you, Lord, and pray that you work through me to do your will."

A woman cackled inside the house. The old man closed his eyes and continued to step forward. A tear rolled down his cheek.

"In the name of Jesus, I pray. Amen."

He wiped the tear and opened his eyes. He reached inside his shirt collar and withdrew a chained crucifix, bringing it to his lips to kiss. He tucked it back in, and it pressed against his heart where he liked to feel it.

After a few more paces he had reached the front porch. He saw the trees that lined his property blowing in the wind before he felt it. The spring breeze was cool in the nighttime. The wind chimes began to play their tunes. The porch swing creaked a ghastly sound as it swayed back and forth. Any other time, he would've found this serene.

The old man took one final, deep breath and placed his foot on the wooden planks below. Without thinking, he marched across the porch and grabbed the flimsy screen door. He quietly opened it and stared at the front door that he'd entered so many times before. All he saw right now were the imperfections—the flaking paint, the cracks in the wood. He knew his mind was just clinging to anything to prevent him from entering the house.

A child giggled from the other side. He pushed open the front door and nearly fell into the house. Save the moonlight flooding through the kitchen windows to his left, darkness enveloped him. Thank goodness he didn't need light to navigate his own home. He stood in the open entryway. The stairs to the second floor bedrooms were ten feet straight ahead of him. The living room was to his right, and the kitchen was on the left. He looked right. The furniture started taking shape in the empty living room as his eyes became accustomed to the dark. The house was too quiet and deceptively empty.

With only one window air conditioning unit in the upstairs bedroom, the house temperature ran concurrently with the outside. Tonight, however, it was unnaturally humid. After only a moment of being inside, the old man could feel sweat beading on his brow. He surveyed his surroundings, noticing nothing out of the ordinary. He took a couple quiet paces across the hardwood flooring.

Still, too quiet.

The old man sidestepped his way into the kitchen. He looked down at the table against the wall to his left where his lone dinner plate still rested, a half-eaten pork chop surrounded by bits of carrots. He reached the cabinets above the refrigerator and popped one door open. The moonlight reflected off the shiny metallic object inside. He pulled the six-shooter down and popped out the cylinder. Still fully loaded like he left it. He cocked it and put it in the side pocket of his overalls.

Using both hands to minimize the sound, he pried open the sticky refrigerator door. The yellow light brightened the room, and he noticed that every knife that he owned had been stabbed into the ceiling above him.

"Lord, have mercy," he whispered.

Even though he'd seen this display of power before, the fact that it was in his home disturbed him on a deeper level. It was much easier for him to walk into someone else's nightmare when called, knowing that he could leave when the job was done and retreat back to the safety of his domicile.

The old man grunted as his way of shaking it off. He looked in the back corner of the open refrigerator at the mason jar neatly stashed away. It housed a clear liquid that anyone else would probably assume was moonshine. There was a sole piece of masking tape stuck to the metal lid. On it, a small cross had been drawn in black marker. He grabbed the jar and shut the door quietly. He looked at the closed basement door at the far end of the kitchen. He knew that's where it came from—the evil. Right now, however, there was only darkness and silence in that direction. *It just wants me to let my guard down.*

After making sure that he was still the only one in the kitchen, he placed the jar on the counter and unscrewed the lid. He withdrew the pistol from his pocket and pushed out the barrel once again. The six .357-caliber bullets fell into his open palm. One by one, he dropped them into the jar of holy water.

The shutters behind him slammed shut from a heavy gust of wind. The old man jumped at the sound and dropped the mason jar. The jar shattered against the hard tile, spilling water, bullets, and broken shards across the floor.

13

"Good Lord."

He strained to get down on one knee. Even though he was more active than most people his age, he still wasn't as limber as he'd like to be. He leaned heavily on his bent knee, grimacing as he snatched what bullets he could locate. Looking down in his palm, he counted three. The others must've rolled out of reach.

"This'll have to do," he said to himself as he painfully stood back up.

Wasting no more time, he dropped each wet bullet into the open chambers. He locked it back into position, cocked it, and slid it back into his pocket. He stepped through the narrow kitchen, side-stepping bits of glass as best he could. As he approached the entrance to the living room, he heard footsteps running up the wooden stairs. His heart froze, and he closed his eyes.

"Heavenly Father, be with me in my time of need. I beg of you. Give me strength," he whispered.

His bedroom door slammed shut above him. Something was walking around directly above his head. He looked up at the knives in the ceiling. There was a loud thud upstairs and the knives swayed back and forth. The old man's eyes widened as another thunderous slam hit the second floor. The knives came loose. He darted out of the kitchen just as the blades came clanking to the tile floor, one landing tip first in his pork chop.

His heart had never given him any trouble in his sixty plus years on this Earth, but he felt like it was struggling now. He did his best to control his breathing and focus on the task at hand. A laugh bellowed from the upstairs bedroom. The sheer bass and volume of the voice didn't sound like anything he'd ever heard emitted from a human being. Just as fast as it started it stopped. *It's in my mind.*

Again, deafening silence. The old man reached into his pocket and pulled out the pistol. He untucked the cross chain around his neck and let it hang openly against his overalls. Ready, he walked through the living room and began ascending the stairs.

One step . . .

Two steps . . .

Three steps . . .

There was a closet door directly at the top of the staircase, a bedroom down the hallway to his left, and his bedroom at the other end of the hall to his right. As soon as he walked up far enough to peer down the hallway, he stopped. His bedroom door was shut, and all was still. His heartbeat reverberated through his ears. He could see moonlight under the crack of the door.

He stared, waiting. The shadows of small feet scurried past the doorway, startling the old man. He stayed quiet and kept his composure. He thought about how many times he'd had to confront evil in the past and momentarily convinced himself that this was no different. He continued up the stairs.

Four steps . . .

Five steps . . .

Six steps . . .

With one final stride he reached the top of the stairs and turned to his right. He extended the gun and began walking toward the closed bedroom door.

"In the na . . . " he coughed before he could finish his sentence. The humidity was thicker upstairs and hung in the air like a dank blanket. He cleared his throat.

"In the name of Jesus, I command you to get out of my home and go back to where you came from!"

There was movement in the room, and the old man looked down at the shadows moving by his feet. Someone was standing just on the other side of the door.

"I said . . . "

"Merle?" a familiar woman's voice spoke softly from his bedroom.

The old man felt his heart doing that freezing thing again.

"Merle, it's me," she said.

It sounded like she had been crying. He couldn't believe his ears. His mind wouldn't let him comprehend what—who—he was hearing.

"Gertie?" he finally replied as he lifted the gun up away from the door.

"Yes, Merle. It's me, Gertie."

Had he not recently endured the tragedy in his basement, he would've been stronger—would've been able to see through these tricks like he always had. But after what happened to that poor girl, he just didn't care anymore. *You got no one, and you can't even do your damn job anymore.* The old man stepped even closer to the door as if he could embrace the woman through it.

"Oh, Gertie," he sighed. "Oh, how I've missed you."

His eyes started to moisten as he closed them and listened to his wife's voice. An amber glow emitted from the crack under the door, followed by a thick, mustard-colored smoke. The old man wasn't looking. He didn't even notice the smell of sulfur rapidly filling the air.

"I've missed you too, Merle."

The old man pressed his cheek against the door and felt warmth from the wood. A child giggled from inside the room.

"Who is that?" the old man asked with excitement.

"You know who it is."

"Is that . . . " the old man couldn't bring himself to say the name of his son who died from a snakebite when he was just eight years old.

"It is," the female voice replied.

"Daddy?" a child's voice spoke from behind the door.

The old man dropped to his knees so that he could be face level with his son who he hadn't seen in decades.

"My boy! Oh, my boy!" he said as he again pressed his face against the door and caressed the wood. The door was getting warmer, but he didn't mind.

"Daddy, will you come in here with us?"

"Absolutely, my boy," the old man said as he stood back up, not feeling the ache in his bones any longer. He held the gun in his right hand and used his palm to press against the doorknob to stand up.

Searing pain shot through his nerves as the blazing metal knob burned his skin. He recoiled and looked at the red mark on his hand that had snapped him out of his delirium. His surroundings were now clear to him. He saw the yellow smoke fuming from under the door; he saw the orange glow of dancing flames; he smelled the pungent odor; he thought about the heat of the doorknob.

Hellfire.

The old man could now hear the sounds of the engulfing blaze in the bedroom. The fire roared as it ate its way up the walls and spread across the ceiling and up into the roof through the bedroom.

"*Devils!*" he shrieked as he raised his gun to the door once more.

He pulled his white undershirt out from the side of his overalls and used it to grip the hot doorknob and push it open. The sudden rush of oxygen into the room caused the fire to flare through the entry and engulf the old man in flames.

He fell to his side and frantically rolled on the floor, screaming for dear life. A charred wooden beam from the ceiling dropped and slammed atop the old man's chest, breaking his ribs. The air was too hot and smoky to breathe, and he was soon coughing in and out of consciousness. A dark figure grinned down from the burning ceiling. Merle knew the wretched thing would crawl back to the basement once he was dead. It was just enjoying the show for now.

"Gertie . . . " His voice trailed off as his head rolled to one side. Bloody saliva dripped from his mouth. Visions of his wife and child took shape in the smoke, and his pain subsided.

17

The flames raged above him until the entire roof collapsed. Smoke twirled through the air until it was caught in a breeze with the fading laughter.

CHAPTER 1

April 1994, Southern Ohio

THIRTY-SIX-YEAR-OLD DANIEL HILL sat across from the crying woman in his office at 2:28 PM. He caught himself checking his watch, which was a major no-no in the psychology field. Never let a patient see you check your watch. If they feel like they're wasting your time, best case scenario, they get offended; worst case scenario, they realize that even the people they pay to listen to their problems couldn't care less, and they go home and have their final pharmaceutical cocktail.

Normally, he didn't do it. His mind was just preoccupied today, and who could blame him? It was closing day on a new house—a thirty-acre plot of land in southern West Virginia. It was on the outskirts of a small developing area of a town about twenty miles from a new chemical plant set to open. More jobs, more people, more money equals higher property values.

He looked down at his watch again: 2:29 PM.

This was the part of the job that he hated. He could tell that this poor lady wasn't even halfway through telling her sob story, and he was going to have to cut her off in one minute. After six meetings with Sarah, the forty-something-year-old crying into a tissue in front of him, she was finally addressing the possibility of her husband's infidelity. Had this been any other day, he would've let the meeting run a tad late.

His phone alarm dinged and made him jump. Sarah stopped talking.

"Sorry. I forgot that I set that alarm."

"It's OK, doctor," Sarah replied.

"Not a doctor," Daniel corrected. "Psychologist with a Master's. Not a doctor."

Daniel smiled uncomfortably at his academic Achilles' heel. Had his wife, Nora, not gotten pregnant sixteen years ago, he would've chased after the doctorate. It's something that's plagued him ever since.

"Is our time up?" Sarah asked.

"Unfortunately, so. I have to head across town for some personal business. We can continue this next week."

He thought about how he must sound just like her cheating husband, and the irony was not lost on him. He suppressed any hint of his dark humor in this setting, though.

"Thank you, doc . . . I mean Mr. . . . "

"Daniel is fine," he said with a smile as he stood up. Sarah followed his lead and turned toward the door.

"Thank you, Daniel."

"Leslie will take care of you on your way out," he said holding his clipboard against his vest.

Sarah exited, and Daniel shut the door behind her. He checked his watch again: 2:31 PM. He had a twenty-minute drive across town for the closing at 3. Nora would no doubt arrive early, and he didn't want to keep her waiting. She was on summer break from her job as a high school science teacher and planned to take maternity leave at the start of the next school year in the fall. Even though he knew she hated the idea of transferring schools and missing the first few months in a new building, she supported her husband, and he was grateful.

Daniel tossed his clipboard on his large oak desk and loosened his tie a bit. He was wearing his favorite blue dress shirt, a vest, and brown slacks. He sank down into his cushioned swivel chair and let out an exhausted sigh.

This was his sixth year in private practice as a psychologist, and each successive year his client base had grown. He looked up at his diplomas on the wall and then over to his massive bookshelf that was filled with volumes of books about human physiology, brain chemistry, emotional disorders, addiction, trauma recovery, etc.

He was taking five minutes to decompress. He'd earned it. He couldn't remember the last time when he didn't collapse onto something soft as soon as his final patient for the day walked out of the door. Even though he made his living talking and listening to people, Daniel was extremely introverted. Constant communication wore him out, but it paid well.

Four more minutes and he'd get up and head downtown. He leaned back in his chair and closed his eyes. Deep breaths. Inhale through the nose, out through the mouth. He felt his heart rate slowing down. His nerves were steadying as he controlled his breath and stilled his thoughts. He focused on nothing but his breathing. Anytime a stray thought entered his brain he redirected back to the steady flow of air in and out of his lungs. The remaining minutes ticked away, and he was now replenished. Mind over matter.

Leslie was finishing up the paperwork for the day when Daniel walked out of his office with his briefcase.

"Good luck with the closing," she smiled.

"Thanks, Les. Do I need to do anything else?"

"Nope, boss. Have a good weekend," she said as she pecked away on her computer.

Leslie was in her late forties and was a consummate office manager. She was the second person to fill the position in Daniel's practice, and she'd been with him for the past five years. She was short, but none of Daniel's patients would ever know it. All day she was behind the desk: scheduling, billing, filing. Daniel didn't know what he'd do without her.

"You have a good weekend, too. Call me if you need anything."

Daniel checked himself in his car mirror. The black BMW 325i convertible was a gift from his wife after the first year of running his own practice. He would've loved any car that Nora gave him in a gesture like that, but the fact that it was a black beamer was a home run. He made sure his light brown hair was decently brushed and checked to see if there was anything in his teeth. Satisfied, he popped a mint and started up the engine. He looked at the digital clock display: 2:39 PM.

Nineteen minutes later, he coasted into an open parking space in the lot for Wetzel & Wetzel Law Firm. He remembered chuckling with Nora about the name. "Weasel and Weasel" he had called it. He smiled to himself when he saw their sign.

Nora watched Daniel pull in and exited her Chevy Caprice station wagon. She was six months pregnant but moved as gracefully as ever. Daniel opened his car door and nearly hit her in the belly.

"Geez, Daniel, watch what you're doing," she said, instinctively backing up.

Daniel realized what he had done and winced.

"Sorry!" he said as he got out and shut the door behind him.

Nora let the moment pass for what it was and forced a smile. Daniel hugged her and kissed her forehead.

"How are you feeling today?"

"Fine. The little gal has been active," she said as she rubbed her stomach.

"Have you?" Daniel asked, kneeling on one knee to speak directly to his unborn daughter. "Have you had a big day, my little surprise baby?"

Nora smiled and looked around the parking lot to see if anyone was watching.

"Surprise baby?" she asked.

"Well, I was going to go with 'mistake baby' or 'accident baby' but thought better of it."

"If I could knee your face right now without hurting the baby I would," she teased.

Daniel turned his attention back to his child.

"Unplanned, but not unloved. Are you ready to help Mommy and Daddy buy a new house in the country? We're moving one state south on a big thirty-acre farm! Are you excited?" Daniel smiled and looked up at Nora who was looking lovingly down at her husband.

"Get up," she said, slightly blushing.

"Honey, your Mommy thinks your Daddy is crazy for buying a farm in West Virginia, but we're going to fix it up real nice and flip it for some money. What's money you ask? I'll teach you all about that when you're older."

Nora grabbed Daniel by his hair to lift him up. He laughed and stood to face her.

"I don't think you're crazy for buying a farm," she started. "I think it's going to be challenging moving over an hour away from your office into a new state in a house that needs a lot of work on thirty acres of farmland that also needs a lot of work. Not to mention the fact that I'm six months pregnant . . . "

"How did you luck out marrying someone with such ambition?"

"Reiterate your ambition to your fifteen-year-old daughter who will be spending her summer break on a farm in West Virginia."

"It'll build character."

Nora's eyebrows went up.

"Where is Alice by the way?" Daniel asked. "I thought she would've wanted to come with you."

Nora laughed with disbelief.

"She doesn't want to support this move in any way. When I left, she was in her room talking on the phone to one of her friends about how unfair her life is."

"You know it's just temporary."

"Temporary is an eternity to a teenage girl."

"I'll tell her I'll buy her a car for her sixteenth birthday. Trust me, that'll smooth it over," Daniel said.

Nora rolled her eyes. Daniel could tell that he had to outline the plan again.

"We sign the papers, hire the contractors to make the major repairs to the house, move in in a few months, enjoy a brief tour of the farm life while the market continues to spike, then we sell. All the while you can be searching for our dream home back up here if you want. Or the beach for all I care. This land was just too good a deal to pass up, and I believe that our sacrifice will pay off nicely."

Nora had heard his spiel before, but he had gotten much better at selling her on the idea. She was comfortable in the small city where they currently lived. She had no desire to uproot their lives, and the idea of bugs and animals and chores and everything else that came with a farm seemed beneath her.

She had done things, though. Things she wasn't proud of. Regretful things. She figured this was her karma, or at least her chance to make things right without having to destroy their marriage. She thought of Steve Clemmons, the assistant principal at her school, and she felt a rush of shame. She was glad to be transferring to a new school. Her face effortlessly concealed her discomfort, and she gave her husband a hug.

"You're the smartest man I know, and I trust your judgment."

She kissed him.

"Go on."

She laughed and broke the embrace.

"Come on. Let's go buy our farm."

"Let's do it," he said, following her lead toward the building.

Two men sat at the absurdly long conference table inside the law office: George Wetzel, Sr., a small, bald man in his sixties, and George Wetzel, Jr., a big, burly man with a lush mane of black hair who must've inherited his mother's genes. Daniel and Nora were escorted into the conference room by a bubbly, young secretary.

"Mr. and Mrs. Hill, welcome," George Sr. said as both men stood up to greet them.

"Pleasure to see you both again," George Jr. chimed in.

"Wetzel, Wetzel," Daniel said with separate nods, humoring only himself.

"Hello," Nora said with a warm smile.

"Have a seat," George Sr. said. "Like I said on the phone, this will be relatively painless. Just a bunch of signatures from you both, and we'll have this thing licked in under an hour."

"Let's do it," Daniel said, pulling out a seat for his wife to sit.

Nora eased herself down, careful not to bump her belly against the imposing table. Daniel sat beside her.

"How's the little one doing?" George Jr. asked Nora and motioned to her baby bump.

"Little one?" Daniel asked with serious offense.

Both George's faces went pale.

"I, uh," George Jr. stammered.

"Daniel, stop it," Nora scolded. "Yes, I'm pregnant, and she's doing just fine."

"Jesus, man!" George Jr. started. "You nearly gave me a heart attack."

Daniel laughed and shrugged.

"You broke the cardinal rule of pointing out a woman's pregnancy," George Sr. said, giving a playful elbow to his son's ribs. "Your mother would've bludgeoned you with your own briefcase if she'd witnessed you do that. To clients, no less!"

"Yes, Wetzel, never address the elephant in the room," Daniel said, looking straight ahead at the two men.

The room went quiet as Nora once again shook her head at her husband's uncomfortable humor.

"Do you all handle divorces here as well?" she asked, breaking the silence.

The attorneys both burst into laughter.

"We're going to have to watch you two," George Jr. said as he refocused and started distributing packs of papers. "Couple of jokesters you are."

Daniel picked up his packet and began thumbing through it. Nora grabbed a pen, ready to make the deal official.

"Green Acres, here we come," she said with acceptance.

CHAPTER 2

Mid-June 1994, Southwestern West Virginia

CARMINE'S CONSTRUCTION CREW had been remodeling the farmhouse since they got the contract in April. It wasn't a big job, but it was delicate. The old house hadn't been updated since it was built in the 40s. The entire first floor—kitchen, living room, and den—all needed new flooring and trim. There were spots in the staircase that needed to be fixed. The smaller bedroom upstairs was fine for now, but the wing where the bigger bedroom was had been destroyed in the fire last March. A new roof would have to replace the temporary tarp that had been put up to prevent further water damage. Any painting, smaller repairs, and work on the land would be completed by the new owners. There was also an unfinished basement that would remain untouched.

The three men composing the crew had put in long days to stay ahead of schedule. There was the owner, Carmine, and his two assistants, Mike and Roy. Carmine was a mountain of a man with buzzed red hair and layers of muscle earned from years of hard work. He was in his early forties and managed to keep his small business booming. He was resourceful and earned a solid reputation around the small town of getting quality jobs finished on time. Mike and Roy were both stocky young men in their twenties who could build, repair, or restore anything put in front of them, so long as they were given enough money to hit the bar after work.

It was lunch break, and the three of them were eating their takeout burgers on the hood of Carmine's Ford truck.

"How many more days would ya say we got?" Mike asked with a wad of burger tucked into his cheek.

Carmine slowly swallowed his bite and took a drink before replying.

"Well, we only have to finish the bigger bedroom and then the roof. We had three weeks total, but I reckon we can wrap it up in the next two or three days. Depends on how late you boys want to stay," Carmine said.

"Don't matter to me," Roy began. "I'd rather finish fast and move on to the next one."

"Same here," Mike agreed.

"Ok, then."

He swallowed the last bit of his lunch and took a final drink of his soda. He lit up an unfiltered smoke and turned to look at the house.

"Sure looks a lot better than it did two weeks ago," Carmine said to the boys behind him.

They acknowledged with grunts as they grazed.

"I've restored a few houses with fire damage, but this is the absolute strangest one I've ever seen."

Carmine was certainly no fire marshal, but he had noticed the odd burn marks when they first scoped out the scene.

"What are you talkin' about?" Mike asked.

Carmine continued to stare at the old man's bedroom from the yard. It had been nothing but a charred cave two weeks ago. Now it was looking mighty fine if he did say so himself.

"If a fire's burning, there's no reason it should just stop if it's got plenty of food to chew," Carmine said.

Mike and Roy shared a confused glance before looking at Carmine's back for more of an explanation.

"Why did only a portion of the roof burn? Why did the fire burn through half of a wall and just stop? Once that blaze got hot enough to do what it did, it should've eaten right through the entire house. There shouldn't be any part of that house left. What do you make of that?" Carmine pondered, more to himself than to his crew behind him.

He took a deep drag off his smoke and turned to face them.

"Odd ain't it?" he asked as the boys were finishing their last bites.

They nodded their heads in agreement.

"Could it have rained that night?" Roy proposed.

"It didn't."

"Think the wind coulda blown it out?" Mike hypothesized.

"Wind don't blow fire out. It spreads it quicker than dandelion seeds."

"What do ya think happened then, boss?" Roy asked as he fumbled for his cigarettes and lighter.

Carmine turned back to the house, took another puff, and contemplated.

"Act of God, I suppose."

Mike and Roy had never heard their boss talk about religion, and they both started to feel uncomfortable.

"Ya think God put out the fire, boss?" Roy asked.

Carmine smiled at the condescension in his employee's voice.

"God or somethin' like Him. Don't you boys know whose farm this used to be?" Carmine asked as he turned back around to face them.

They both shook their heads as they smoked.

"Thought not," Carmine said. "Something of a local legend the old man was. He supposedly operated as a backwoods exorcist of sorts. Can you believe that? Makin' house calls like some kind of supernatural doctor?"

"An *exorcist*?" Mike exclaimed, suddenly intrigued. "Like spinning heads and floating beds and that kinda shit?"

Carmine chuckled.

"Ahh, hell," Roy chimed in. "Boss is just pulling our leg, Mike. He watched *Ghostbusters* on cable last night and is just fuckin' with us."

"I assure you I'm not. Just repeatin' local legends, boys."

"Keep your legends to yourself next time. Shit's freaky," Mike said.

"I had no interest in telling you at all. Wasn't interested in old hillbilly gossip in the slightest when we first started this job. But boys, the longer we work on this house, the more uneasy I feel," Carmine admitted. "Either one of you set foot in that basement?"

"No, sir," Mike replied while Roy shook his head.

"I did and wish I didn't," Carmine said. "Creepiest damn place I've ever been."

He stubbed his cigarette on the grass and put the butt in his pocket.

"I'm with you boys. Let's finish this job quick and move the hell on."

Two days passed, and the crew was poised to finish just as Carmine had predicted. The three men had worked like machines, completing the remaining major jobs first and then going back through and touching everything up. The bedroom was one of Carmine's best jobs, and he was proud of his helpers for their efforts.

Carmine finished the final shingle of the roof that he was applying. He looked around at his completed section for anything out of the ordinary. Satisfied, he looked down the other end of the roof where Mike and Roy were working. Their area looked flawless, and they would soon be finished as well.

"You boys nearing the end?" Carmine hollered to the other end of the roof.

Mike turned around and gave a thumbs up.

"I'm going to head down and start roundin' up the debris."

"Got it, boss," Roy replied. "We'll be done in ten minutes, tops."

Carmine shimmied down the extended aluminum ladder and hopped off at the bottom. He lit a cigarette and walked to his truck to retrieve the industrial trash bags. His watch read 8:44 PM.

Another long day—another long job—coming to an end. He put his cigarette in his mouth and stepped up into the bed of his truck. He looked around at the various supplies and tools but saw no trash bags. He turned to the men still on the roof.

"Hey! Where are the trash bags?"

He heard them talking.

"Check the kitchen!" Roy hollered back.

Carmine remembered that Roy had brought the roll of bags in there the day before when they were rounding up all the pieces of broken trim. He sighed and stepped down out of the truck, making it wobble under his weight.

The sun was tucked behind the rolling hills surrounding the farm. A slight breeze blew over the land, lightly cooling the sweat on his brow. Carmine took in a quick scenic view as he strolled and smoked his way toward the porch. The evening sky was a colorful swirl of maroon and orange. It would be dark within the hour. They needed to get busy cleaning up. He stubbed out his smoke in the front yard and added the trash to his pocket.

The inside of the house looked fantastic. It retained its original rustic integrity but now had some modern amenities. They had repaired and cleaned up nicely, and he knew that Daniel guy from Ohio would be pleased. Carmine headed left into the kitchen. There was movement coming from the roof above him, and he knew he was right under Mike and Roy. He saw the roll of trash bags on the counter and grabbed them. Just as he turned back around, he felt something blow on the back of his neck causing the hairs to stand erect. He put his hand under the base of his skull and rubbed away the odd sensation. He swung around to see what was behind him.

It dawned on him that this was the first time he had been in the house alone, and he was now staring at the door leading to the basement that was slightly ajar. Carmine examined the old wood hanging from the hinges. He could've sworn that he had shut the door and bolted it after he ventured down that one time, but now it was revealing a slight opening.

The dark crack held his attention. He could feel his heart start to race and his hands clam up. The temperature in the kitchen felt like it had just gotten ten degrees warmer. The air was thick and humid. Carmine wiped the sweat from his eyes with his shirt. When he pulled the shirt away, he saw orange eyes in the darkness through the crack.

"Jesus!" he shrieked and stumbled backward.

He fell on his bottom and scrambled to get back up. There was a loud pounding on the roof directly above him.

"Boss? You OK down there?" Roy's muffled voice asked.

Carmine heard a quiet *latch* and looked at the basement door that was now completely closed. Without giving it a second thought, he turned and stormed out of the house with the trash bags in tow.

Mike and Roy were climbing down the ladder when Carmine stepped off the porch. Mike released the ladder extension and converted it to its mobile size. Roy looked over at Carmine, noticing the obvious flush in his face.

"Did you scream, boss?" Roy asked.

Carmine started to speak but coughed on his saliva. He swallowed and started again.

"Yeah. It, uh, it was nothin'."

Mike looked over at his boss.

"You don't look so hot."

"Yeah, boss. You look kinda pale," Roy agreed.

Carmine pulled out his cigarettes and plopped one in his mouth. He didn't realize how badly his hands were trembling until they were in front of his face with the lighter. He lit the smoke and shoved the lighter in his pocket before his crew had something else to analyze. He took a deep drag and released a slow exhale.

"I told ya both I'm fine," he asserted as he ripped three trash bags off the roll and handed one to each of his employees. "Let's get these old shingles cleared off this lawn and get the hell outta here. This job's done."

The three men went to work while the wind played with the screen door, creating a taunting squeak that Carmine spent the rest of the evening trying to ignore.

CHAPTER 3

Late June 1994, Southwestern West Virginia

THE DRIVE FROM the Hill's old house to their new farm had taken about sixty-five minutes so far, and they were still about ten minutes away. Daniel accepted that his morning commute had grown forty-five minutes overnight. He drove the moving truck along the curvy road that ran parallel with a river. Alice was riding shotgun, and the fact that she chose to ride with him over her mother shocked him. He thought she was still angry with him for making her move in the first place.

Nora followed behind in the station wagon. At some point tomorrow, she'd have to give him a ride back north to pick up his beamer. Although Nora thought he was crazy for renting the biggest U-Haul truck available, she was glad he did when she saw how snugly everything they owned fit in one load.

They passed a small, developing subdivision on the left called River's Edge. Daniel looked at the cozy little neighborhood as they went by and thought that that would be a nice place to raise a family. He was impressed with all the riverfront properties that he'd seen so far. He knew that once this new chemical plant opened later this year, it would only boost the local economy. His property value would soon follow.

Nora was even impressed with the scenic rural area as she trailed behind the rest of her family. Bright green trees lined the road and spawned out exponentially across the rolling hills surrounding the valley. The summer sun gave the vegetation an amber aura. For the first time since agreeing to this endeavor, she realized that this might not be so bad after all.

Daniel turned on his blinker and checked his side mirror to make sure that Nora did as well. Her blinker flicked on, and he turned right onto a gravel road passing a small green sign that read, "Sunny Branch Way." He liked his new street name.

"Sunny Branch Way?" Alice said, unimpressed.

"Has a nice ring to it, doesn't it?" Daniel replied.

"I guess."

"We're a half mile up here on the right," he said as he pointed.

Before Alice said something bratty, she stopped herself. She knew there was no point. She had put up her initial fight and stated her case and quickly realized that she was outnumbered. It was a nice compromise that her dad said he'd let her pick out a car for her sixteenth birthday, so she did her best to not be a downer. She realized how much her parents did for her.

Her best friend, Molly, had made her feel better about the situation too. Molly came over to help her pack her things the day before and to say their hopefully temporary goodbyes. Alice vented for a good twenty minutes about how this was the end of her life and how she would be the new kid with no friends and had no desire to start her high school social life from scratch. Molly told her to look at it as an opportunity to have two sets of friends now. She also highlighted the fact that there could be all sorts of hot farm boys nestled away in these woods. Now, looking at the beautiful scenery through the window of the moving truck, she was starting to think about how this might just turn out to be something good.

The truck wobbled over low spots in the road, releasing

a trail of dust behind it. Nora kept her distance. She noticed that the rock station on the radio was cutting in and out. She hit the scan button, and it skimmed through the dial and stopped on a screaming preacher, raving about our sins. Nora turned the volume knob to silent so fast that she almost broke it off.

An image of Steve Clemmons, her old boss, looking at her in that way *with that smile* appeared in her head. She looked at the farmland through her window to focus on something else—anything else. The last thing she wanted to be reminded of was secret sin.

"This is us!" Daniel exclaimed to Alice as the farmhouse came into view on the horizon.

Daniel was the only one of them to have seen the completed house before now. Nora saw it when they came down to buy it at auction before it was restored, but Alice had not seen the house or land at all.

"The house up there?"

"Yep, but all this is our property."

He lowered his voice to do his best James Earl Jones impression and said, "Someday, Simba, all of this will be yours."

"Thanks, Mufasa," Alice replied with a smile.

They had had a family outing the night before to go watch the new movie *The Lion King* in theaters. Even though Alice was older, she never acted too cool for school when it came to new Disney movies. Even Nora enjoyed it, smiling in the dark theater while she rubbed her belly. Both ladies were subjected to Daniel's theoretical critique of the movie's connection to *Hamlet* on the car ride home from the theater.

"Seriously," Daniel began. "That house and barn are ours. We have about ten acres going that direction and about twenty going that way. There's tons of land to explore."

"It sounds cool, Dad."

Daniel looked at her and saw that she was being genuine.

"I'll make sure it is. Just don't go falling into any rabbit holes and winding up in Wonderland."

"Alice jokes," she said while nodding her head. "Can something never get old if it was never funny to begin with? Just curious."

Daniel laughed at his daughter's response. He felt proud to have passed down his treasured wit. He flicked on his blinker and turned right onto the long gravel driveway. They pulled up beside the front porch, and Alice jumped out before he could even put it in park. She stared wide-eyed at the two-story house; it was so much nicer than she had anticipated. She noticed the trees to her left that gradually got denser the further up the hill she looked. Slowly turning until her back was to the house, she stopped and stared out at the rolling, open field that was glowing green in the sunshine.

"Wow, Dad."

Daniel smiled from inside the car.

"Not bad, right?"

Nora pulled in behind them. Daniel looked in the rearview mirror and saw that she had a similar response admiring their newly remodeled home. They got out of their vehicles at the same time.

"Daniel, it looks so good! I can't believe it. Is this even the same house?"

He was all smiles.

"Now imagine you're someone who's actually trying to buy a nice place in the country, and you pull up on this."

Nora still hadn't taken her eyes off it. No matter how hard she tried, she could find no fault in the renovations. Daniel walked up beside her and put his arm around her as they both took it in.

"We're going to make out like bandits when we sell it," she said.

"If ever there was an I-told-you-so moment . . . "

She elbowed her grinning husband in the ribs.

They unpacked for six hours, pausing only to have lunch in the early afternoon. Daniel was pleased with how willing Alice was to help. She hadn't complained once about having to carry heavy boxes or be Daniel's moving partner when it came to the bulky furniture. She simply listened to her new CD Walkman that he had bought her the day before and did as she was asked. It was an easy bribe even though he knew he was now going to have to replace her extensive cassette tape collection with CDs. He smiled as he watched her seem to enjoy the manual labor as long as she could jam out to her new tunes. His plan had blossomed perfectly.

Nora went through boxes that were brought in the house but kept her work light. With the precious cargo she was carrying inside her, she and Daniel had insisted on it. It was nearing 5 PM, and everyone was getting hungry once again. Nora had no intention of trying to cook anything with the majority of their belongings still in boxes, so she decided to just have pizza delivered. She was grateful that Daniel had had all of the utilities turned on and working for them before they arrived. He had even picked up a local phone book. There were pros and cons to the way Daniel's analytical mind worked, but his ability to thoroughly prepare was definitely beneficial. Just as Nora found the phone book, Alice came backing in through the front door carrying one end of a loveseat.

"Careful," Daniel instructed from outside. "Tilt it to your right."

"I am, Dad. Just push it."

Daniel gave it a firm shove, and it slid through the doorframe.

"What would you do without me," he said to his daughter as he winked at his wife.

Alice rolled her eyes as she carefully made her way to

the living room with the loveseat. Daniel followed, attached to the other end. After a few seconds, Nora heard a thud and knew that they had placed the piece of furniture.

"Are you all getting hungry?" she asked.

Daniel and Alice walked back into the kitchen.

"You bet," he said.

"Yes," Alice agreed.

Nora slid the phone book across the counter to her daughter standing in front of the refrigerator.

"You pick where we order from," Nora said.

"Sweet," Alice said, snatching up the book and heading back toward the living room.

Daniel walked over to his wife and gave her a light hug. "Are you overwhelmed yet?"

"Yet?"

"Just breathe. We'll be settled in before you know it."

"I never want to see another moving box. This may become our forever home just so I don't have to go through this again," she sighed.

They heard Alice calling one pizza place after another trying to secure some food. After several failed attempts, she stormed back into the kitchen.

"No one even delivers out here!"

"I guess we better order takeout," Daniel said with a smile. "Call wherever, and I'll go pick it up."

Alice, frustrated, walked back into the living room and placed an order to go.

"Need anything while I'm out?" he asked his wife.

"A masseuse, a bartender, and a housekeeper."

"Poof," Daniel said, mimicking a magician. "You got all three in one right here."

Nora rested her head against Daniel's shoulder.

"I'm going to hold you to that."

Nora's gaze was disrupted by a shiny metallic object behind Daniel.

"What's that?" she asked as she squinted at the

basement door over Daniel's shoulder. He turned around to see what she was looking at.

"The basement? Oh, that's right! You didn't go down in there with me when we first looked at the house."

"I know it's a door to the basement," she said. "What's above the doorknob?"

Daniel looked and finally noticed what she was pointing out. There were six nails that had been hammered into the door between the doorknob and the door frame. They were meticulously placed with four nails making a vertical line and one nail on either side of that line making a horizontal row of three. The resulting shape was a cross. Daniel walked across the kitchen to investigate. He crouched down on one knee to look at the odd construction.

"I definitely don't remember seeing these the last time I was here," he said.

Nora stood behind him just as perplexed.

"Why would someone do that?"

Before Daniel could say that he had no idea, he figured it out. He grabbed the doorknob and gave it a quick twist. The knob wouldn't budge, just as he had suspected. He looked back at his wife.

"These three horizontal nails are all piercing the latch through the wood, pinning it in place. Geez, you'd have to use some high-powered nail gun to do that. I don't know what the reason for the column of nails is other than whoever did this just wanted to make a nice cross," he said.

"I thought you said you went in the basement?" Nora said with confusion.

"I did. There's nothing down there but a bunch of junk and cobwebs. This door opened the day we first checked out the farm. When I came down last week with the construction guy, he gave me the grand tour and showed me everything he did. I came in the kitchen and checked it out. I'm telling you that these nails weren't here. No one else should've been in this house between then and now."

"Do you think someone broke in and did thi . . . "

"Holy shit!" Daniel exclaimed, cutting off his wife. "I *know* these weren't here when I was in here with Carmine because I walked over here and turned the knob when he and I were in the kitchen. I said something like 'I'd check the basement, but I know it's still a shithole,' but he just gave me a weird look. I didn't go down there, but, Nora, I turned the knob and *it worked* . . . just a few days ago."

"Then who would've done this, Daniel?"

Daniel stood up and stared down at the glimmering cross, his face frozen in a perplexed gaze.

"I have no idea," he said as the two of them stood in silence.

"Pizza!" Alice exclaimed walking back into the kitchen.

Both of her parents jumped and spun around. Her mom shrieked and caught her breath.

"Jesus, Alice!" Daniel said as he placed his hand on his heart.

"Sorry. The pizzas can be picked up in twenty minutes."

Her parents were obviously still startled.

"Jumpy much?" she muttered to herself as she walked back into the living room.

Daniel and Nora looked at each other and couldn't help but laugh.

CHAPTER 4

Late June 1994, Southern West Virginia

ABOUT TWO WEEKS after Carmine had finished the farmhouse job, his crew was midway through their new contract of replacing the roofs on several apartment building units near the Virginia border. He and his two helpers were put up in a small motel near the job site since it was over two hours from where they lived. Even though he hadn't set foot on that farm in thirteen days, he couldn't stop thinking about it.

Mike and Roy knew something was bothering their boss, and he knew that they knew. At least once per day, one of them would ask him if everything was all right. He would lie, nodding and just claiming exhaustion. He was getting more irritable by the day. The last thing he wanted when he was battling something internally was to be reminded that something was wrong.

Even though they were getting on his nerves, he didn't fault them for questioning his behavior. He was actually a bit surprised that they weren't more forthcoming. Twice now he had been careless on the job and nearly caused one accident. The first time he had left half of the needed supplies for the day on his other work truck. The second and nearly disastrous error was when he was walking across the roof of one of the units and got distracted by the setting sun. Something about the lighting—he'd heard it called 'magic hour' before—had reminded him of being at that farm on Sunny Branch Way.

Then came the slight breeze. Carmine closed his eyes as the gentle wind lured him forward. He was unaware that he was walking and bumped into Mike who was bent over removing an old shingle. Mike toppled face-first and rolled down the declining slope. Luckily, Roy had been near the gutter and grabbed Mike before he could pick up the necessary momentum to send him over the edge to a three-story fall. The two workers looked up at their boss in shock. His daze was broken, and he was instantly brought back to a sobering reality. He blinked for a few shocked seconds and then made sure that the men were OK. Of course, he apologized repeatedly.

That was earlier this evening. It was just after 9:30 PM now, and Carmine needed a drink. He snuck out of the hotel and drove his truck to the nearest drugstore to pick up a bottle of whiskey and a pack of smokes. His commute was dark, and streetlights were scarce. As soon as he finished one long curve in the road, another one started. He wound back and forth through the mountainous terrain that was a hallmark of the southern part of the state.

He reached the drugstore in about fifteen minutes. The glowing neon sign and fluorescent lights inside were a warm comfort in the middle of the Appalachian wilderness. He was in and out, picking up exactly what he had set out for. Normally, he was not in the habit of drinking and driving, but he figured one little swig wouldn't do much other than steady his nerves. The lid twisted off, and he guzzled a hefty gulp of the amber liquid. It warmed his belly and numbed his throat. He pulled the last cigarette out of his old pack and lit it before starting up his truck.

Driving at night never used to bother him until recently. In fact, he had developed a complete repulsion to the dark in any setting. Even in his hotel room, he would sleep with the bathroom light on. Something deep down inside of him knew that he should be on guard. After speeding through the rest of his drive, he pulled the truck back into the motel parking lot. As soon as he stepped out of his vehicle, he noticed a red cherry glowing in the darkness. He recognized Roy standing beside the building puffing away on a cigarette. He smiled as the two men made eye contact.

"Had to pick up some essential supplies," Carmine said as he held up his brown paper bag.

"I hear ya."

"Want a toot?"

"Sure, why not?" Roy answered and took a mouthful.

He handed the bagged bottle back to Carmine and made a face of repulsion.

"Shewee, that's some straight rot-gut ain't it?"

Carmine smiled and took a drink himself.

"I'd have it no other way," he said, unfazed by the strong kick of the bourbon.

The two men stood in the empty lot saying nothing for what seemed like an eternity to both of them.

"Hey, boss . . . "

"I swear, Roy, if you ask me if everything is OK, I'm going to break this goddamn bottle overtop your melon."

Roy smiled.

"You just ain't yourself lately, is all."

"Fine," Carmine started. "You want the truth, do ya?"

Roy was all ears.

"The last day of that farm job back home, when I walked back into the kitchen by myself, I swear I saw something I ain't got no business seein'."

"What'd you see?"

"It was somethin' in the basement. I, uh, I'm not sure what it was."

"What do you mean? Did you go in the basement again when you went to get those trash bags?"

"Hell no. I walked in the kitchen and grabbed the bags and turned around to walk my ass right back out when I felt somethin' blow on my neck."

Roy looked scared now. Carmine continued.

"I turned around and saw that the basement door was open, just a crack. There was somethin' inside it, *lookin' out at me.*"

"Jesus, boss. What was it?"

"I didn't get a very good look, but I know it was lookin' back at me. I felt like I was gonna shit myself right there. It was the most God-awful feeling I ever felt, and that's the truth."

The two men stood in silence as the story settled in with both of them.

"Boss, I'll take another shot of that," Roy said gesturing for the liquor.

"You and me both."

Carmine took a big swig and handed the bottle to Roy who did the same.

"I think it's just one of those things that'll get better with time," Carmine said, nodding his head. "I appreciate your all's concern, but I'll be fine. Hell, just talkin' about it with you now has me feeling like a big load has been lifted off my chest."

"That's good, boss."

"We better turn in. We got another long day tomorrow with an early start."

"OK, boss."

"And keep what we talked about between us, will ya?"

"Yes, sir."

Both men stubbed their smokes in the ashtray and went their separate ways to their rooms for the night. Carmine shut the door to his room and emptied his pockets on the nightstand beside his bed. He turned the knob on the TV and watched the fuzzy glow in the screen come to life and start to form pictures. He changed the dial to channel four and settled for the final act of some cop drama.

The shower beckoned him. He peeled off his sweaty work clothes, grabbed the bottle of whiskey, and hobbled to the bathroom, sore from a hard day's work. He stepped inside the sliding glass shower door and shut it behind him. The scalding hot water stung at first, but then got to work on his joints. The booze helped, too. He slid his back down the tile wall of the shower, letting the stream of water pelt his face. He sat there with his eyes shut, trying to relax.

The basement door appeared in his mind's eye. It floated there, surrounded by darkness, growing as it slowly came toward him. When it was just a few feet away, it swung open and contorted into a mouth, swallowing him whole.

"Goddamnit!" Carmine screamed as he opened his eyes, his voice bellowing in the small shower.

He unscrewed the lid of his bottle and drank three hefty gulps. Holding the bottle up to the light he could see that he'd nearly polished off half of the fifth, and he was feeling it.

"Can't even relax in the shower."

He bent his knees and sank even further down into the tub until the spraying water hit the wall above his head. He kept his eyes open, afraid of what he might see if he didn't. He took another drink and used his foot to wedge the drain stopper in place so that the shower water would begin filling up the bath. He sat the bottle on his chest and started to read the history of the bourbon on the label.

Steam permeated the bathroom. The glass door was completely fogged up. The atmosphere was thick with moisture. He immediately thought of the warm air that seemed to flow from that basement and how that kitchen was unnaturally humid. He took another gulp from his bottle and placed it beside him.

He wiped the moisture from the glass and regarded the bathroom door. It was pushed shut just the way he had left it, but he realized that he hadn't closed it all the way. There was a sliver of darkness in the crack between the doorframe and the door. He stared at it through the foggy glass. The bathroom door gradually started to open.

Carmine leapt up from the tub and threw open the

sliding glass shower door. He grabbed the bottle by the neck and turned it upside down, ready to swing it if needed. The bathroom door hadn't moved. It was still in the same position that it was when he first got in the shower. He quickly righted his bottle to avoid spilling the rest of his booze. He realized that looking at it through the shower glass must've tricked his eyes. He took a deep breath and shook his head. One more drink, and then he cut off the shower.

He sat the nearly empty bottle of booze on the nightstand and fell back onto the flimsy pillows. The queen-sized bed was firm and uncompromising, but he was too drunk to give a shit. He clumsily yanked at the tightly tucked-in sheets as he wrestled his way underneath them. Finally in an acceptable sleeping position, he closed his eyes.

The lamp on the nightstand blazed orange behind his eyelids, but he didn't want to turn it off. The first few nights he only slept with the bathroom light on, then he added the TV, and tonight he was leaving this light on as well. It was too bright in the room, but it made him feel more comfortable.

With his eyes still closed, he grabbed the bottle and finished it off. He knew he was going to feel it in the morning, but right now he just needed sleep. He tried to set the bottle back on the nightstand but ended up just dropping it on the floor. With enough booze in his system, his mind finally became weary.

Something in the air vent above stirred. His eyes shot open just as he was drifting off. He looked up at the grate near the ceiling above the TV. There were several dark slits in the metal. He stared into the darkness, at what, he did not know. After nearly a minute of not blinking, he disregarded the sound and closed his eyes again.

There was a tap on the grate. Carmine sat up in bed and saw a face behind the grate looking at him with bulging, orange eyes. Carmine screamed with primal rage as he jerked the bottle off the floor and flung it at the air vent. The bottle missed its mark, clanged off the forgiving wall, and rolled on the floor back beside the bed.

The vent was empty again. Carmine sat there trying to catch his breath. His heart was fighting to break through his chest. He swung his legs over the side of the bed and sat up. Bowing his head and clasping his hands together in his lap, he began to pray between sobs.

"God, help me. I don't know what's wrong with me. Please, just help me," he cried.

He opened his eyes and saw that he was facing the louvered closet doors. He saw the abundance of cracks housing a black abyss. Something in the closet moved, and then he noticed the tall silhouette standing inside. He looked in a crack near the top of the door at the two glowing eyes peeking out at him and screamed in terror.

Roy had heard the liquor bottle hit their shared wall when Carmine threw it. He had just fallen asleep and had to get up early. Naturally, he was a little fed up with Carmine's craziness. He lay in bed, debating on whether or not to get up and confront his boss. He decided that he should. It may cost him his job, but Carmine's behavior was en route to jeopardizing that anyway. Besides, Carmine felt comfortable enough to confide in him already, so maybe he was willing to listen.

Roy slid his jeans back on and walked out onto the cement sidewalk with no shoes or shirt. He stepped up to the door next to his and lifted his hand to knock. Before he could do so, Carmine screamed from inside. It was the type of scream he had only heard in scary movies. He shook the locked doorknob.

"Carmine!" he yelled as he pounded on the door.

There was commotion inside.

"Boss!"

Roy heard glass break and then there was a thud. He

grabbed the knob again and heaved his shoulder into the door trying to break it down, but it didn't give.

"Boss!" he screamed, trying one more time.

The night manager came running out of the main office with a flashlight, looking understandably startled.

"What's going on?" the small, old man asked.

"I think my friend is in danger in there! Can you open the door?" Roy pleaded.

The night manager grabbed a keychain from his belt loop and stepped up to the door. He unlocked it, and Roy shoved him out of the way to run into the room. He screamed at what he saw.

The confused old man stood outside in shock and watched Roy run back out of the room and vomit all over the parking lot.

"What . . . what is it?" the night manager asked.

Roy dry heaved and dropped to his knees, sobbing. Lights in the other occupied rooms started to turn on. The old man walked to the open door.

"Don't . . . " Roy warned as he held his chest.

The manager poked his head in the room. There was black and white static on the TV screen, the bathroom light was on, and the bed was messy. He took a few steps inside and saw the open closet doors. He walked around the bed and noticed two legs on the floor poking out of the closet, feet pointing up in the air.

The old man felt his stomach turn to knots as he inched his way forward and looked inside. Carmine sat with his back against the closet wall with shards of the broken glass bottle protruding from his eyes. Ribbons of blood trickled down his bare torso and were still puddling on the closet floor.

The night manager didn't make it as far as Roy before he, too, vomited.

CHAPTER 5

DANIEL HAD TAKEN two weeks off from his practice to devote to settling into the house. He had his office manager arrange for emergency teleconferencing if needed. They had been at the farm for almost a week, and the house was finally unpacked. All of the rooms were coming together in their own unique way. The house was stocked with food, cleaned, and was beginning to feel more like a home.

It was around 11 AM on a Saturday when they all heard what the doorbell sounded like for the first time. Nora was upstairs in their bedroom folding laundry. Alice was in her room moving her bed from one side of the room to the other, unable to settle on a final arrangement. Daniel was in the kitchen with a new circular saw that he had bought to cut through the lock in the basement door. The doorbell chimed three times in different tones. Daniel turned around and walked out of the kitchen toward the front door.

"I guess that's the doorbell," he yelled to the ladies upstairs.

Nora poked her head out of their bedroom to see who it was. Alice continued working, uninterested. Daniel looked through the peephole in the door and saw a man in his mid-twenties standing on the porch. He opened the door.

"Hello, can I help you?" Daniel asked.

"Hey, uh, Mr. Hill?" Roy asked.

"Yeah, I'm Daniel Hill," he said stepping out onto the porch.

"Hi, Mr. Hill. I'm Roy Harris. I worked on the remodelin' contract for this here house."

"Oh, OK. You're one of Carmine's crew?"

"Yes, sir. Well . . . no. I mean, not anymore," Roy said uncomfortably.

Daniel could tell the man was trying to figure out what to say. He was trained to recognize precise emotional cues, and Roy was obviously agitated.

"Everything OK?"

Roy stopped fumbling and just came out with it.

"Mr. Hill, my old boss, Carmine, killed hisself in a motel down near Bluefield last week."

"Oh my God," Daniel said, letting the screen door shut behind him. "That's horrible."

"Yeah . . . yeah."

Roy just rubbed his scruffy chin and stared at the porch nervously.

"Does anyone know why he did it?" Daniel finally asked.

"We was down there on a roofin' job, and he just kept gettin' worse and worse."

"How do you mean?"

Nora opened the door behind them, and Daniel turned to make room for her. Roy took a step back uncomfortably.

"Howdy, ma'am," Roy said.

"What's going on?" Nora asked Daniel after eyeballing Roy.

"Carmine, the man I contracted to work on the house apparently committed suicide," Daniel explained.

"Oh, that's terrible," Nora said as Roy nodded.

"Yes, ma'am," Roy agreed. "I was just about to tell your husband that the reason I came here today was on behalf of the parent company over top of Carmine's business. I know that our contract on your house included a twenty-year warranty, and I wanted to make sure that you knew that the job was still insured."

Roy withdrew a business card from his jeans pocket and

handed it to Daniel. Daniel looked down at the cream-colored card with green lettering that spelled "Armor Home Warranty" with additional contact information.

"If you have any problems, contact them and they'll take care of it," Roy said.

Daniel looked back up at Roy.

"I appreciate that, Roy, but you didn't have to come all the way out here just for that."

"Well, I recently took a job with them, so technically I did," he grinned.

"Oh, OK then. Congrats on the new job."

Roy shuffled his feet as he looked back down at the creaking porch. A warm breeze blew over them all.

"Was there something else?" Nora asked bluntly.

Daniel looked over his shoulder at her and then back at Roy.

"Yeah, I reckon there is," he answered. "Look I don't know if my boss just lost his marbles or what, but he was just scared silly from somethin' that happened here at your house."

"What happened?" Daniel asked.

"He said he went down in your basement and . . . got the creeps, I suppose," Roy began without making eye contact. "He said on the last day that we worked that he actually *saw* something hidin' behind your basement door lookin' out at him."

Roy finally looked up to gauge their reactions. Daniel and Nora were staring at him, obviously unsure of how to take in this information.

"What did he see?" Daniel asked.

"Some eyes, is what he said. I know it sounds crazy. It *is* crazy. He even told us that the old man that used to live here was some sort of an exorcist," Roy said.

"*Exorcist?*" Nora echoed with shock.

"Yeah, I don't know how much of that is true, but it sure did bother my boss," Roy continued. "The night Carmine killed hisself, he told me all about it. My co-worker, Mike, and me was noticin' that Carmine's behavior was gettin' weirder and weirder. He damn near knocked Mike off the roof of an apartment building on accident, but I caught him at the last second. But last night, he got plum drunk, went in his motel room, and gouged his eyes out with a liquor bottle."

Nora gasped and covered her mouth. Daniel turned to her and put his hand on her shoulder.

"That is just so awful," Daniel said. "How are you holding up?"

"I ain't never seen nothing like that in my life, mister. Never want to think about it again. But I wanted to tell you about it. I didn't know how or the appropriate way to go about it until I took this new job and they made me come out here."

"Why did you feel like you had to tell us about Carmine?" Daniel asked, already knowing the answer.

Roy looked him dead in the eyes.

"I had to tell ya just in case there's a one percent chance that my boss wasn't crazy," he said. "I reckon I felt like I had to warn ya about the basement . . . just in case. I personally don't believe in any of that ghost-type shit—pardon my language—but I felt like I had to pass on the message."

"Did you tell him about the cross?" Nora asked Daniel.

"Hadn't gotten to that, yet. Thanks, honey," Daniel replied with a sarcastic tone that was only detectible to her.

"Cross . . . ?" Roy asked.

"Yeah, when we first got here, we noticed that someone had taken the liberty of nailing our basement door shut, and it just so happened to be in the shape of a cross," Daniel explained.

Roy's eyes widened.

"I think we can safely identify the one responsible for that now, can't we?" Daniel said to Roy.

"Reckon you can. If you want me to fix that for ya, I can do it right now."

"That won't be necessary," Daniel said. "I picked up some new tools that I needed anyway, and I was just about to take care of it myself."

"I'm sure my new company would reimburse ya for the expenses."

Daniel waved it off.

"Roy, I want to thank you for personally coming by to give me the card and relaying the information about Carmine. I truly am sorry about what happened to your boss. It sounds like he had some underlying issues that required professional help. I wish someone could've helped him out before all this happened."

"Yes, sir. Me too," Roy replied as he awkwardly backed away from the porch. "Y'all have a nice day now and just reach out if ya need anything."

"Thank you," Nora said. "Drive safely."

Roy nodded to her and turned to walk toward his new company truck as Daniel and Nora went back inside.

"That was bizarre," she said before shutting the front door behind them.

"Yeah," Daniel began, not sure what to make of the situation. "Can you imagine the sheer will it must take to jab shards of glass in . . . "

"Stop, I don't want to imagine that again."

"Sorry," he said, giving her a hug. "Hey, want to watch me saw my way into the basement?"

"I'll pass. Yell up to me when you get the door open."

Nora broke the embrace and walked back upstairs.

"What's wrong? Is the image of me with a power tool too much manliness for your quivering loins to endure?" Daniel taunted up the stairs.

"Eww, Dad," Alice said walking out of her bedroom at precisely the wrong time. Daniel's face reddened, and he abruptly turned toward the kitchen.

"That's your father for you," Nora said over her shoulder as she entered her bedroom.

Alice walked down the stairs and opened the front door.
"Where are you off to?" Daniel asked from the kitchen.
"I'm going to install the new porch swing."
"By yourself?"
"Yes, Dad. Girls can do things like that too."
"OK then, knock yourself out," Daniel said, impressed.
"I'll try to prevent my quivering loins from distracting me," she said as the screen door shut behind her.

"This is my life," Daniel muttered as he picked up the circular saw and approached the basement door.

His new pair of safety glasses that he almost forgot to wear were on the counter. After sliding them on, he felt much more prepared. He plugged in the orange extension cord and then connected it to the saw. He flicked the power switch, and the blade loudly spun to life. He shut it back off.

"Good God, that's loud," he said to himself as he examined the tool like it was a piece of extraterrestrial technology.

"Did you cut your finger off already?" Nora yelled from the bedroom.

"How about I cut a hole in the floor under your side of the bed . . . " he said before remembering that she was pregnant and immediately regretted his joke.

He got down on his knees and looked in the crack of the door, eying the bolt keeping it locked. Feeling confident, he turned the saw back on and carefully lowered the blade into the dark crevasse. Bright orange sparks started emitting as he felt a jerking resistance on the blade. The saw's sharp teeth loudly chewed through the dull metal. He applied more pressure as the blinding shower increased. Just then, the sparks stopped and he almost dropped the saw. The basement door popped free, and he knew that he had cut completely through. He placed the saw on the floor out of the way and stood up.

"Hey, honey. I did it!" he yelled up to Nora.

He could hear her moving around in the bedroom and then walking down the stairs. She entered the kitchen.

"Well, that was easy enough," she said as she looked around the room to make sure that Daniel hadn't accidently sawed the wall in half.

He grabbed the loose basement door and pulled it open revealing a set of wooden stairs descending into darkness. He turned to her.

"Ready to go check out our haunted basement?"

"Should I get a flashlight?" Nora asked.

Daniel looked in the open doorway and saw the light switch on the wall to the left. He turned it on, and a series of yellow light bulbs flickered to a steady glow.

"Our ghosts aren't Amish, honey."

She couldn't have rolled her eyes any harder if she tried.

"You walk down those stairs first. If you don't break your neck, then the baby and I will follow you."

"Good idea," he agreed and took a step into the basement.

The wave of warm air wafted in his face.

"My God, it's dank down here."

He continued taking slow steps down the stairs.

"I don't remember it being this humid the last time I came down here."

"Aren't basements supposed to be colder?" Nora asked, poking her head in the basement door.

"Yeah, something's not right here."

"Great, we bought a money pit," she sighed.

Daniel shook his head without reply, unaffected by Nora's tendency to always dwell on what could go wrong. The steps creaked under his weight as he moved downward. When he reached the concrete floor, he turned back to his wife.

"I think you're good," he said, and she followed him down.

He extended his hand when she neared the final step, and she took it, stepping onto the solid ground beside him. She looked around at her illuminated surroundings that were more akin to a cave than a basement, even an unfinished one.

"I'm pretty sure this was the cave Plato wrote about," she said, nodding her head.

"That's what the locals told me. I'm pretty sure Batman keeps a cowl or two in that corner as well when he's not in Gotham."

"I sure hope he's careful not to wake the bears that hibernate here," she replied, straight-faced.

Daniel broke and finally smiled. He kept hold of Nora's hand as they walked around the relatively large basement to investigate. The walls were thick wooden planks that looked like they were struggling to keep the heavy earth from caving in. The ceiling was a combination of running beams, pink insulation, sewage pipes, and ductwork. There were a few spots where light shone through from the kitchen above them. Scattered all over the floor were random pieces of wood and other construction materials, rolls of chain-link fencing and wire mesh, farming and gardening tools with which they were both unfamiliar, and three antique chests stacked on top of one another.

"What do you think are in those?" Nora asked, pointing to the chests.

"Let's find out," Daniel replied as he grabbed the top chest and heaved it off.

He had underestimated the weight and nearly dropped it but managed to keep control. Nora bent down, undid the latch, and opened it.

"Clothes," she said, flipping through a pile of ladies evening wear.

There were silk nightgowns, shawls, and pajamas.

"All women's clothes."

Daniel grabbed the second chest and sat it on the ground beside the third one. He opened both and lifted their lids.

"Winter clothes in this one," Nora said as she looked through chest number two.

"Looks like summer clothes over here," Daniel said looking through the remaining chest.

"Did the guy who lived here before have a wife?" Nora asked.

"I would assume so. I'd say she passed first and then he kept her belongings down here."

"So not only did our exorcist burn to death in our bedroom, but his wife probably died somewhere in the house too," she said nodding her head in understatement.

"It could've easily been the basement . . . " he said as he widened his eyes in heightened terror. "She could even be the ghost that scared poor Carmine to his untimely doom."

He reached down and picked up a white, silk undershirt and dangled it toward his wife.

"Her haunted linens are coming for you."

"All right, I'm done," Nora said as she turned away from Daniel unamused and approached the stairs.

He chuckled to himself as he dropped the clothes back into the chest. Something shiny caught Nora's eye in the darkness under the stairs. She stopped and peered at it.

"Daniel, what is that?" she asked as she pointed toward the object that looked like a metallic snake.

He looked at her and then at the area to which she was pointing. He saw the glimmering thing and walked over to it. He crouched down and stared.

"What is it?" she asked impatiently.

Daniel reached under the stairs and gave it a poke. The dangling chain made a jangling sound.

"It's a metal chain," he replied.

The light bulb was slightly illuminating the chain in front of him.

"That is creepy as shit," Nora admitted. "Why would there be a chain hanging on the wall?"

"Because we have apparently bought Edgar Allan Poe's summer retreat."

She looked at her husband with a smile and noticed

something else odd in the basement. Behind Daniel, where the three chests were previously stacked, was a small wooden door about four feet tall and three feet wide.

"What does that lead to?" she asked.

Daniel turned around and saw the door.

"Well hot damn," he said.

He grabbed the small doorknob, gave it a twist, and pulled, but it wouldn't budge. There didn't appear to be any lock on it.

"The wood may have swelled," he pontificated as he looked at the area surround the door and then to the ceiling. "There can't be hardly any room in there. We're practically at the edge of the house."

"So we have a secret room in our basement?" Nora asked.

"Looks like it." He turned around to face her. "I wouldn't get your hopes up. There can't be much room in there. No buried treasure."

Daniel crossed the basement and caressed the chain on the wall as he walked. A shimmering ripple flowed across the hanging loop.

"I can move this to our bedroom if you like?" he offered. "I'm sure we could find a use for it."

Nora sighed and walked up the stairs above Daniel's head.

"I am trying to not kill you, Daniel, but it gets harder every day," she said as she stepped out of the basement and into the kitchen.

Daniel smiled to himself as he continued to wonder about the chain. He realized now how eerily quiet it was in the basement all alone. His fleeting humor made room for concerned thoughts. He quickly stood up and looked behind him, just to make sure that he was still alone. Satisfied, he turned to go upstairs but stopped a few feet from the first step. The hidden door in the corner of the room caught his eye. He suddenly felt hot and sweaty, but he could not break his gaze from the small door that was stuck shut. His heart began beating faster and louder. The door held his focus as everything else in the world faded away. The smell of rotten eggs broke him from the trance. He looked away from the door, feeling faint and confused.

"What the hell was that?"

He took a deep breath and wiped the moisture from his brow. Wasting no more time, he hurried up the stairs and shut the door behind him.

CHAPTER 6

L ATER THAT EVENING, Alice was reclined in their newly installed porch swing. She swung back and forth in the setting sun, listening to music in her headphones. Her eyes were closed, and her legs dangled off one end. She was in a relaxed state bordering on sleep when she felt small vibrations that disturbed her serenity.

She opened her eyes and saw a tall young man standing at the front of her porch. The sun was setting over the hills behind him which gave his silhouette a glowing aura. Alice shielded her eyes from the rays, and she sat up in the swing. For the first time, she got a good look at him, and that instant infatuation only a teenager could muster rushed over her.

He wore tight jeans and a white T-shirt. He was skinny but muscular in the way one gets from manual labor. His dark hair hung over his ears and accentuated his eyes. When he smiled at her, she temporarily forgot how to breathe. He waved and said something, but she couldn't hear his voice. She squinted in confusion and shook her head but then realized that she was still wearing her headphones. Red-faced, she took them off her ears.

"I said that I'm sorry to disturb you. My name is Luke." He smiled again, and Alice felt her heart flutter.

"I'm Alice," she finally said.

"Hi, Alice. It's very nice to meet you."

"You're welcome," she said and instant mortification set in.

He contained his laughter.

"I mean, it's nice to meet you too."

She could feel her cheeks flushing in that annoying way that they did.

"Did you just move in?"

"Yes, from Ohio."

"Ohio, wow. Do you like it here so far?" he said as he stepped up onto the porch.

"It's very beautiful. We haven't left the farm much since we got here. Just busy moving in and fixing things up."

"That's kind of why I stopped by, actually," he said. "I used to mow Old Man Merle's grass and help clear the land for him." He could tell that she had no idea who he was talking about. "The guy that lived here before you."

"Oh, OK," she said. "Were you wanting to still do that or something?"

"I was hoping to at least ask. Mowing lawns is a good way to bank some cash over the summer. Plus, having someone to mow the grass on big farms like this one frees up whoever lives here to do other jobs. Old Man Merle liked to tend to his goats and chickens a bunch. Wonder what happened to them?"

"I wouldn't know," Alice began. "My dad hasn't said anything about farm animals. I know he's just planning on fixing up the house and land and trying to flip it."

"Cool, cool," Luke said as he brushed the hair out of his face behind his ear.

He looked up and caught her staring at him. She quickly looked down at the porch.

"How old are you, Alice?"

"I'll be sixteen in August."

"I just turned seventeen. Looks like we'll be going to school together in the fall."

She smiled and nodded.

The front door opened, and Nora stepped out onto the

porch. Luke took a step back from Alice and smiled at whom he presumed was Alice's mother.

"Hello," Nora said, unsure of what to make of the strange boy on the porch with her daughter.

"Hello, ma'am. My name is Luke Simmons." He extended his hand.

Nora shook it.

"Nice to meet you, Luke. I'm Nora Hill, Alice's mom."

"Yes, I just met Alice. She said you all moved from Ohio?"

Nora nodded her head.

"Sure did. Do you live nearby, Luke?"

"Yes, ma'am. About a mile down the road. I was out walking just now and saw y'all's cars in the driveway and wanted to speak with you."

"That right? What can I help you with?" Nora asked.

"Luke wants to mow our grass, mom," Alice said, still sitting on the swing.

"That's right," Luke concurred. "Plus, anything else you may need. I was just telling Alice that I used to work for Merle Blatty, the man who used to live here. I would mow his grass and clear the land, help with fencing, anything he needed, really."

"Oh, well, I think you should definitely speak with my husband. We both have a lot on our plates at the moment, and I'm not much help when it comes to heavy lifting," Nora said as she rubbed her pregnant belly.

"I'd love to speak with him," Luke smiled.

"Just a second," Nora said as she poked her head back in the house. "Daniel!"

"Yeah?" he called back from upstairs.

"Come out on the porch!"

Daniel came walking down the stairs carrying a paintbrush, his sleeveless T-shirt covered in flecks of paint.

"What is it?" he called from the stairs.

"Can you just come out on the porch? Someone wants to speak with you."

Daniel walked outside and saw Luke standing there with his friendly smile.

"Hello, sir," Luke said.

"Hello, young man," Daniel replied. "What can I do for you?"

Before Luke could speak, Nora answered for him.

"Luke's going to be mowing our grass this summer," she said as she winked at Alice on the swing. "And anything else that you need help with on the property."

Daniel looked at Alice and Nora and then back at Luke.

"OK," he said, knowing that his approval was not sought or needed. "Hi, Luke. I'm Daniel Hill."

Daniel shook Luke's hand.

"Nice to meet you, sir." Luke pulled his hand back, and Daniel saw that it was covered in beige paint.

"Ah, shit, Luke. I got paint all over you," Daniel said.

"*Daniel*," Nora scolded in reference to his language.

Luke looked down at his hand.

"Don't worry about that," he smiled as he wiped it on his jeans.

Daniel noticed a spider web tattoo on the back of the boy's hand.

"Interesting tattoo you have there. How old are you, kid?"

"He's seventeen, Dad," Alice said, wanting her father to go back inside before he became even more embarrassing.

Daniel looked over at Alice and then back at Luke.

"Seventeen, huh? Stevie Nicks over there is on the edge of seventeen herself."

"Oh, I thought she said she was about to turn sixteen," Luke said.

"*Sixteen*, yeah that's right," Daniel said looking over at Alice with a smile. He patted Luke on the shoulder and said, "You're helping me out already. I'll tell you what, whatever deal you had with Mr. Blatty, I'll honor it."

"That'd be great Mr. Hill! I'll keep this place looking

good for you. You won't regret it," Luke said, brushing the hair out of his face and extending his hand again to seal the deal with a shake.

Daniel gripped his hand and looked him dead in the eye.

"I know I won't, Luke," he said as he squeezed the bones in Luke's hand.

Luke held back from flinching but felt the warning loud and clear. Daniel released his hand and turned to walk back in the house.

"I've got to finish painting. Feel free to come by and start mowing whenever you're ready."

"Yes, sir."

"Call me Daniel," he said as he ascended the stairs.

"Thank you for coming by, Luke," Nora said.

"Thank you. It was nice to meet you both," Luke said as he stepped off the porch.

"Goodbye," Nora said with a smile.

She looked over at Alice who was watching Luke walk away. "Can you help me start making dinner, honey?"

"Sure, Mom."

Nora walked inside and into the kitchen. Alice looked back at Luke who was now near the end of their driveway.

"See you later!"

He turned back, smiled, and waved with his tattooed hand.

Later that night, Nora was lying in bed staring at the ceiling fan. Daniel was sound asleep beside her and had been since 11 PM. She looked over at the digital clock under the TV and saw that it was 3:10 AM. Her head dropped back onto her pillow, and she felt the cool moisture on the back of her neck from sweat. She wiped her forehead and sighed with frustration.

Their brand new air-conditioning system was not doing

the job. On top of the muggy atmosphere on the second floor, she had not been sleeping well overall since they moved in. The bedroom was big, and at night it looked like a cave that she couldn't see all the way through. She couldn't get used to the layout yet because they kept unpacking or moving things around. She didn't like opening her eyes in the darkness and seeing unfamiliar shapes. A stack of boxes at the foot of the bed or a tall lamp standing in the corner of the room might momentarily trick her eyes into seeing something that wasn't really there. There were also the sounds that come with a new house. The creaking wood, the way the wind blew against the building, the porch swing, the ambiance of living in rural WV—the crickets, the owls, the tree frogs—all of it contributed to the auditory stimulation that did not help her fall or stay asleep.

And those were just the physical aspects of her insomnia.

At night, her guilt came out to play. As soon as Daniel would drift off to sleep (which was normally only a few minutes after he laid his head down) and Nora realized that she was the only one in the house still awake, her mind would replay events from the past. After living with a psychologist for so long, she knew what was going on in her head. By revisiting mistakes, she was subconsciously controlling the situation. She was able to change decisions made and alter the outcomes. But, sometimes, she just relived the memory, no matter how shameful it made her feel afterward.

As she stared at the slowly spinning blades of the ceiling fan, she thought of the miniature oscillating fan on Steve Clemmons's desk back in Ohio. She was right there in his office again on the day that it happened, staring at the metal desk sign that said, "Assistant Principal."

Their relationship was professional at first, and she was even a bit intimidated by him. He was tall, young, and broad-shouldered. She was tall herself but felt completely overpowered when he stood in front of her looking down. He always dressed in a sharp suit that fit his form. It started at first with him dropping by her room after school ended to see how she was doing. They would discuss work, naturally, but then she'd start venting about her family, or he'd romanticize his life as a bachelor.

One day when they were alone in her classroom, he put the ball in her corner. She had just admitted to going weeks without affection from her husband, and Steve said that he would gladly fill that role if she wanted. All she had to do was come by his office after school. Less than a week later, she was bent over his big wooden desk.

As soon as it was over, she felt a level of disgust and regret unparalleled to anything she had experienced in her life up to that moment. Sensory details from the minutes immediately following the act were forever seared into her memory: her hands pressed against the hard and flat desk; the massive desktop calendar filled with scribblings of various meetings and appointments; the slow-motion sound of Steve zipping up his pants behind her; the way his miniature fan on the corner of his desk spun back and forth like it was denying something; the sound of him peeling off the condom and dropping it in his small wastebasket.

She stood up and walked out of the office without saying anything. He had called her name as he struggled to tuck his shirt back in and buckle his belt, but she fled. In the weeks following the incident, she had heard rumors that Steve Clemmons had slept with coworkers in the past, but as far as she knew, her adultery had gone unnoticed. She continued working at the school and treating Steve in only a professional manner but always felt uncomfortable.

Daniel never found out, which only made her guilt that much more unbearable. Every good thing he did for her was magnified in her brain to make her feel even worse. Nothing he had done pushed her away. She had chosen to fulfill a desire outside of their marriage instead of putting in the effort at home. She knew she had messed up but decided to only be honest about it if Daniel found out. In her mind, it was unethical to unburden herself through confession if the knowledge would crush the man she still loved. She would table her sin and make amends through action.

Their love life quickly improved, and their marriage felt fresher than ever. Most days, she didn't even think about what she had done. She could convince herself that they were happy, and Steve Clemmons was nothing but a speed bump on her lifelong journey. As long as she was distracted, she was OK.

Perhaps the biggest distraction came in the form of a positive pregnancy test months after her affair. It wasn't possible for the child to belong to anyone but Daniel. The shock of being pregnant was intensified by the fact that she was thirty-five-years-old and already had a fifteen-year-old daughter. Initial doubts crept in as soon as her doctor confirmed what she already knew to be true. She thought briefly of driving to the nearest clinic and never telling Daniel about it, but knew she couldn't successfully live with two dark secrets. No, she accepted her situation, told Daniel about the baby, and after brief shock and disbelief, they rejoiced.

It was only months after that Daniel had sprung the idea on her about flipping the farm. She was skeptical and less than thrilled about the business venture, especially being pregnant, but she felt like she owed him. For the first time in her life, she felt like events were lining up beyond her control or comprehension. She had gotten pregnant, Daniel had put together this farm deal, and they suddenly had the opportunity for a new beginning. She convinced herself that this was what she really wanted.

Now, having moved a state away from the act, she thought she would feel better, and, for the most part, she did. It was only in these late nights, this time of isolation where every fleeting thought was amplified, that she had to watch her transgressions again and again like a film projector on an endless loop. She didn't know how much longer she could keep up the façade. Something had to give because the lack of rest was only accelerating her agitation during the day.

Daniel stirred in his sleep, and she was sucked out of the dark tunnel of her memories in a split second. She looked over at his bare back as he breathed in and out. She extended her arm and carefully placed her hand on his shoulder. He twitched but did not wake. She didn't know she was crying until a tear ran down her cheek and dampened the pillow. She rolled over on her side and draped her arm around her husband.

"I'm sorry," she whispered as he slept.

CHAPTER 7

I T WAS A little after 9 AM on Monday morning. Daniel sat in the living room with the cordless phone checking his messages from work. Nora was in the kitchen making breakfast and listening to the radio. Alice was still asleep upstairs. None of his patients had any pressing issues that needed to disrupt him from his vacation, so he tossed the phone on the couch and walked toward the smell of bacon. Nora smiled at him when he entered the kitchen.

"What's on your agenda today?" she asked.

"Breakfast. I might walk the property in a little bit and see if I can put together a list of jobs for our new pool boy."

"Luke?" Nora laughed.

Daniel smiled.

"I figure the busier I can keep him, the less time he has to put the moves on our daughter."

"Let the girl have some fun, Daniel. The more pressure you put on her now, the more she'll rebel."

Daniel looked at her curiously.

"I'm speaking from experience," Nora went on. "My dad was super strict during my teenage years, and I snuck out every chance I got. I didn't feel like I could ever confide in him without getting in trouble. You don't want to push Alice away."

"Maybe you should be the psychologist. I've always said you're a natural at it," he told her as he filled his coffee mug.

Nora stirred the eggs in the pan and then scooped them onto a plate with bacon and toast. She handed it to Daniel.

"I'm just saying that if she wants to date Luke, kill him with kindness. She'll know you care, and she'll trust you. Once you have that, you can prevent fires instead of putting them out."

Daniel smiled, genuinely impressed with her thought process.

"Speaking of putting out fires, you might want to move that paper towel."

She turned around and saw the paper towel that had fallen on the burner when she moved the eggs. It was blackening and starting to smoke.

"Shit," she said as she grabbed it and tossed it in the sink under running water.

"OK, Lady Macbeth, I'll play nice," he said as he took a big bite of toast. "I defer all plans of action regarding the teenage female to your judgment."

He took a bite of his eggs.

"Mmm, these are good. Thank you, honey."

"You're welcome," she said as she sat down beside him with her own plate.

"What are you going to do today?"

"I was thinking of taking Alice shopping. A little girl time, you know?"

"I think that's a great idea. Get a little retail therapy," he said, adding some pepper to his food. "You know what else I was thinking of doing?"

"What's that?" she said with a bite of bacon.

"Start cleaning out that basement. Might even explore the secret room down there," Daniel said motioning to the basement door behind Nora.

"I'll lend you moral support from afar."

"I don't want you down there anyway. Might be fumes or something."

Nora looked at Daniel with concern.

"I mean, I doubt there are. Just being safe is all."

"Mhmm," Nora groaned. "Money pit."

The doorbell chimed its trademark three tones.

"You expecting anyone?" he asked with a mouthful of eggs.

Nora shook her head as Daniel got up and walked to the front door. He looked through the peephole.

"It's the pool boy."

Luke jumped a little when Daniel jerked open the front door.

"Morning, Luke."

"Hi, Mr. Hill."

"Daniel."

"Hi, Daniel."

"You here to work?"

"Yes, sir. I drove my mower over."

Daniel looked down the gravel driveway at the impressive riding lawnmower Luke had.

"Wow, is that yours?"

"It's my dad's. He lets me use it as long as I throw him a piece of my earnings."

"Smart man."

Alice, woken by the doorbell, came scampering down the stairs. She stopped midway when she saw Luke and realized that she hadn't even brushed the sleep out of her eyes. Luke saw her, and she knew that it was too late to flee.

"Good morning, Alice," Luke said, looking over Daniel's shoulder.

She gave a half-grin and an awkward little wave.

"Oh, I'm sorry for waking you. I didn't even think about you all still being asleep. I suppose we keep early hours in the country."

"It's OK," Alice said from the stairs.

"Yeah, don't worry about it," Daniel said. "She needed to get up anyway. Say, are you hungry? We have some breakfast in here if you want something."

"No, thank you. This is an all-day job. I want to get a good jump on it if you don't mind."

"By all means. I might meet you outside here in a bit. I

was planning on taking a stroll through the land to see what else I could use you for."

"Sounds good, sir, uh, I mean, Daniel," Luke said as he walked down off the porch and awkwardly headed toward his lawnmower.

Daniel stood in the open doorway with his coffee and watched the boy. He admired a strong work ethic. He turned around to face his daughter on the stairs.

"Seems like a nice young fella," Daniel said with an intentionally obnoxious sip of coffee.

"Yeah, he does," Alice said with a smile as she turned to go back to her room.

"Happy fuckin' day," Daniel muttered to himself as he strolled back into the kitchen.

Nora and Alice went to the mall a few hours later for some shopping and lunch. Daniel had been in the basement since they left going through all of Merle's old possessions. Most of what he found was junk. He was hoping to at least find some salvageable tools or something that would prove useful for the farm life, but it was either trash or sentimental items belonging to the former inhabitant.

He had accumulated a neat row of loaded trash bags against the wall by the stairs, each filled to the max with a lifetime's worth of clutter. After he emptied the chests with the clothes, he examined the containers to see if they were worth keeping, but they were coming apart with rot. He stacked the empty cases neatly on top of one another by the trash pile. The single piece of treasure that he did find was a large wooden push broom that was tucked away under the stairs by the chain. Once he carried all the trash upstairs and to the end of the driveway, he went back to the basement and swept up the debris.

He used his shirt to wipe the sweat from his brow. It

dawned on him that it wasn't nearly as humid in here as it was the other day when he and Nora had come down. The sweat he was dealing with now he had earned from humping heavy loads up and down the stairs.

He looked around to gauge his progress. The room was now completely empty except for him, his broom, and that big ass chain under the stairs that he pretended wasn't even there. It gave him the willies, but he didn't know why. Old Man Merle had probably just used it to haul stuff around the land. Still, it made him uneasy.

Satisfied with what he had accomplished so far, he leaned the broom in the corner opposite the stairs and turned around to leave. Just as he was halfway up the stairs, he heard the broom topple to the ground with a loud clang. His nerves startled in that way that kicked in the fight or flight response. He lowered his head to look into the basement and saw the broom on the floor. He sighed and walked back down to get it.

After picking the broom up and putting it back in its place, he realized that he had forgotten about the other half of his basement job for the day: exploring the secret room. He looked at the bottom of the corner where the broom was resting and saw the small door. He moved the broom and crouched down to get a good look.

Daniel grabbed the doorknob and tried to pull it open, but, again, it didn't budge. He noticed that the top of the wooden door had swelled and was catching on the frame. Gripping the knob with two hands, he jerked and leaned back to use his body weight. It opened, and he tumbled backward, landing on the broom handle.

The small open doorway revealed nothing but cobwebs and darkness. A breath of dust particles blew through the atmosphere as if the secret room awakened with a yawn. Daniel crawled back over to it and peered in. It was too dark. He couldn't see a foot in front of him, let alone make out the dimensions of the room.

"I'm going to need a flashlight," he mumbled. He got up, bolted up the stairs toward the kitchen, grabbed his flashlight from under the kitchen sink, and giddily sped back into the basement. He slid across the floor like he was stealing third base and turned on the flashlight. He poked it into the darkness.

"Holy Christ."

The walls of the small secret room were made of cinder blocks, the ceiling was made of rows of wooden planks, and the floor was dirt. He shone the light from one end of the room to the other. Cobwebs adorned every corner like a long abandoned Gothic manor. In the center of the room was what looked like a cube of bricks, and in the corner was another one of Merle's antique chests.

Daniel crawled through the open doorway and was hit by a pungent wave of humidity. The thick air coated the back of his throat, forcing out a cough. Whatever was causing the odd heat waves in the basement was coming from this room.

He pointed the light first at the brick construction; they were arranged in a square shape five bricks long, five wide, and five tall, making a fence with something in the middle. He saw a piece of plywood lying on the floor, perfectly fitting inside the bricks. On top of the plywood lay a silver cross about six inches long and three inches wide.

"What the . . . ?"

Daniel slowly backed up and away from the shiny object and felt something graze the top of his head. He let out a shriek as he jumped back and pointed the light at whatever had just touched him. He saw it and immediately felt like a giant pussy.

Dangling from the wooden ceiling directly above the bricks was a rosary made of black beads and a black cross. He inched closer and examined the object with the flashlight. It was a pretty piece of jewelry and appeared old. He looked back down at the silver cross on the plywood. In each corner of the wood were large metal bolts the size of railroad spikes that pinned the wood to the ground. Daniel sighed as he realized that he'd have to crawl back out of the room and go upstairs to get another tool. He crab-walked out holding the flashlight under his chin.

A few minutes later he was back with a crowbar. He chucked the heavy piece of steel through the little doorway, and it thudded into the earthly floor. He crawled in after it with his flashlight in tow. After carefully placing the light on the top of the brick wall so that the beam shone down on the plywood, he picked up the crowbar.

Just before he slid it under the wood, he noticed the shiny cross still lying freely. He picked it up and examined it. It was lighter than it looked, and Daniel realized that it could be made out of solid silver. He carefully placed it on top of the dirt beside him.

The tip of the crowbar did not want to go under the wood, but Daniel persisted. He angled it back and forth as he gradually wedged it underneath. As soon as he shoved enough of it in, he pushed the opposite side down and jarred loose one of the corner bolts a half an inch. It was much harder than he anticipated. Whatever these bolts were beaten into was not earth. Judging by the friction against the crowbar, he guessed that it was concrete. He moved the wedge closer to the bolt and repeated the action until it was completely out.

The newly exposed crack under the wood released a waft of heat. Daniel recoiled at the putrid smell and temperature of the air. He leaned back and extended his hand over the opening and felt that it had passed. Convinced that it was just a pocket of hot air, he resumed his job and worked feverishly to remove the remaining three bolts.

After ten minutes, the last bolt came out. He tossed the crowbar to his side and grabbed the piece of wood. He gripped the edges and gently lifted it off the ground and placed it on top of the crowbar. There, encased in a fortress of brick and now freely exposed, was an open well. *What the hell is a well doing down here?*

Daniel picked up the flashlight and explored his discovery. Although there was nothing but dirt for flooring everywhere else in the room, inside the brick construction it was concrete with a perfectly round hole in the middle that was nearly three feet wide. He pointed the light down into the well but could only see the cement edges running straight down into the earth.

"Hello," he said as his voice echoed back to him.

He picked up one of the loose bolts and held it directly above the well's opening. After making sure he was perfectly centered, he released it into the abyss and carefully listened. The bolt dinged several times off the sides for what seemed like an eternity, but then there was a faint splash.

"Good God, this thing's deep," he said as he relaxed back into a sitting position and thought about what he had just found.

Daniel wondered why this room existed, why the well was so securely closed off, and most of all, why the crucifix and rosary were purposefully placed where they were. The more he thought about the separate elements of the equation, the more concerned he became by the solution: someone had gone to great lengths to keep this part of the house sealed off and they obviously felt that they needed God's help to do it. Although he didn't believe in the supernatural, deep down in the dark recesses of this basement his wondering mind was getting the best of his rationality.

Daniel looked up at the dangling rosary swaying ever so slightly over the open well. In one violent invisible jerk, the beads ripped off the ceiling and disappeared into the hole beneath. Daniel leapt backward and banged his head against the doorframe. He felt the air thicken like some unseen liquid was filling up the room. That putrid smell came back and stayed this time.

He looked at the untouched antique case across the room and knew that exploring that could wait for another day. Right now, he just needed to get the hell out of this basement. He grabbed the piece of wood and re-covered the well, picked up his flashlight and crowbar, and clumsily shuffled out of the opening. He shut the door behind him and hurried upstairs.

CHAPTER 8

L UKE HAD BEEN mowing grass for a few hours by the time Daniel finally caught up with him. Daniel was impressed by the boy's job so far. There was a wooden fence that ran along the property line that separated freshly cut grass from a robust forest. Luke was currently weed-eating underneath the fence, wearing protective sunglasses and listening to music on his Walkman while he worked. He didn't hear Daniel approaching, hollering his name. Daniel extended his arm into Luke's line of vision and waved. Luke smiled and cut off the weed-eater. He motioned for Luke to remove his headphones to chat, and Luke obliged.

"Doing a heck of a job so far," Daniel said.

"Thanks. I'm sure tryin'."

"How much longer do you think it'll take?"

"Oh, I only have the western plot over there to mow, and then I was gonna finish weed-eatin' along the fence. Probably an hour at the most, I'd say."

"Wow. It would've taken me double that. I'm glad to have you."

"My pleasure," Luke said with a smile as he wiped away the steady glaze of sweat.

"Hey, speaking of the fence, I noticed that there are quite a few spots that need replacing or repair. I'd also like to paint it white. Do you think you'd be up for that?"

"Absolutely. I'll take all the work I can get!"

"Great. When would you want to start?"

"I can do it as soon as I finish mowin'," Luke said as if it was obvious.

"Good God, son. You're a workhorse," Daniel laughed. "I tell you what, when you finish mowing, come back to the house and I'll give you some money to run in town to get lumber and paint. You can start whenever you want. Does $200 for the whole job sound fair?"

"For sure!"

They shook hands.

"Good deal," Daniel said. "I'm going to keep exploring this way. Who knows? Might find some bubblin' crude in this here holler."

Luke smiled but clearly didn't get Daniel's outdated reference.

"OK then," Daniel said and continued on his path.

Luke cranked up his tunes and started up the weed-eater again.

It took Daniel longer than he expected to scope out the rest of his land. He found a small area where Merle had kept some animals. He suspected chickens, judging by the small wire fencing and lingering smell. When he looked inside the coop, he discovered a pile of small bones cleaned of all their meat. *Something had its way with the chickens*, he realized.

"I hope we don't have coyotes around here."

There was another area near the chicken coop that also looked like it had once housed animals. A taller, wire fence enclosed it, and the land inside looked heavily traversed. Daniel remembered hearing something about the old man having goats.

He took a nice leisurely stroll through the open meadow admiring the scenery. The sun's rays warmed his skin, but just when it got to the point where it became too hot, a nice breeze would swing by to cool him down. He had lost count of how many rabbits he'd seen scurrying along the fence during his walk.

He thought that this was something he could easily get

used to but let that thought pass right through his head; he knew where Nora and Alice stood on the issue. It was obvious that Nora was only willing to temporarily stay. She wasn't even the one who brought up the fact that it was a two-bedroom house. Daniel pointed out that they wouldn't have a room for the baby. Nora brushed it off like it wasn't a big deal and said that the baby would be sleeping in their room for the first few months before they gave her a nursery at the new house that they'd purchase.

Daniel couldn't help but think of how perfectly in place everything had to be when Alice was born. He remembered how careful Nora was with her diet while she was pregnant; how she listened to classical music while Alice was in the womb; how the nursery had to be just right for her new baby girl. To go from that to letting the baby temporarily crash in their room was quite the difference.

Daniel brushed it off as the usual cycle of how the experience with the first-born child is majestic and unknown, and then it just becomes more routine with each successive child. He had counseled enough parents of multiple children to know that each child was raised differently, but that didn't mean they were loved any less.

No, there was no way that Nora wasn't completely ecstatic about this child. There was no way. She's a seasoned parent and pragmatic is all. That's all it is. In fact, this was all *his* idea, and she was going along with it. He had to remind himself of that. There was just no chance that the child was unwanted in any way. *None.*

Just as Daniel rounded a corner of imposing trees, the house came into view. He saw Nora's car in the driveway and knew they were back from the mall. He could faintly hear Luke's weed-eater running somewhere on the property behind him.

There was commotion on the porch. Daniel could see movement but was unsure of what was going on. He saw Nora and then Alice beside her. Nora appeared to be bent over while Alice was on her knees. There was something between them moving around. It was jumping and rubbing against them both, back and forth. Daniel put his hand to his brow to shield the sun and squinted.

A dog. Nora and Alice were petting a dog on his porch, and a big one at that.

"What the hell?" Daniel muttered and picked up the pace.

Nora rubbed the dog's back as it licked Alice on the face. Alice laughed and petted it behind its ears. They saw Daniel approaching the porch, tanned and sweaty.

"What is that?"

The big dog whipped its head around, and Daniel saw some gray on its mature snout. It bounded toward him.

"Woah, boy!" Daniel warned, but it just increased its speed. "Hey, stop!"

The dog came to a dead stop.

"Sit!" Daniel instructed.

The dog obeyed with military discipline.

"Wow," Nora said from the porch. "That's a well-trained dog."

Daniel studied the dog. It was a purebred bloodhound. Big, but malnourished.

"At least it knows who the alpha is around here," Daniel said, looking up to his gallery of eye-rollers.

He patted the dog on the head.

"At ease, boy."

The dog relaxed and let its tongue flop out as it caught its breath. Daniel grabbed its collar and looked at the dangling metal tag attached.

"The dog's name is Buck," Daniel said to his family. "And this is his home address."

"That's the old man's dog?" Alice asked.

"Looks like it."

"He was sniffing around the porch when we pulled up," Nora said. "I was nervous to get out of the car, but then he came and started licking the windows like a big baby."

"How you doing, Buck?" he asked the dog.

He could tell by the dog's eyes that it was exhausted.

"You want some food?"

The dog panted with approval.

"How has that dog survived for months out here by itself?" Nora wondered.

"A seasoned bloodhound like this would have no trouble getting by. Have you been busy eating chickens, Buck? Did you find a stream around here to drink from?" Daniel asked as the dog seemed to smile between floppy breaths.

Buck suddenly came to attention as he focused on something over Daniel's shoulder.

"What is it, buddy?" Daniel asked as he turned to look.

"Hey, it's Luke," Alice said as she stepped off the porch and waved at the boy riding the mower across the meadow.

Luke waved back as he drove forward. Buck lunged past Daniel, knocking him down on his back. The dog barreled across the yard with the speed of a racehorse.

"Jesus," Daniel said as he picked himself up off the grass.

He looked at Buck, who was now about twenty yards from Luke and closing in quickly. Luke saw the dog and shut off the mower. He jumped on top of the seat so the dog didn't have access to his dangling legs. Buck started barking ferociously at the mower, barking up at Luke like a cat in a tree.

"Buck, *no!*" Daniel shouted.

The dog looked over at his new master with hesitation.

"Get over here!"

Buck snarled once more at Luke and then retreated to the Hill family. Daniel grabbed the dog by the collar and held tightly. Luke still stood on the mower's seat, unsure of what to do.

"I got him. Come on over," Daniel shouted and waved the boy over. "What was *that* all about?" he asked turning to his wife.

"Buck doesn't like Luke," Nora replied.

"It was probably just the loud mower," Alice said.

"Could be," Nora agreed.

Daniel looked back at them skeptically and then to Luke, who was pulling up in their front yard. He shut off the mower's engine and carefully approached the family.

"Wow, that woke me up," Luke said with a nervous laugh.

"Sorry about that," Daniel said. "This dog appeared out of nowhere."

"Weird," Luke said. "I'm glad he likes you though."

"You recognize this dog, Luke?" Daniel asked.

"Is that Old Man Merle's dog?"

"That's what I'm asking you," Daniel replied.

Luke nervously studied the dog.

"I figured if it was, you'd know since you were out here so much."

"Yeah, that's him," Luke finally said. "That's Old Man Merle's dog."

"Buck," Daniel informed.

"Yeah, that's Buck. It took me a minute to recognize him."

"It took you a minute to recognize a pure bloodhound?"

Buck growled behind Daniel's leg.

"They say dogs can sense evil, you know?"

"Dad!" Alice interrupted, annoyed by the interrogation.

Daniel smiled.

"I'm sorry. He just looks different than the last time I saw him is all," Luke clarified.

Daniel nodded.

"Yeah, I imagine he's pretty malnourished after being left behind," Daniel said.

He turned to face his wife.

"Luke's going to head to the store and get some supplies to start repairing our fence, honey."

"Oh, that's very nice of him," Nora said. "Luke, I'm so sorry about the dog."

"It's really not a big deal. It looks like you guys got a good guard dog though."

"Yep," Daniel replied. "Better pick us up some dog food while you're out."

CHAPTER 9

THE DAY WAS OVER, and night descended on the farm. Luke had worked well into the evening. Daniel had to go out and tell him to go home before he would stop the job. He'd probably still be out there hammering away well into the night. The boy had fixed quite a few spots on the fence, not to mention his stellar lawn mowing job. This was the first time Daniel had seen the place in top form. He was pleased. After a late dinner and watching a new episode of *Home Improvement*, they all went to bed.

This was one of those rare nights when Nora conked out before Daniel. He had tried to go to sleep, but now that he was alone in the dark with his thoughts, he kept thinking about the rosary that was yanked into the well. He replayed the scene over and over until he temporarily convinced himself that he hadn't seen what he knew he had seen. There must've been a pocket of air that gusted up from the well and knocked the fragile beads off their hook. That's all it was. He was in the dark and didn't have a good view anyway. Anything could've happened. As soon as he accepted this reality, his mind was hijacked by the image of some invisible force gripping the rosary and jerking it until the string of beads exploded.

Daniel sat up in bed and looked at the clock. It was nearly 3 AM. He watched Nora snoozing away in a peaceful bliss. After she had complained about not getting enough sleep since the move to the farm, he was starting to worry about her and the baby. Her serene state right now gave him some relief. She was going through a lot, and that's how he convinced himself not to tell her about the strange experience that he had had in the basement.

He rubbed his temples in a feeble attempt to relax his thoughts. He just couldn't quit thinking about that one antique chest still in the secret room in the basement. He wondered what was inside it. If it was important enough to keep stored away like some dirty secret, then he wanted to know why.

There was a strange clicking sound coming from downstairs. Something was crawling across the hardwood floor. Daniel felt a brief chill until he heard their new dog loudly lapping water from its bowl. He knew that he was going to have to get used to Buck sharing residence with them now. He listened as the dog finished its midnight drink and slunk back to its bed of blankets.

Everyone was asleep, and they had a new guard dog: Daniel decided it was time to head back to the basement. He quietly maneuvered his legs to the side of the bed, slid on a pair of gym shorts and a T-shirt, and snuck out of the bedroom. As soon as he descended the creaking stairs and rounded the corner to the kitchen, he was staring at an open basement door.

Only a few hours ago he had closed it. He knew that he had. It was part of his nightly routine to walk the first floor turning off all the lights, shutting windows, and locking the door. He remembered turning off the light above the stove and specifically checking to make sure that the basement door was shut before heading upstairs for bed.

Now, it stood agape like an open mouth into an abyss.

Daniel felt his heart rate return to normal as he told himself that this was an old house that was still unfamiliar to him. The door could simply have a faulty latch. He could've damaged it when he sawed through the bolt the other day. Focusing on rational thoughts was much easier in the daytime.

He turned on the small light above the stove, giving him just enough light to feel comfortable. Without overthinking it, he stuck his hand into the darkness of the basement stairwell and felt for the light switch. His fingers felt all around the area of the wall where he knew it was, but he felt nothing. He took another step closer and moved his hand back and forth against the wall, covering as much area as he could.

"What the hell?"

A warm hand gripped his wrist and jerked him forward.

Daniel toppled down the wooden steps in a thunderous roll that seemed to last a lifetime. He saw nothing but darkness as he tumbled over and over like laundry in a washing machine. The hard wall at the base of the stairs stopped him abruptly; he fought to maintain consciousness.

His vision was blurry, but he was alive and awake. He had landed in a position where he was leaning against the wall staring up the stairs at the kitchen door. The stove light he had turned on was now off, leaving only faint moonlight in the kitchen. That abruptly disappeared as the door slammed shut. He now sat in complete darkness.

The sounds of his breathing and heartbeat were amplified by the dead silence surrounding him. He moved his arms and legs and realized that apart from an aching back and a throbbing knee, he was uninjured. He listened to see if his fall had awakened his family but heard nothing above him—not even the dog.

"Ahh, shit," he winced as he slowly tried to sit upright.

Something stirred in the dark corner near the little door. Daniel's eyes shot toward the sound hidden in the pitch blackness.

"Wouldn't do that if I were you," a grizzled voice whispered from the corner.

Daniel felt his blood run cold. He thought of speaking

but was paralyzed by fear. He listened to whomever was in the basement with him fumble around for something. A match struck, and the flame glowed in the darkness.

Daniel saw the illuminated face of a charred corpse in a pair of smoldering overalls leaning against the corner of the room. From what he saw in that brief flash of light, the corpse was an older man with globs of dead flesh hanging from his face like hot wax. There were patches of white hair on the parts of his scalp that hadn't been seared off. His skin had the texture of chewed-up steak. Both of his eyelids had melted shut.

The old man brought the flame to the tip of a tobacco pipe that was hanging out of his mouth. He sucked a few puffs. The burning tobacco glowed, which gave Daniel a better view.

"This isn't real," Daniel said.

The old man pulled the pipe from his mouth which eliminated the light source. His burned face again disappeared into the shadows.

"It's no more pleasant for me than it is for you. I can assure you that," the old man said.

Daniel could only see the floating cherry of the tobacco moving around in the old man's hand.

"I can still feel every burn. I do apologize for the unfriendly welcome. Didn't mean to cause such a tumble."

"I'm delirious. I'm hallucinating. I banged my head, and I'm not thinking clearly . . . "

"The name's Merle Blatty," the old man said as he brought the pipe back to his mouth for another toke. "And you're in my house."

Even though Merle's eyes were sealed shut, Daniel could feel him staring at him.

"But you're dead," Daniel said.

"You're a quick one, fella. What gave it away? My Laffy Taffy complexion or the fact that my clothes are still smoking?"

Daniel didn't know how to respond. He rubbed his eyes and looked back at Merle, but he was still there like a dying ember in the corner of the room.

"I don't have much time, son. It was hard enough for me to figure out how to cross that barrier in the first place. I need you to listen to me like ya never listened before."

Daniel instinctively nodded his head.

"Your entire family is in danger. Won't do ya no good to pack bags and kick rocks at this point. You're all already infected."

"*Infected?*"

"In a manner of speakin', yes."

He hit his pipe again, and Daniel could see the smoke seeping out of his ripped flesh like a macabre incense burner.

"I don't have time to tell ya my life's story right now, and I doubt you'd believe me anyhow. Lucky for you, I've left behind a box of just that."

Daniel listened to Merle as he pulled out another match and struck it. The flame's glow lit up the room. Merle bent down and used the burning match to illuminate the chest that was between his legs. Daniel realized that it was the same chest that was inside the secret room.

"I even crawled back in there and brung it out for ya," Merle said.

He dropped the match on the floor and smeared it with his foot. "Better ya don't go in this room anymore until ya know exactly what you're dealin' with," he said as he tapped the secret room's wall.

"You're giving me homework?"

"In a manner of speakin', yes."

Above them, something clicked and clacked its way across the kitchen floor. Buck could be heard sniffing the basement door and then emitting a low growl. Merle looked up in the direction of the sound.

"Take care of my old Buck up there. He's a good dog, and he'll help keep ya safe. Heed his warnings."

"Well, it sounds like he's not too thrilled that you're here right now, Merle," Daniel replied. "Maybe you're not really Merle at all. Seems odd that such a loyal dog would be growling at his former master."

Merle chuckled and then coughed on strands of throat.

"Now, you're usin' your noggin. Fact is, he ain't growlin' at me, son."

Daniel felt the thick humidity that was quickly filling up the room. It had that dank earthy smell like death spewing up from beneath him. Sweat started to bead all over his body as a third presence began to let itself be known in the room.

"Then what's he growling at, Merle?"

"You opened up the doorway, son. That's how I was able to get here. But I'm not the only one hangin' around these parts. Reckon it's time for me to go."

"Wait. What the hell is a well doing in our—your—basement anyway?"

"Drinkin' water. What else? Used to be a hand crank on the kitchen sink, but I broke it off when I realized what I done by diggin' that well."

"What do you mean by that?"

"There's no bottom to that well, son. The gateway was already there. All's I did by diggin' the well was take the lid off."

An orange light started to glow through the cracks in the little door like there was a bright, growing fire on the other side. Whatever the hidden light source was started to brighten the basement room where Merle and Daniel were. Daniel looked at the old man's shoes and could see that they were fuming smoke now.

"Ahh, shit. Not again," Merle said as he took one final puff from his pipe.

He winced as his shoes ignited into flames.

"This doesn't hurt any less the second time around. I can assure ya that."

Daniel coughed as the smoke filled up the room. He saw the flames run all the way up Merle's overalls and nip at the exposed flesh of his face.

"Listen now," Merle struggled to say. "Go through this chest. It's my life's work."

Merle coughed and slid down the wall to his bottom. The heat began to melt his already mangled face.

"Pick up where I left off."

He fell over on his side as the fire consumed his entire body. His flesh bubbled and popped until he was little more than a simmering skeleton. Somehow, he managed to say, "Finish this."

The doorknob turned easily. Something inside knocked the door off its hinges, sending it flying across the basement and exploding against the opposite wall. Daniel felt his guts turn to knots as he stared at the open doorway. He could see the well inside the secret room and the flames bellowing out of it.

A burnt arm jutted out of the opening and gripped the brick enclosure. Daniel jumped off the floor. He darted to the chest beside Merle's charred remains. He gripped it on both sides and heaved its heavy weight off the ground, nearly straining his lower back.

"Jesus Christ," he winced as he turned toward the stairs with the heavy payload.

He waddled as quickly as possible, fueled by pure adrenaline. Snarling sounds came from behind him, but he dared not look. He lifted one foot on the first step and tossed the chest on the steps in front of him. He ducked down and pushed the chest with his shoulder as he ascended the stairs. Something behind him slithered across the floor of the secret room.

He ignored the increasing orange glow in the room and the approaching sounds. He pushed harder until the chest touched the door leading to the kitchen. He looked up and saw his escape. Pinning the corner of the chest under his knee, he extended his arm until he touched the hot doorknob ahead of him. His fingertips twisted the brass and pushed the door open. With his last burst of energy, he used all his body weight to slide the chest over the last step and into the dark kitchen where Buck was holding his position, growling timidly.

Just as Daniel stood upright to make his escape, he felt the rickety stairs shake. He froze in disbelief. He listened as claws dug into the wall and then up to the ceiling, slowly creeping toward him. His mind told him to run, but he couldn't get his limbs to move. The burning entity now hung motionless above him. Drool dripped on his right ear and oozed down the side of his neck.

The sulfuric stench of rotten eggs finally snapped him out of shock. He flung his body across the open threshold. Just before hitting the floor, a clawed hand swiped at his back, removing strips of shirt and flesh. The fall knocked the breath out of him, but he managed to flip over in time to see the bloody, clenched fist protruding out of the basement. Moonlight shone on the steaming, blackened arm with its elongated fingers. Whatever it was connected to was not human.

Buck's fur stood on end as the dog exposed his teeth in a snarl. Daniel watched through dazed vision as a grinning face with orange eyes and its outstretched appendage receded back into the darkness. His eyelids were getting heavy as the world spun around him. He used his foot to gingerly shut the basement door and then lost consciousness.

CHAPTER 10

DANIEL WOKE UP in bed screaming at 7 AM. Nora shot up with a confused look on her face, trying to figure out what was going on. She looked over at her husband who was violently shaking and shrieking as he writhed in the sheets.

"Daniel!"

He had never had night terrors, but it was obvious that he was trapped in a dream. She slapped him across the face.

"Daniel, wake up!"

Daniel rolled to his left and fell out of the bed with a thud on the hard floor.

"Oh my gosh, are you OK?"

Daniel scrambled to a sitting position and crawled backward until he hit the wall. His eyes were wide open as he frantically looked around the room, unsure of where he was. He was hyperventilating, and sweat poured down his face, saturating his shirt.

"Daniel, it's OK. You were having a nightmare," Nora soothed from the bed. "Take some deep breaths. It's OK."

He made eye contact with her and realized that he was in his bedroom, not in the kitchen. Once his nerves steadied a bit and his adrenaline subsided, he accepted that he had just awakened from a terrible dream.

"Dear God! That was the worst fucking nightmare I've ever had!"

"Shh!" Nora scolded, not wanting him to wake up Alice.

He wiped the sweat from his brow with his soaking wet shirt.

"That felt so real," he said, still in disbelief. "I've never experienced anything so lucid before."

He exhaled deeply. Nora climbed off the bed on his side and knelt beside him. She pressed his head into her chest and hugged him.

"You're OK. I'll go make some coffee. Maybe you should take a shower and cool down."

"OK," he said as he watched her get up and head downstairs.

As soon as he caught his breath, he pushed himself up off the floor and winced with pain.

"Oww, shit."

His whole body ached like he'd tumbled down a mountain hitting every rock on the way down. He peeled off his sticky shirt and gym shorts and tossed them in the dirty clothes hamper. The bathroom floor tiles were cold and stuck to his sweaty feet. He stopped dead in his tracks when he looked at his nude body in the full-length mirror. There were blue and black welts on his ribs. He turned to look at his back and nearly collapsed with dread. Running down his spine were three long, deep gashes.

"That was no dream," he said to his reflection.

He turned around and grabbed the shirt out of the hamper and examined it. The back of it was torn and blood-stained like it had been clawed by some wild beast. He ran across the room and looked down at his side of the bed. There were sweat and blood spots all over the mattress cover.

Without really knowing why, he yanked all the sheets off the bed and threw them in with the dirty clothes and tossed his ripped shirt in the trash. He wondered why he was hiding this—why he was acting like he was cleaning up the scene of a crime. He knew why. He didn't want to worry his pregnant wife.

Daniel walked back into the bathroom and looked again at his body. He stared into his own eyes and tried to center his thinking. With each passing breath, he got more into psychologist mode.

"Get a grip, Hill. What's more logical? You spent the night talking to a human s'more in the basement and then you were attacked by a fire demon, or you simply had a night terror. Night terrors can manifest later in life under the right set of circumstances. You moved into a new home, you have a pregnant wife, you're under a lot of self-imposed pressure to flip this property, and then some stranger shows up telling you that your haunted basement is the reason that the contractor killed himself. It's your subconscious, Hill. You scratched your own back in your sleep. Who knows how you did it? Humans display superhuman strength under extreme circumstances all the time. You know that. Those bruises could also be self-inflicted from spasming all night and falling out of bed."

Daniel gripped the sides of the mirror and pulled his face nearly nose to nose with his reflection.

"It was just a dream, man."

He nodded with satisfaction and then pushed himself away. He turned on the shower and started brushing his teeth while the water warmed up. The longer he was awake, the more the nightmarish event seemed like a distant memory. He spit out the toothpaste and stepped into the hot water.

Nora had already made coffee and was working on breakfast when he entered the kitchen wearing clean clothes and feeling fresh. He grabbed his favorite mug and filled it to the top with black coffee. He took a sip and sat it down on the counter to retrieve the bottle of ibuprofen. He popped a couple and washed them down with the hot beverage.

"When did you bring that up from the basement?" Nora asked.

"Huh? What?"

"That chest," Nora clarified. "When did you bring it up here?"

Daniel spun around and looked at where she was pointing. Sure enough, Merle's antique chest from his nightmare was neatly placed in front of the closed basement door. Daniel felt his throat dry as a cold sensation nestled in the pit of his stomach. He couldn't remove his eyes from the black chest sitting right there on the floor staring back at him. The self-therapy pep talk that he had just administered washed away in a millisecond.

"Last night, I suppose."

"You suppose? You're not sure when you brought it up?" Nora asked as she moved her head into Daniel's line of vision, breaking his gaze from the taunting chest.

He swallowed hard and quickly put on a brave face.

"Last night or early morning. I always get confused on what to say. What do you call 1 AM anyway?"

"You moved a chest up here at 1 AM?"

"Yeah, I couldn't sleep. It was stupid. I even fell down the stairs. Here, look at this," he said as he lifted up his shirt to show her the bruises.

"Oh my gosh, Daniel!" She bent over and examined him closely. "Did you break a rib?"

"No, no," he chuckled. "It's really not that bad. I just took a tumble to the bottom and hit the wall pretty hard. That chest was actually in the secret room in the basement. There's a little concrete well in there but nothing else. I had to use my back to push the chest out of there, and I scratched the shit out of myself," he said as he turned around and lifted his shirt.

"Daniel! Why? You did this in the middle of the night?" Nora was in disbelief at her husband's bizarre antics.

"I couldn't sleep and really wanted to check out that secret room. I thought if I'd get up and move around, I'd get tired. I didn't anticipate beating myself to sleep though. I'm weird, and I'm sorry."

"You need to go get a tetanus shot and have a doctor check you out."

"Might be a good idea," he agreed. "A trip to town could do me some good."

Daniel walked past her and over to the chest. He crouched beside it and looked at the two heavy padlocks hanging from the latches. "I doubt this one has old lady clothes in it."

The doorbell rang, and Buck started barking from the living room. Daniel jumped in shock.

"Jesus, I forgot we had a dog. It's barely 8 o'clock. That has to be the pool boy." Daniel said as he stood up and stormed to the front door.

He pulled it open and saw Luke standing there. Buck came running up behind Daniel growling.

"Go lie down," Daniel scolded and Buck reluctantly obeyed. "Luke, if you're going to get started this early in the morning, please don't ring the doorbell. You have my un-expiring permission to get started even if we're still asleep."

"Darn it, I did it again. I'm sorry, Daniel."

"It's OK. Do you want breakfast or coffee?"

"No, thank you. Already ate. Pumped and ready to go."

Daniel stared at him like he was from another planet.

"OK, then. Let me know if you need anything for the fence."

"Will do, sir. I mean Daniel," Luke said as he backed off the porch and headed toward his pile of supplies.

Daniel shut the door and looked up the stairs at Alice's room. Her door was still shut, and she had somehow slept through all of the morning's loud events. He walked back into the kitchen. Nora had made a plate for him and placed it on the table. He sat down and started eating, staring again at the chest by the basement door.

"I guess my plan today is to break into that thing."

"I guess I'll have to find out when I get home," Nora said as she sat down in front of her husband with her food.

"Get home?"

She looked at him, annoyed that he had forgotten what she had reminded him of just last night.

"OB/GYN appointment in Ohio," she said.

"Oh, yeah. Sorry, I forgot. Are you sure you don't want me to drive you?"

"There's no need. This is one of the uneventful ones."

"OK," Daniel said as he took a bite of food. "It seemed like they were all important with Alice."

Nora looked up from her plate to gauge where Daniel was coming from. She detected no ulterior motive in his questioning.

"It's just a quick check-up. I'll be in and out. There's no need for everyone to drive up to Ohio for that. There's too much to be done around here."

"All right then," he replied, returning to his food.

He was trying to maintain a calm exterior, but his thoughts were all over the place. For the first time in his life, he felt like he was losing it.

About an hour later, Daniel opened Nora's car door for her and was giving her a kiss goodbye when Alice stepped out onto the front porch. Nora noticed her daughter first and rolled down her window.

"I'll see you in a bit," she yelled across the yard.

"Where are you going?" Alice asked, stepping off the porch.

"Doctor in Ohio. I'll be back in a few hours. Need anything while I'm out?"

"No, thanks."

Nora noticed that Alice wasn't wearing her usual slumming-around-the-house attire. She had on a cute summer outfit and even her face was lightly dolled up. Daniel put his arm around his daughter. He was unaware of her change of appearance, but Nora immediately detected it.

"Where are you off to?" Nora asked Alice.

"I was going to take a walk. Explore a bit, I guess."

"I think that's a great idea," Daniel said as he rubbed his daughter's arm.

Nora sensed that Alice was going to go see Luke. She gave her a knowing look and the smile of a co-conspirator.

"OK. Have fun then," Nora winked.

"We'll see you when you get back," Daniel said as Nora started the engine.

"Bye, guys," she said, rolling up her window.

Daniel and Alice stepped back as Nora coasted down the crackling gravel driveway and turned left onto the main road.

"I guess I'm off too," Alice said.

Daniel removed his arm from her shoulders.

"Be careful out there."

"Careful of what?"

"Never know. Could be snakes. Spiders, even."

Alice judged her father to see if he was making a reference to Luke's hand tattoo. She saw that little upturn in the right corner of his mouth that was his tell-tale sign. He had a good poker face to those who didn't intimately know him.

"Very funny."

"I don't know what you're talking about," he said as he turned to head back to the porch. "I'll be in here. Holler if you need me."

"OK, Dad," she said as she started walking across the yard.

She heard the front door open and shut behind her. After just a few more steps, she heard it open again and turned around to look. Daniel stood on the porch holding the door. He whistled, and Alice watched Buck come sprinting out of the house. The old dog ran up to her and began orbiting her like a canine moon.

"Why don't you take him with you," Daniel said with a grin. "He needs his daily exercise."

Alice rolled her eyes. She was going to bring up the fact that Buck hates Luke but couldn't resist the dog's glee on full display.

"*You* need some exercise," she teased her father.

"Love you, honey!" He waved and walked back inside, letting the screen door slam behind him.

As soon as Alice and Buck rounded the corner of the fence line, she saw Luke across the valley unloading wooden beams from his four-wheeler's trailer. Buck started to growl beside her.

"No, Buck. That's just Luke. He works for us. He's a friend."

Buck looked at her and back to Luke and growled again.

"Hey, knock it off."

Buck let out a defeated whimper and trudged along beside her.

Luke lifted one side of a beam and wedged it into the small opening in the fence post. He turned around and picked up the other side and saw Alice walking across the freshly cut grass with Buck beside her. She smiled and waved at him.

"Hey there," he said as she walked up to him.

Buck made a displeased grunt.

"Stop it," she scolded and then looked back up at Luke. "Hey, yourself."

"I don't know why that dog hates me. He always has. Old Man Merle would let him run free, and he'd come barking at me as soon as I stepped foot on the property."

"Maybe it's because you're tall and threatening," Alice teased and then felt awkward for saying that.

"Am I? Never heard that before. Tall, yeah, but not threatening."

"I meant being tall might threaten Buck."

"I'll take it as a compliment," he smiled.

"How's the fence coming?"

"You tell me," he replied and took a step back from his

handiwork. "Everything from this point to the house is finished. I'm just working my way around the loop."

Alice looked at the rebuilt, freshly painted section running under the trees toward the house.

"It looks great. I'm sure my dad will be happy."

"Good."

Neither one of them said anything, and the awkwardness of the silence grew by the second.

"Hey, I wanted to ask you somethin'," Luke finally said.

Alice looked in his eyes, thankful to be conversing again.

"Yeah?"

"There are a bunch of four-wheeler trails around here that lead to some amazing sights that you have to see to appreciate. Tons of little spots hidden in the forest that are fun to explore. There's a really cool waterfall and a swimming hole about a mile past my house. I'd love to show you around."

She felt butterflies in her stomach as she nervously looked back down at the ground.

"What do you say?" he asked. "Would you like to take a tour of the backcountry with me this evening?"

She smiled and looked back up at him.

"I'd love to."

"Killer," he said as he brushed the hair out of his face.

CHAPTER 11

L ATER THAT AFTERNOON, Alice came walking through the front door smiling ear to ear. Daniel was sitting on the living room floor staring at the unopened chest he had moved from the kitchen. Alice was floating so high on the clouds of her thoughts that she didn't notice her motionless father. She skipped up the stairs looking for him.

"Dad?"

Daniel finally broke from his trance when he heard his daughter's voice. He blinked several times, unsure of how long he had been sitting there. He had completely lost track of time. In fact, he didn't even remember moving the chest from the kitchen to where it was now.

"Dad?" Alice said again upstairs from his bedroom.

Daniel got off the floor and walked toward the stairs.

"Down here, honey."

Alice turned around and walked out of his bedroom.

"I didn't see you down there," she said as she descended the stairs.

"Yeah, I was in the living room trying to get this chest open. What's up?"

"Is Mom home yet?"

Before Daniel spoke, he realized that he didn't even know if she was home. The last thing he remembered was telling Alice to take Buck with her when she went to see Luke. But he guessed that if Nora had returned, she would've spoken with him long before Alice did. He looked down at his watch and saw that it had only been a little under two hours since Nora left. He knew she wouldn't be home for at least another hour.

"No, not yet," he finally said.

"Dad, are you OK?" Alice asked when she noticed how pale and clammy her father's skin looked.

"Of course, honey. Why?"

"You look . . . sick."

"I feel fine. Just a little exhausted, I guess. Thanks for checking in on me," he smiled.

Alice thought hard about asking her dad about the date with Luke before her mom but did so anyway. Even if he said no, she had no doubt that she could convince her mom to come to her defense.

"Question," she began.

"Shoot."

"Do you care if I go four-wheelin' with Luke this evening?"

"'Four-wheelin'?'" Daniel repeated, taunting his daughter's recently adopted regional dialect. "You've lived in southern West Virginia for less than a month, and you already sound like a local. 'Four-wheelin','" he said smiling.

Alice was not amused so Daniel dropped the smirk from his face immediately.

"Four-wheeling . . . I'm assuming that's where you travel on the back of Luke's four-wheeler somewhere?"

"Yes, Dad. Luke says there are some really cool trails and stuff around here. He asked me if I wanted him to show me around. I said that I did."

Daniel sensed his daughter's vulnerability, and the advice that Nora suggested on how to relate to her flashed through his brain.

"Well, that seems very nice of Luke to offer to do that," he said as Alice looked up, surprised that her dad didn't completely blow her off. "If you want to get out of the house for a little bit with your new friend, then I certainly don't want to get in the way of that."

"Thanks, Dad."

"Just wait until after dinner to go and be home by ten," Daniel said sternly.

"Deal," she said and turned to go back outside.

"Where are you going now?"

"To tell Luke that I can go," she said as the screen door shut behind her.

He heard Buck follow her off the porch.

"Oh, goody."

As soon as Alice was out of sight, he remembered the chest in the living room. He turned around and stared at the dark, aging wood housing a mystery. He walked to it and bent over to examine the two large padlocks keeping the lid shut. He stood back up and put his hands on his hips.

"I guess it's time to get some more mileage out of my saw."

Not a second after he spoke did he realize that the saw, along with all of his other tools, were neatly tucked away in the basement under the stairs. The thought of going back down there gave him a shiver, but he knew what he had to do. He turned and walked toward the kitchen.

The basement door was shut. There was nothing imposing or intimidating about it in broad daylight. Sunlight shone through the open kitchen windows, filling him with a renewed sense of bravery. He grabbed the doorknob and pulled it open. The light behind him lit up the stairs leading into the darkness. He saw the light switch to his left and flicked it on. The basement illuminated beneath him.

"You've got this, Hill."

He took one step down and didn't spontaneously combust into Hellfire, so he stepped again. Quickening his pace, he marched all the way down, focused only on the basement floor at the foot of the stairs. He took the final step and then turned to look at the room, fearing what he might see. To his surprise, there was no charred corpse of Merle Blatty smoldering in the corner. The little door wasn't smashed to smithereens. Most importantly, there was no demonic creature lurking anywhere in the shadows. It looked like your run of the mill, normal basement. Even the temperature was cool. He let out a deep sigh of relief.

Wasting no more time than he had to, he turned to look under the stairs. Sure enough, his tools were in their place underneath the chain still hanging on the wall. He picked up the circular saw and confidently walked back upstairs like he owned the place; which, in fact, he did.

He stepped up into the kitchen, turned the basement light off, and shut the door behind him. The saw was heavy, so he switched hands as he walked through the room, not noticing Nora's purse on the kitchen table. He passed the stairs to his left, heading toward the chest in the living room.

"I know you're not going to use that thing in our living room," Nora said from the top of the stairs.

"Agghh!" Daniel shrieked as he jumped at the sound of his wife's voice and dropped the weighty saw on the ground.

"Jesus, Daniel, you probably just dented the hardwood floor!"

He grabbed his chest and tried to steady his nerves. His newfound sense of courage dissipated by the second.

"I didn't know you were home. You scared the shit out of me. Why are you home so early?"

"I'm not home early. It's past five."

Daniel looked down at his watch and saw that an hour had passed since he last looked at it.

"This can't be right," he said. "I just checked my watch a few minutes ago, and it was four. I walked down to the basement to get my saw and came right back up here."

"You obviously misread your watch, Daniel. It happens."

Just as she said that, Alice walked out of her bedroom. Daniel felt more confused than ever.

"You just left to go meet Luke. How are you back already?"

"Dad, that was like an hour ago."

Daniel could see the mounting concern on their faces. He felt the panic building in his pulse, but he did his best not to let his family notice.

"Shew, I must be more exhausted than I thought," he said with a fake laugh.

The two ladies shared a worried glance.

"You look awful," Nora said.

Daniel waved it off and started walking up the stairs to meet her.

"I'll be fine. I think I'm just tired and hungry," he said as he stepped onto the second floor.

Nora examined his pale, sweaty complexion and the dark circles forming under his eyes.

"I'll make dinner soon. Why don't you go lie down until it's ready? Between this and last night, you're giving me a lot to worry about."

Those words filled Daniel with guilt. The last thing that he wanted to do was to give his pregnant wife anxiety.

"That's probably a good idea," he said as he kissed her on the cheek. "How'd the appointment go?"

"Everything's fine," she said. "Routine check-up."

"Good, good."

"Go lie down, Daniel."

"You got it," he said as he walked into the bedroom, shut the door behind him, and collapsed on the bed.

About an hour later, Nora was almost finished preparing their meal. She called for Alice to go wake her father and tell him dinner was ready. Alice, in the middle of fixing her hair for the date, poked her head out of the second floor bathroom and shouted at Daniel's closed bedroom door.

"Dad, dinner is ready!"

Daniel opened his eyes and sat up in bed. He looked at the clock and saw that he hadn't been asleep very long but could tell that he had gotten some quality rest. The power nap worked wonders. He walked into the bathroom and checked himself in the mirror. The paleness of his face and dark circles under his eyes had slightly cleared up. He walked out and headed downstairs.

Nora turned to him as soon as he entered the kitchen. She could tell that he felt better.

"How was your nap?"

"Great, thank you," he said as he gave her a kiss on the cheek.

He sat down in front of his plate of food.

"Alice, get down here!" Nora shouted upstairs.

Alice finished her hair and came down to join them. She had obviously spent a lot of time on her makeup and was wearing a revealing tank top with a pair of jean shorts that barely covered her thighs. Daniel immediately noticed his daughter's drastic change in appearance and couldn't help himself.

"Is that standard four-wheelin' apparel?"

"Daniel," Nora warned.

"It's summer, Dad. Chill out."

Daniel bit his tongue and reminded himself that his baby girl was rapidly becoming a young woman. He grunted and took a bite of steak. Nora began talking about the drive home from Ohio and how she had passed their old house, but Daniel zoned out. He cut another piece of meat and brought it to his face. Just before he took a bite, an image of Merle's seared flesh popped into his mind. He dropped the fork and abruptly ran out the front door to vomit off the porch.

Nora and Alice scrambled to follow him out. He was bent over with his hands on his knees, dry-heaving onto the grass.

"Daniel, are you OK?" Nora asked as she touched his back.

He stopped retching and spit out what was left in his mouth. He stood up and wiped his brow.

"I'm sorry, honey," he said. "My stomach is just upset. Steak may not have been the best thing to try and eat."

He saw that they were both highly concerned.

"Do you want me to make you some soup?" Nora offered.

Daniel wasn't thinking about food in the slightest, but knew that if he refused, then he'd cause more worry.

"Sure, that'd be great."

"OK," Nora said as she turned to walk back inside. She looked at Alice. "Come on and eat, honey. Luke will be here soon."

The two ladies entered the house. Daniel struggled to keep his composure out there alone on the porch. He looked at the setting sun and knew that he couldn't wait another night to know what Merle was hiding. He looked over through the living room window at the chest on the floor.

Nora heard Daniel walking through the house as she heated his soup. When it was finished, she carried the hot bowl on a plate toward the living room, but it was empty.

"I'm out here, honey," Daniel said from the front porch.

She turned around and went out there. She saw the chest now on the front porch and the saw beside it hooked up to an extension cord. Daniel took the soup from her and sat down on the porch swing.

"Mmm, thank you so much," he said as he began to take careful sips of the hot liquid from the spoon.

"Are you sure that you're feeling up to breaking into that chest?"

"Sure. I'm fine, really," he said. "It'll take me two minutes to cut through those."

A faint engine buzzed in the distance and got louder as it neared them.

"Sounds like a four-wheeler," Daniel said, taking another sip of soup.

Nora watched as Luke appeared in the distance riding down the road.

"Yep, it's Luke," she said.

"Tons of people die every year on those things," Daniel said.

Nora shot him a look.

"Then tell him to be careful. Give him the dad talk . . . a tame version."

Daniel smiled and then tilted up his bowl, drinking what was left. Luke turned and drove up their driveway. Buck came bounding out from behind the house barking his head off. Luke slowed down, unsure of what to do about the incoming bloodhound.

"Buck, come!" Daniel shouted and the dog altered his course and ran to his master. "Get in the house and lie down!"

Buck lumbered inside. Luke continued up the gravel and came to a stop in front of the porch.

"Hello, Hill family," he said with a smile.

"Hi, Luke," Nora said warmly. "Alice is just finishing her supper."

Daniel listened to Alice hurriedly empty her plate and put it in the sink. A minute later she appeared at the screen door.

"I'm finished," she announced. "We can go."

"I stand corrected," Nora said.

Alice walked off the porch and hopped on the back of the four-wheeler. Daniel felt his nerves blaze as he watched his daughter wrap her arms around this tattooed boy's torso.

"Ready," Alice said.

"Hey, guys," Daniel began.

Alice looked at her father knowing that some kind of pre-date talk was coming. Daniel looked at Luke and then over to Alice.

"Home by ten. Got it?"

"Yes, sir," Luke said.

"Yes, Dad."

"And Luke . . . that's the most precious cargo in the world on the back of that machine," Daniel said. "Drive carefully."

"You have my word."

Daniel couldn't help but like the boy. He was the most hard-working and respectful kid he'd ever met.

"OK, then," Nora said, ending the awkward pause. "You kids have fun."

Luke smiled and revved up the engine. Alice held on tightly as they started down the driveway. She turned and waved to her parents.

"I think I'm going to barf again," Daniel said.

"Oh, stop it," Nora laughed as she walked over to him still sitting on the porch swing. He put his arm around her and pulled her on top of his lap.

"Daniel we're going to break this thing," she giggled.

"You don't trust your daughter's craftsmanship?" he said as he gave the metal chain a tug.

"You know what I just realized?" she asked.

"That Alice is one heck of a swing installer?"

"That we have some alone time," she said, looking up at him.

"Say no more," he said as he stood up with his wife in his arms.

"Daniel, be careful. You were just sick," she laughed as he carried her across the porch.

"I've suddenly been reinvigorated. I don't know what's come over me," he said, crossing the threshold of their home. "I'll get a swig of mouthwash on the way though, but that's only because I love you."

Nora laughed again as he carried her up the stairs to their bedroom. He kicked the door shut and they made love.

Not once did Daniel stop thinking about the chest on the porch.

CHAPTER 12

AROUND 8 PM, Daniel stood in front of the porch with the power saw. He started up the whirling blade and slowly brought it down to the metal padlock. Sparks shot in all directions like thousands of fireflies in the evening sky. The saw slowly chewed through the metal. In a few moments, the lock was severed and hung ajar from the chest.

Daniel moved on to the next one. He sawed straight through the arching bolt until it cut loose. He turned off the power to the blade and placed it on the ground beside him. Carefully, he gripped the hot metal lock and knocked it off the latch. At last, he stared at the unlocked, unopened chest in front of him.

"Time to see what you've been hiding in here, Merle," he said into the warm night.

A cool breeze blew through the trees, across the open yard, and ruffled Daniel's hair. He looked up at the playful wind and then back down at the chest. He reached forward to unhitch the latches, but Nora opened the screen door and poked her head out. Daniel stopped and looked up at her.

"Did you get it?" she asked.

"I did," he said with some annoyance.

He felt protective over this chest. For some reason, he felt like she was interrupting a private moment.

"Let's see what's in it," she said.

"OK . . ."

Nora walked onto the porch to get a better look. Daniel again leaned forward and grabbed the latches. He used his thumbs to try and pop them open but struggled. They were old and rusty and did not want to move. He applied some more force, feeling the metal indenting his thumbs. Just before the pain became too much to bear, both latches flung upward.

"There we go."

Nora took another step closer and put her hand on Daniel's shoulder. He gripped both top corners of the chest and lifted the lid open. A musty, stale odor wafted out.

"Yep, this belonged to an old person," Daniel recoiled.

The stench was carried away in the breeze, and both of them leaned forward to examine the contents. The chest was packed full of composition notebooks and VHS tapes.

"That's it?" Nora asked.

Daniel lifted a few notebooks out and placed them on the porch.

"Well, I'll leave you to that. I'm going to go take a shower. Let me know if there are any bars of gold at the bottom of that thing."

She kissed him and went back inside. Daniel counted fifteen notebooks. He thumbed through one and saw that it was completely filled out. He picked up another one and saw more writing. One after another—hundreds of pages of rambling scribbles. He pushed them aside and started carefully examining the VHS tapes.

They were blank tapes used for making home movies or recordings. There were three of them stacked in the bottom of the chest. He noticed the labels on the sides of each tape. Each label had a different name and year written on it: "Clayton '88", "Edmond '90", "Amelia '92." He stacked the tapes on top of the composition notebooks and went back to the chest.

There was a cardboard box and a small black satchel no bigger than a purse. Daniel grabbed the satchel first and lifted it out by the handles. It was plain leather and deceptively heavy. It reminded him of a bag that a doctor making house calls would carry back in the day. He unzipped the top and inserted his hand. The first item he withdrew was a heavy, metal cross similar to the one from the basement, but this one was much denser. He sat it to the side and pulled out a Ziploc bag containing several small plastic bottles that looked like travel-sized shampoo, but they had no label and contained what appeared to be water. He noticed something drawn with black marker on the bag itself: another cross.

"Holy water?"

He slid the bag of bottles aside and reached back in the satchel. He felt another metallic object and then gripped it, knowing fully what it was before he pulled it out. The pistol in his hand was heavy. Daniel looked at it closely. He had some experience with handguns, mostly from a gun safety class that he took before purchasing one himself for home protection. He released the magazine and saw that it was fully loaded. He pushed it back in and carefully placed it with the other items.

The bag was nearly empty now. He felt around the bottom of it until he grabbed the final item. It was a small, leather-bound Bible that had seen better days. The corners were worn and mashed, some of the pages were bent and beginning to yellow—it was not the typical decorative Bible that classed up a bookcase. He placed it beside the other items and double-checked that the satchel was empty before shoving everything back inside it.

The last item in the chest was a box housing a VHS camcorder. Daniel pulled it out and looked at the faded picture of the product on the side. He opened the top and peered in at the device still in the box. Looking back and forth between the camcorder and the recordable VHS tapes sitting on his porch, he assumed that Merle had made some interesting home movies that he needed to see.

Daniel packed everything back in the chest in the same way that he found it. After loading up the camcorder box, the black satchel, and the VHS tapes, he began stacking the notebooks. He stopped when he suddenly had a renewed interest to see what was written inside them. He opened the one he was holding and looked for a second time at its contents.

Within moments of flipping through pages, he knew exactly what it was: a journal. It looked like a lifetime of journals. He was overwhelmed by the sheer amount of writing in just one of the notebooks. He grabbed another one and opened it. While thumbing through it, he could see that every entry occurred in 1973. Another one was 1975. 1976. 1974. He put them in chronological order. There was one for every year from 1973-1988.

"Why'd you stop at 1988?"

As if on cue, the label on one of the VHS tapes caught his eye.

"'Clayton '88.' You started recording instead of writing."

He looked at the most recently dated artifact—the tape that read "Amelia '92."

"Amelia was in 1992, and then you died in 1993."

He picked up the Amelia tape and looked closely at it like some hidden clue would reveal itself.

"Amelia," he whispered to himself before setting the tape back down with the others.

Daniel finished packing the notebooks in the chest and shut the lid. He latched it closed and picked it up. Using his foot to fling open the screen door, he carefully carried the bulky chest through the kitchen and placed it on the floor by the basement door. He took a moment to give his muscles a rest, opened the basement door, picked the chest back up, and then walked it downstairs.

CHAPTER 13

A T THE SAME TIME that Daniel was walking out of the basement to rejoin Nora upstairs, Luke and Alice were swerving up an ATV trail on a ridge about two miles away. It was dark, but the lights on the front of the machine lit their way. She wrapped her arms around his torso and held on tightly as the four-wheeler climbed up a steep incline. They had already explored two trails on separate hills. Luke had shown her several campsites and scenic overlooks that put postcards to shame. The path they were currently ascending was the longest, but he promised her it would be worth the ride. She rested her head against his back and closed her eyes, enjoying the moment.

Alice felt the four-wheeler level out and knew they had reached a plateau. There were few trees on the top of the hill. The moonlight teased a view of the rolling farmland that surrounded them for miles. She wished they had arrived early enough to see the sunset.

Luke drove across the flat ground toward a makeshift campsite in the center of the clearing. He pulled up to an area with a firepit that was surrounded by large rocks used for seating. A hammock hung between two skinny trees. Cigarette butts, beer bottles, and other litter was scattered across the area. He killed the engine.

"Here we are."

Alice released her arms and sat up. Luke hopped off first and then helped her down.

"Is this another one of your secret spots?" Alice asked.

"Well, it's a great spot that me and my friends like to come to, but it's not really a secret. The best part about this place is that we never have to worry about the law being called on us," he smiled.

"No, I guess not."

"It's getting pretty dark. I better grab this," Luke said as he opened a compartment on the four-wheeler and pulled out a heavy-duty flashlight.

He clicked it on, and the massive beam shot through the darkness like a burst of energy. He shined the light around, scoping out their location, and then turned back to Alice. With a playful look, he extended his open palm like he wanted to escort her somewhere. Alice smiled and surrendered her hand.

"Come check this out," he said, leading the way toward the far end of the cliff.

They walked thirty yards across mulch-covered rocks and exposed tree roots without talking. Alice decided to break the silence.

"This has been great, Luke. Thank you for getting me out of the house tonight."

Luke gave her a quick smile but was focused on something up ahead. Alice heard a noise that was getting progressively louder as they approached it.

Running water.

Luke stopped just short of the edge of the cliff and let go of her hand.

"Careful now," he warned.

Alice stopped and let Luke inch closer to what appeared to be a straight drop. She was terrified of heights but was doing her best to play it cool. Luke peered down at something that she couldn't see.

"OK, come here."

Alice looked at him, unsure. Luke glanced back at her and sensed her reluctance. He extended his open hand.

"You can trust me."

She took his hand for the second time. He helped her walk up beside him so that she could look over the edge. About six feet below them was a boulder the size of a minivan jutting out of the cliff. Alice could hear water splashing but couldn't see it, especially in the dark.

"Check this out," Luke began as he pointed the flashlight down onto the boulder. "See that rock?"

"Uh-huh."

"You slide down onto that rock and then walk over that way," he said as he dragged the beam of the flashlight over to a dirt path that gradually descended into darkness along the wall of the cliff. "You get on that path and follow it down."

"Down to what?" Alice asked, already terrified of this plan.

"Well, you kind of have to see it to appreciate it," he smiled. "Follow me."

Luke jumped from the edge of the cliff and effortlessly landed on the rock. Alice felt like she was going to have a panic attack.

"Are you crazy!" she screamed from above him. "You could've fallen!"

He laughed and put his hands on his hips.

"Do you know how many times I've done this? Come down here with me."

"I am not jumping down there."

"You don't have to. Sit on your butt and slide. I'll catch you."

Alice looked around and felt the fear creeping in. The last thing she wanted was for this older boy to think she wasn't cool. She didn't want to start the next school year with a reputation of being the timid city girl that didn't know how to have fun in the country.

"Fine."

Luke moved closer to the cliffside and extended his

arms like a parent waiting for their toddler to come down the slide.

"Well, get out of my way, would you?"

Impressed, Luke raised his eyebrows and took a step backward. He made a sweeping motion with his hand.

"The floor is all yours, m'lady."

Alice focused on nothing but the spot where she would land. She ignored the treacherous drop at the edge of the boulder. She ignored the fearful voice in her head telling her what could go wrong, and she leaped.

She landed on both feet and immediately grabbed hold of Luke. She couldn't stop herself from laughing in that hysterical way that one does after stepping off a roller coaster or jumping during a scary movie.

"*That* . . . was impressive," Luke said.

"Oh, my God. I've never done anything like that."

"Now, you have," Luke said, still holding her.

She looked up into his eyes, hoping that he would kiss her right then and there. She sensed his hesitation, and he quickly broke free.

"Here, check this out."

He walked to the edge of the boulder and sat down letting his legs dangle into the abyss. He looked over his shoulder at Alice who had her back to the cliff, obviously wanting no part of that straight drop.

"Come sit with me," he said as he turned the flashlight back on and sat it beside him. "Take a look."

Alice's curiosity overrode her fear, and she inched her way to the edge. She carefully sat down next to Luke. Not only could she hear a torrential rush of water, but she felt vibrations in the rock beneath her. He picked up the flashlight and handed it to her.

"Take a look."

Alice carefully held out the flashlight and peeked over the edge. The light glimmered on the hidden waterfall spilling out beneath them.

"Woah."

The steady flow of water shot straight out into the darkness and crashed against the rocks below.

"I know you can't see that far down, but the waterfall empties into a swimming hole down there."

Alice imagined Luke walking her down the path, hand in hand, them getting in the warm pool of water at the bottom of the cliff, illuminated only by the moonlight. She thought about clutching onto his body as they swam together and . . .

"Are we going down there?" she abruptly asked.

Luke looked caught off guard by the question. He didn't reply. Alice could tell there was something that he wasn't saying.

"What's wrong?"

"If we went down there, we'd never make it back by your curfew. It's probably close to nine now."

"You brought me all this way to show me this, and we're not even going to get in? I'd like to," she said as she touched his forearm.

Luke looked down and withdrew his arm.

"I'm sorry," he said as he pushed himself up. "This wasn't a good idea. I should get you home."

Alice looked up at him, confused. He stood, waiting impatiently.

"I have to boost you back up before I can climb out," he said.

Alice got up and walked over to him.

"What just happened? I thought we were having a good time."

Luke looked down at his feet and then turned his back to her.

"I'm sorry."

"For what?"

"You're really pretty, and I think you're really cool, but I shouldn't have brought you here."

Alice closed the gap between them and extended her hand halfway to touch his back but didn't.

"Why?" she asked.

"This was one of the places where I used to take my last girlfriend."

Alice suddenly felt uncomfortable and let her hand fall.

"Are you saying that you're not over her or something?"

"I have no choice but to be over her," Luke blurted out as he struggled to hide the fact that his eyes were tearing up. "She's dead. She got sick last year and died."

Alice was overcome with sadness, confusion, and shock as she struggled to find the right words to say. She finally placed her hand on his back.

"I'm sorry. What was her name?"

"Amelia," Luke said as he discreetly wiped his eyes and turned to face Alice. "Her name was Amelia. Now, let's get you home."

CHAPTER 14

LIGHTNING CHISELED ITS way through the night sky and lit up the farm below. All three Hills were sleeping, but Buck nervously circled the living room as rain pattered the roof. The dog put his paws on the windowsill and nosed open the curtains, staring out into the night. Thunder detonated, rumbling through the house and sending Buck to his blanket in the corner. Torpedo rain assaulted the exterior. Buck put his paw over his snout and closed his eyes.

Down in the basement, the secret room door slowly opened. No one was awake to witness the putrid wave of humidity roll across the floor and waft its way up the stairs. Buck's ears shot up when he heard the basement door creaking in the kitchen. He let out a low whine as he stared from the living room.

Lightning flashed and gave Buck a clear view of the empty living room. He stood up and slowly crept across the wooden floor, passing the second-floor staircase and then poking his head into the kitchen. The basement door was wide open revealing nothing but darkness. Buck immediately detected the foul odor emanating from the doorway, and the hair down his spine electrified. Another explosion of thunder and Buck lunged forward, teeth bared, into the abyss. The basement door slammed shut behind him.

Nora shot up in bed. She didn't know if it was the

thunder, the loud noise from downstairs, or a bad dream that had startled her, but she was wide awake now. She looked over at Daniel sound asleep as usual. The rain beat against the roof above her head. Normally she found thunderstorms at night relaxing, but this one was too forceful to be anything but disturbing.

Lightning illuminated her bedroom like a camera flash. She reached for her bottle of water but found it empty. Her throat was parched in that way that only sleep can produce. She quietly got out of bed and made her way downstairs.

Halfway down the stairs, she covered her mouth and nose with her hand.

"Yuck," she said, trying not to gag from the sulfurous smell.

She took a few more steps and felt the drastic rise in temperature. A marsh of moisture filled the first floor. She stepped off the stairs and walked into the kitchen where it only got hotter.

"My *goodness.*"

It felt like someone had cranked up the furnace and let all the space heaters burn since they had gone to bed. She opened the refrigerator, grabbed another bottle of water, and walked out of the kitchen. It was hard for her to take a drink and not inhale a nose full of the rank atmosphere.

She knew she couldn't just go back to sleep without figuring out what was going on with their house. She walked to the thermostat underneath the stairs thinking maybe Daniel had turned it on by mistake when he meant to adjust the AC. The heat setting was off, and the AC was set to seventy-two degrees. She looked at the thermometer that read that it was currently seventy-two degrees in their house.

"What the heck?" she said as she tapped the obviously broken thermostat.

She turned around and decided that she should go wake Daniel. Perhaps there was something seriously wrong with their house. She would rather be safe than sorry. Just as she walked out from under the stairs and turned to go back up to her room, she heard someone whisper her name from the kitchen. She stopped, unable to believe what she couldn't possibly have heard.

"Nora," the voice said again.

She felt goosebumps spread across her forearms. It sounded like it was coming from the kitchen, yet simultaneously whispering into her ear. The heat and stench aided in the confusion. All of the sudden she felt woozy. Her eyes were starting to burn, and she had to blink over and over to keep them moisturized.

"Nora," it said again.

She sat her bottle of water on the stairway banister and walked through a hypnotic fog into the kitchen. The basement door now stood completely open. A whirling smoky substance twisted around the doorframe like some dreamlike decoration.

"Nora," the now louder voice said from the darkness of the basement.

"I'm dreaming," she said as she continued to walk toward the sublime scene.

Lightning flashed outside and she briefly saw a figure standing on the basement stairs. Her heart fluttered as she recognized the man's silhouette but knew that it couldn't possibly be true.

"I'm here, Nora. Come closer."

Sweat accumulated on her forehead and started to dribble down her body. Her nightgown quickly saturated with perspiration as a shot of excitement electrified her insides.

"Steve?" she asked the darkness.

Two elongated hands stretched out of the basement along the kitchen floor, enshrined in mist. The pointy fingers walked over to and then across her bare feet like spiders. Nora became paralyzed by the scalding hot fingertips slowly creeping up her legs. The burning pain was numbed by the adrenaline rush that she felt. She tried to breathe but couldn't remember how. The flaming fingernails lightly scratched their way up her thighs and then around to her bare behind. She moaned with agonizing pleasure as each hand cupped her buttocks and slowly lured her into the open doorway.

Thunder boomed over the house, masking the sound of the basement door closing.

Nora felt herself floating through a hazy abyss. She had the feeling that she was falling but couldn't find the will to open her eyes. Whatever this force was that had completely overpowered her soothed her into a blissful sedation. She imagined lifting her heavy eyelids and seeing a tunnel to the center of the earth rushing upward on all sides as she descended.

Just when she felt like she would completely dissolve into oblivion, she felt a solid, flat surface rise up from the depths and press against the back of her body. After a moment of confusion, she realized that she was lying on solid ground. The hands retreated, and she found the will to open her eyes.

She was drenched in sweat in complete darkness. She could see shapes, but nothing detailed. There was a straight object going up at an angle toward the only faint source of light that she could see. She realized that she was in the basement looking at the stairs going up to the kitchen; the light she saw was moonlight coming under the kitchen door.

Her paralysis subsided like she had just been administered laughing gas and was slowly being brought back to reality. She painfully pushed herself up to a sitting position and froze again when she saw the figure standing in the corner.

"Nora," the masculine voice whispered.

The tall shape of a man stepped into the middle of the room. A glowing amber light from inside the secret room intensified. The basement illuminated ever so slightly. Nora hazily studied the man standing before her. He was wearing what looked like an elegant business suit and tie. In his right hand was a briefcase. She looked up at his face, barely lit by the light behind him, but she knew without a doubt that it was her former boss, Steve.

"I came all this way to see you."

Nora smiled as she struggled to keep her droopy eyes open.

"I've missed you so much," he said.

Nora tried to focus on his blurry face. She saw that beautiful smile of his, the shape of his supple mouth, but there was something not right about his teeth. His nose seemed pointier than it had been, and every few seconds his eyes would burn bright orange. She knew the light must be playing tricks on her.

"Steve, why are you here?" she asked with a sedated normalcy.

"Aren't you happy to see me?" he replied.

Nora recognized enough of his voice to know that it was him, but there was something odd about it. There was a deep bass that hung in the air after he spoke. An other-worldly reverberance made it sound like she was listening to a recording of him.

"You know that I am," she slurred, slouched against the wall.

"You don't regret what we did that day in my office do you, Nora?"

An image of Daniel and Alice smiling appeared like a photograph in her mind but was suddenly engulfed in flames. She instantly forgot about her entire family.

"Of course not, Steve. I think about that day all the time," her lips said while her soul squirmed.

Steve's out-of-focus head nodded with delight.

"Good, good."

Nora licked her parched lips and blinked slowly. The

smell of sulfur began to break her from the trance, but Steve snapped his fingers with a spark, and her focus returned only to him. She smiled like she had just hit the button on a morphine drip.

Steve took another step closer and knelt down in front of her.

"Why are you here?" she asked again.

"To answer your prayers," the hypnotic voice replied matter-of-factly.

Even though she was just a few feet away from him, his face was still a blurred image, baring only enough resemblance of Steve to retain the ruse.

"What prayers?"

Steve chuckled as he reached toward her and brushed a few strands of hair out of her face. She closed her eyes and felt the heat from his fingers.

"Can I be blunt with you, Nora?"

"Yes."

"I know what you want, and you know what you want. You just don't want to admit that's what you want."

"And what do I want?"

"Me," Steve smiled.

She looked at the flashing orange eyes and shining teeth.

For a moment, she remembered being in the bathroom of her old house sixteen years ago with Daniel as they gleefully hugged beside a positive pregnancy test. Again, her mind turned back to flames, and she snapped right out of the reverie.

"I *do* want you," she said to the glowing eyes.

"I'm glad to hear you say it, my love," he said as he brushed her cheek.

She quivered under his burning touch.

Steve pulled back his hand and turned his attention to his briefcase on the floor beside him. He entered a combination on the lock and opened it. Nora tried to see what was inside, but the light from behind the little door wasn't bright enough.

"What do you have there, Steve? Did you bring some toys for us to play with?" She smiled as drool dribbled from the corner of her mouth.

He looked over his shoulder at her and grinned.

"Before you can have what you want," he began, "you must get rid of that which you . . . don't want. I can take it from you."

Something growled from under the basement stairs. Nora looked toward the sound. For a split second she saw her dog, Buck, tied up in the chain on the wall like a gnat in a spider's web. Only his head poked through the entanglement, and he furiously shook his snout back and forth trying to break free. He growled again.

Steve snapped his fingers, creating another spark. The chain wrapped tighter around Buck and pulled his head back within their confines.

"Nora," Steve said as she felt a warm force jolt her head back to the man in front of her.

She stared into his beautiful, burning eyes and forgot all about the dog under the stairs.

"Yes, my love?"

He withdrew a shiny metallic object from his briefcase. He lifted it up in front of him and examined it, letting Nora get a good look as well.

"What is that?" she giggled as she stared at the long, phallic object.

It was a metal rod with what looked like a point on the tip.

"Do you like it?"

Nora felt her head nod.

"Watch this," Steve said as his eyes gleamed.

He pressed a button on the bottom of the twelve-inch device, and the pointed tip opened into four tiny blades that whirled like a helicopter propeller. Nora was mesmerized by the mechanism and reached out to touch it. Steve playfully batted her hand away.

"Careful. You don't want to hurt those lovely hands of yours."

"Can I . . . see that?"

"Do you know what you have to do with it, Nora?"

Nora followed one of the spinning blades around and around its axis and knew. She nodded her head.

"I have to get rid of what I don't want, and you'll take it away from me," she said robotically.

"And what's that?" Steve asked, his smile inhumanly stretching up and around his head.

"The baby . . . " Nora said with a smile as a tear rolled down her cheek.

Steve released the button, and the four spinning blades came to a standstill. He handed it to her, and she gratefully accepted it. A tear fell from her other eye as she admired the device with reverence.

"Now," Steve began as he placed one hand on each of Nora's knees and gently spread her legs apart. "Do what needs to be done. I'll take it once it's out."

She slowly lowered the device and inserted it inside herself.

"Careful," Steve cautioned as he caressed her thighs.

She gently pushed the phallic instrument deeper until it would go no further. Tears were now pouring down her cheeks and into her smiling mouth. She looked into Steve's glowing eyes, unable to see his hideous face.

"Now . . . turn it on."

Just before she pressed the button, the basement door swung open, and a beaming ray of light burst through the darkness.

"Stop!" shouted a voice from the top of the stairs.

The Steve figure hissed and then vaporized in front of Nora. The particles were sucked through the cracks of the little door and back into the well. The fire behind the door extinguished immediately.

The person holding the flashlight ran down the stairs toward Nora, but she only saw a bounding light. The chain under the stairs rattled and slacked as Buck fought his way free. Nora felt like she had just awoken from a bad dream. Confused, she looked at the basement around her. A tall figure pointed the flashlight away from her eyes and jumped off the stairs.

"Mrs. Hill, are you OK?" Luke asked as he looked her over.

Nora was too delirious to respond in anything other than panicked whimpers. Buck trotted over to her and licked her hand.

"Mrs. Hill, it's OK. He's gone now. You can put that down."

Nora sobbed as she looked down at the twisted wire coat hanger she held in her hand, inches away from herself. Sheer repulsion filled her soul as she threw it across the basement.

"Oh my God," she sobbed hysterically. "*Oh my God!*"

Luke hugged her as she cried. After a moment, he helped her up.

"It's OK, Mrs. Hill. Come upstairs. I'll explain everything."

CHAPTER 15

NORA FOLLOWED LUKE onto the front porch, still in shock from what had just transpired. Buck sorely walked across the front yard to go relieve himself. The thunderstorm still raged but was moving east. Lightning flickered on the horizon, and the thunder made a distant roar. Luke knew that the clamorous weather was the only reason Alice and Daniel had slept through all the commotion in the basement. He closed the screen door softly behind them and escorted her over to the porch swing, helping her sit down. He took a step back and looked around nervously.

"Are you OK?" he finally asked as she stared at something a thousand miles away.

Nora snapped out of it and looked over at him.

"That wasn't a dream," she said with red, puffy eyes.

The wind blew across the porch, swaying her white nightgown. She folded her arms across her lap and clasped both of her elbows.

"That's true . . . somewhat, I guess," Luke replied.

Nora looked up at him for clarification.

"What do you mean by that, Luke?"

"I mean, whatever it was you were seein' down there was entirely in your head, but you weren't asleep."

Nora was bewildered. The more she thought about what he said, the more annoyed she became.

"Are you saying that I'm crazy?" she asked, glaring up at him.

"No, no . . . not at all," he said taking a step closer to her. "This is hard to explain without soundin' crazy myself," he chuckled.

Nora did not find any amusement in the situation.

"Right. I'll just put it all out there."

Nora leaned forward in anticipation.

"The old man that lived in this house," Luke began.

"Merle," Nora said.

"Yes. Merle Blatty. He was an exorcist."

Nora stared at him blankly.

"You're the second person to show up on my porch and say that."

"Really? Who else?"

"A guy that remodeled the house. He said that his boss had gone down into the basement and said that it was haunted," she explained as Luke nodded his head.

"And what happened to his boss?"

"He killed himself in a motel shortly after."

Luke closed his eyes and let out a deep sigh. Lightning flashed so far away that it was barely a flicker.

"Storm's nearly gone," he said.

"Luke, I know you just saved me, but what the hell are you doing at my house this late?"

"Making sure you and your family don't end up like that man in the motel," he replied, still staring at the storm.

"You came back to check on us?"

"I never really left."

Nora was baffled.

"There's so much that you don't know," he said.

She detected something deeply tragic about his tone.

"What do you mean?"

"Ever since you all moved in, I've stayed close to this farm. I knew it wouldn't be long before what's in that basement let itself be known to y'all. The last few nights, I've just hung out in the woods just up on the hill. I use my binoculars to get a good look through those kitchen windows."

Nora was becoming visibly uncomfortable.

"I swear I'm not a creep. I only look in through the kitchen to make sure no one goes in the basement. I thought I saw you walk by but wasn't sure. I heard some sounds and saw an orange glow in the kitchen. That glow that looks like fire. I knew you had gone in the basement."

"Your parents don't mind you staying out all night?"

"My mom left us right after I was born. Dad's a truck driver. He's gone half the time. The other half he's so drunk that he don't even notice that I'm not there. Our house down the road ain't my home. The only time I ever felt at home was when I was with Amelia, but she's gone now too."

Nora felt bad for the young man. She had no clue who Amelia was and was too much in shock to ask for elaboration. She only thought about Luke running through the woods, into their house, and then coming to rescue her.

"Luke, what did you see when you opened the basement door?"

Luke's face reddened, and he looked at his feet.

"What did you see, Luke?"

"I saw you, Mrs. Hill," he began. "You was sittin' on the floor, leanin' against the wall."

"And what was I doing?"

"You had your legs spread and . . . "

"And what?"

"You was about to stick a coat hanger inside yourself."

Nora's eyes got watery again. Luke looked up and saw her upset again.

"I know that wasn't you doin' it though, ma'am. It was the thing in the well. It poisoned your mind and was trickin' you."

"How is that possible?" she sobbed.

"I don't exactly know. It did the same thing to Amelia, but I wasn't able to save her. It did the same thing to that construction man in the motel. He got exposed to it when he went in the basement and it . . . latched on."

"'Latched on'? Are you saying that whatever is in that well is haunting our house?"

"I'm saying that you live on top of something evil. It doesn't just haunt your house. If anyone comes in contact with it—that well—it haunts their *mind*. Makes them crazy . . . suicidal even. And sometimes, it possesses them entirely. Damnedest thing is that there ain't any rhyme or reason for what it does."

Nora didn't know what to think. She leaned back in the swing, attempting to process the information. Out of habit, she pushed it backwards with her feet and let herself coast forward. The wooden porch roof emitted a loud creak, and she immediately put her feet back down to stop the momentum. She knew that their bedroom window was right above the porch. With the storm now miles away, there was no natural sound to mask her disturbance.

Buck came trotting around the side of the house to investigate the sound. He ran up on the porch, looked at Nora, and then rubbed his head against Luke's legs.

"I guess we're friends again, are we?"

"Did you all have a falling out?"

Luke smiled as he massaged Buck's floppy ears.

"Yeah, I blamed Old Man Merle for what happened to Amelia. I popped him in the jaw in front of Buck. I've never seen a dog turn beast so quick. He chased me off the farm and has held that grudge ever since. He's loyal, but boy can he hold a grudge."

Nora stood up from the swing.

"Luke, you have to promise me not to tell Daniel or Alice what you saw in the basement tonight."

Luke hesitated before responding, contemplating her request, careful not to give his word to something that he couldn't honor.

"Yes, ma'am," he finally said.

Some night creature scurried across the yard, catching Buck's eye. The dog began barking furiously and lunged off the porch, giving chase until both animals disappeared over the hill.

"Shit," Nora said as she realized the dog probably just woke up Daniel. "Luke, you've got to get out of here. We'll talk more about this later. You were never here."

"OK," he said as he hurried into the front yard.

He turned around and whispered, "Stay safe," and then disappeared into the trees.

Nora heard Daniel walking around on the second floor and then down the stairs.

"Nora?" he asked from inside.

"I'm on the porch, honey."

Daniel pushed open the screen door, rubbing his eyes. "What's going on?"

"I heard Buck pacing down here and let him out to pee. Some animal took off across the yard, and he chased after it. I'm sorry that we woke you."

Daniel looked at the yard but saw no sign of the dog.

"Come on in here. He can stay out. It's only a couple hours until dawn," he said, holding the door open for her.

The last thing Nora wanted to do was to go back in that house. She stayed on the porch swing.

"I think I'll just sit out here for a little while. I'm wide awake now."

Daniel looked half concerned and half asleep.

"I'm fine, Daniel."

"OK. I'm going back to bed."

"OK, honey," she replied as he walked inside and up the stairs.

She leaned in the swing and swayed gently back and forth, wondering where Luke had run off to. Something on the porch railing where he had been standing caught her eye. It was a black, shiny object with a handle. She walked over and discovered that it was Luke's flashlight. She picked it up and turned it on, pointing it toward the yard. The beam had something odd about it, like there was something smudged on the lens. She turned it off and looked into the bulb.

"OK . . . " she whispered to herself, unsure of how to react to what she saw.

There was a small cross made out of black electrical tape on the clear plastic covering. She pointed the light on the floor of the porch and turned it back on. The circle of light that appeared had a shadow of a cross in the middle of it. She remembered how Steve evaporated as soon as Luke's flashlight hit him, and she immediately began to weep.

The moon had finally emerged from behind the storm clouds and lit the way for Luke as he trudged up the ridge beside the Hill's farm. He could see so clearly that it didn't dawn on him until just then that he had left his flashlight on the Hill's porch. It was closer to dawn than dusk; he would get it in a few hours. His clothes were soaked, and his boots were caked in mud. With each step up the steep hill, the squishy earth below him clung to the base of his shoes like it was trying to get him to stop.

He reached the top of the hill and walked over to his hideout. There were four trees close together nearly forming a circle with a makeshift tent tied to them. The thick canopy of the trees had kept everything relatively dry through the brutal storm. He only got wet when he ran after Mrs. Hill. He sat down on a log that he had scavenged and withdrew a bottle of water from his backpack. He took a long chug and screwed the lid back on.

The binoculars were right where he had left them beside the log. He picked them up and looked down at the Hill's house. All of the lights were still off. He assumed everyone was back in their beds for the night. His vantage point gave him a straight view into their kitchen. He stared through the binoculars at the dark kitchen window. Satisfied, he pulled them away from his face and placed them beside the log.

He looked down at his wristwatch and saw the neon 4 AM display: time for bed. He stood up and took off his wet clothes and hung them on a low branch. Wearing just his boxer shorts, he crawled under the green tarp tent and onto his blanket, rolling on his side so he faced the Hill's house. Finally, he shut his eyes. All the things he didn't get to explain to Mrs. Hill flooded his mind. Soon, he was thinking about Alice, and his mind started to relax.

Just as he was drifting off to sleep, he heard a twig snap somewhere in the woods between him and the Hill's house. His eyes shot open, but he didn't move. He heard more footsteps that were getting closer. The way they moved didn't sound like an animal recklessly bounding through the forest. Whatever was making those sounds was moving slowly, deliberately. He heard the leaves rustle as something took two more steps toward him and stopped. Luke stared into the night looking for the intruder. A fiery-eyed, smiling face was staring back from behind the tree in front of him. He gasped, and it vanished. He stayed perfectly still, wide-eyed, with his ears perked up for any sound of it coming closer.

"Luke?" a girl's voice said from behind the tree.

Luke's blood ran cold when he realized who was speaking. He remained motionless, staring at the tree, unblinking.

"Luke, it's me," the girl said.

Amelia, Luke thought but dared not speak. He knew it wasn't her, and to speak her name was to make it real.

"Luuuuke," the voice cooed and then giggled in a way that Amelia never did.

Luke shut his eyes and thought about the last time the thing in the well came to him. It was right after Amelia died when he and Old Man Merle were in the basement. The two of them got into the only fight they ever had, and Luke punched him in the jaw and ran away with Buck hot on his tail. Later that night he was home in his bed when he heard "Amelia" clawing at his window. Old Man Merle had told him that if that ever happened to him, he was to use the flashlight he had given him. Luke shined the flashlight at the window, and the thing disappeared before he could even see what it really looked like.

Luke opened his eyes. His heart sunk to the pit of his stomach when he remembered that he had no flashlight. He didn't even have time to curse himself for being so careless.

The tent flaps behind him parted. Luke instantly perspired from the acute heat wave. He couldn't bring himself to move as he listened to something scoot up to his back. He felt its breath on his neck as a warm, wet arm draped across his chest. His eyes started to water, so he shut them.

"What's the matter?" a version of Amelia's voice whispered and then became increasingly hoarse. "Forget your night light?"

Luke opened his mouth to scream but was silenced when the clawed hand gripped his lower jaw and snapped it from his face.

Down on the porch, Nora rubbed her stomach and continued to rock back and forth until dawn.

CHAPTER 16

THE SUN ROSE, ushering in the start of a new week. Daniel sat in his office in Ohio staring through someone who was paying him to listen. It was his first day back since his self-allotted time off to move into the new house. This was his third patient of the day, and he hadn't taken a single note or offered any substantial feedback other than his fail safe response: "Mhmm, tell me more about that."

Joe Huff, a young man who had seen Daniel on a weekly basis for the last year, knew his psychologist well enough to detect that something else was on his mind. He stopped in the middle of his story about losing his temper at work and started talking about how he had developed a habit for compulsory masturbation while in line at the grocery store.

Daniel, thinking only about driving home and opening the chest in his basement, looked up from his blank notepad when he detected that Joe had stopped speaking. Joe was waiting on a response.

"Mhmm, tell me more about that."

Joe burst out laughing.

"Did I say something funny?"

"No, but you haven't heard a single thing I've said this session, have you?"

Daniel felt his face redden as he struggled to remember something—anything—that Joe had said.

"Yes, you were, uh, telling me about, uh," Daniel tried but just gave up. "You caught me, Joe."

He was thoroughly embarrassed. He had never let something like this happen in his career before.

"I'm so sorry. My body is here, but my mind stayed home today, I suppose."

Joe was more amused than offended and just kept giggling.

"Don't worry about it, man. I needed a good laugh. That's the best therapy there is," Joe said.

"Oh, good, then I can still bill you for services."

Joe laughed, but Daniel assured him that this session would be free.

"It would be unethical for me to do anything otherwise," he said.

Daniel spent the remaining twenty minutes doing his best to ignore the intrusive images of the chest and the mysteries scrawled in those notebooks and recorded on the tapes. As soon as the hour was up, he told Leslie to reschedule all remaining appointments for the week. Leslie was visibly flustered after having just put together a crammed schedule because of his previous time off.

"I just need another week, Leslie. You're invaluable, and I'll make it up to you," he smiled.

She just shook her head from behind her desk.

"You still have three more appointments today. One of them is here, Daniel," she said and gestured toward the woman sitting alone watching the lobby TV.

He rolled his eyes and walked over to her.

"Sarah!" he began with mock enthusiasm. "I'm so terribly sorry to do this to you since you're already here and all, but I've got a bit of an emergency at home and need to take off right now."

"That's OK, Dr. Hill," the meek woman replied.

She was obviously let down by the news and seemed to have something she needed to discuss. On any other day

Daniel would've picked up on her demeanor, but his mind was already busy scanning the pages of Merle's journals. She stood up from her seat and started for the exit.

"Oh, Sarah, you can reschedule with Leslie at the front desk. She'll get you in for early next week."

Daniel pulled into his driveway around 3 PM, much earlier than he was expected from a full day's worth of work. He cut off his engine and noticed that Nora's car was not in the driveway. He got out and walked across the front yard while checking out the fence in the distance. There was not a broken or unpainted spot in sight. Luke had apparently made some progress since yesterday.

Daniel walked through the yard to the bend in the fence line to scan the rest of the meadow. As soon as he rounded the corner, he saw Luke at the far end of the farm painting the last little section.

"Good God, that boy is a monster."

He turned around and headed back toward the house, walking along the newly painted fence. It was a beautiful, sunny afternoon, and he was glad to be home. All day he had not felt right being away from this place. Now that he was back on the farm, thoughts of work and responsibilities floated away.

Just before he stepped onto the front porch, he heard Buck growling from the side of the house. He turned toward the noise but didn't see the dog. He walked around the house and saw Buck recoiling and snarling at something in the distance. He had never seen the dog this terrified and aggressive before. Buck looked like a feral beast being apprehended by animal control.

"Easy, boy, easy."

The dog wasn't looking at Daniel, but at something in the meadow beyond the front yard.

"What is it, Buck?" he asked as he turned to see what was in the dog's line of sight.

He tried to find something that would trigger this response in the normally docile hound, but saw nothing. No birds, no bears, no mountain lions, no humans, nothing. He looked back at Buck who was definitely fixated on something. Daniel noticed the tell-tale hair spiking down the dog's spine. He turned back to the yard again, but still saw nothing.

"There's nothing there, boy," he said.

Buck continued to growl. Daniel snapped his fingers and stomped his foot and shouted, "Hey!" to break the dog's trance. Buck jerked with a startle and then bit Daniel's forearm.

"Shit!" he screamed as he pulled his arm back and looked at the purple indentions in his flesh. The dog didn't break the skin.

"Why did you do that?" he shouted, but Buck stood up and bolted the other way, sprinting nonstop until he reached the tree line in the back yard.

Daniel shook off the pain and turned to walk back toward the front of the house. He saw Luke standing by the bend in the fence line, motionless like a statue. Daniel stared, wondering what he was doing. He waved at the boy. Luke slowly smiled and gave a slight head nod before disappearing back from where he had just come.

Daniel entered his house and heard music playing from Alice's bedroom. He walked upstairs and was just about to knock on her door when he heard her start singing along with the song at the top of her lungs. He smiled and listened to her belt out some new pop song that he'd heard on the radio a few times when she was in the car. Just as the chorus was about to come on, he burst through the door, matching her harmony like an overzealous backup singer.

Alice was in the process of putting on her bathing suit when her dad exploded into her room. She screamed while desperately trying to cover herself. Daniel's face turned blood red as he did an instant pivot and marched out of the room saying, "I'm sorry. I'm sorry. I'm sorry."

"Dad! What the hell?" his daughter screamed as he shut the door behind him and marched down the stairs.

He slid his briefcase under his corner desk in the living room and loosened his tie. He walked into the kitchen and grabbed a beer from the refrigerator. He popped the top, took a swig, and headed outside to check the mail. When he approached the porch with a few bills in hand, he saw Alice standing there in her bathing suit, arms crossed, giving him a death stare.

"Can't you knock?"

"I know. I'm sorry, honey."

"What are you doing home so early? I thought you were working all day."

"I had to rearrange my schedule to get some stuff done around here," he smiled. "Are you going swimming somewhere?"

"Yes. Luke is taking me up to the waterfall when he's finished with the fence."

Daniel nodded his head and pretended not to be annoyed by this. He didn't want to push her away.

"Sounds fun," he said forcing a grin.

"Luke's a good guy," Alice reminded her father.

"I know, honey," he said as he took a step toward her and placed his hand on her shoulder. "More importantly, you're the most level-headed teenager I know. Seriously, have fun with Luke."

She smiled and then noticed Luke about one hundred yards away walking across the meadow carrying his work supplies. Daniel turned around to see what she was looking at.

"Speak of the devil," he teased, causing Alice to give him a slight elbow to the ribs.

Daniel waved and Luke nodded his head. He turned back to Alice.

"Hey, where's your mom?"

"She just said she had to run errands," she said. "She's been gone for about an hour."

"Ah, OK. Well, I've got some things to sort through in the basement. Have fun with Luke but not too much fun, OK?"

"OK, Dad."

Daniel turned and gave Luke one final wave before walking back into his house. He tossed the mail on the counter and headed down into the basement with his beer, shutting the kitchen door behind him.

The light flickered as he descended the steps. The air was cool and earthy with nothing out of the ordinary in sight. He walked around the staircase and saw the chest underneath the stairs where he had left it. He felt the anticipation building as he stared at the unopened case.

"OK, Merle. Talk to me," Daniel said as he grabbed the chest by the sides and dragged it out into the middle of the room.

He opened it and spread the contents across the floor, putting the notebooks in chronological order followed by the tapes. He picked up the notebook nearest him and turned to the first page.

"April 19, 1973," he read aloud, taking a sip of beer.

While Daniel was reading the journal, Nora was sitting in her car outside of her old school in Ohio trying to find the courage to go inside. It was mid-June, and the parking lot was empty with the exception of a few of the administrators' vehicles. She didn't have a foolproof plan for coming up here to find Steve. If he wasn't at the school, she guessed she was going to look him up in the local phone book and go to his home. Whatever she had to do to speak to him, she was willing to do it.

After she talked with Luke on the porch the night before, she had stayed up trying to piece together what he had said and what she had experienced in the basement. The longer she was awake, the less she remembered from either occasion. As the hours passed, memories faded away like a waking dream. Somehow, she had forgotten most and rationalized the rest. She had accepted that Luke was just a deeply hurt young man who was struggling with the trauma of having an alcoholic father and losing a girlfriend. She had planned on talking to him when he came by for his morning check-in before reporting to the fence, but he never showed. What little she remembered from being in the basement she attributed to nightmares brought on by intense guilt from her previous infidelity. Images of the Steve apparition in the basement, the botched abortion, and details of Luke's confession burned from her consciousness and blew away like smoke. The only truth she was left with was that she had had a nightmare about Steve and could no longer go on with the incident swept under the rug.

After she and Alice ate lunch, she lied that she had to go run some errands and drove an hour up the road to the school parking lot. Now, she stared at the only two vehicles remaining. Luckily, one of the vehicles was Steve's truck. She looked at the truck and took a deep breath. Her vision drifted over to the main entrance of the building and then to his office window beside it. The light was on, and someone moved around inside. She knew what she had to do. For her own sanity, she knew what she had to do.

She approached the main entrance and tugged on the glass door. Locked. She turned to her right and saw the window and the back of the man's head inside. She took a deep breath and walked over to it, sidestepping a prickly bush. The man inside jumped when she tapped on the glass. The shock from the sound was nothing compared to the look on his face when he turned around and saw Nora Hill standing outside his office.

Nora mouthed, "Can I come in?" and pointed toward the main entrance.

Steve nervously nodded and walked out to let her in.

"This is crazy. This is crazy," she said to herself as she waited by the door.

After a few minutes, Steve appeared on the other side of the glass and pushed the door open for her.

"Hello, Nora. What brings you here?"

His tone told Nora that he didn't know if she was here for round two or to shoot him where he stood. He looked down at her bulging belly and went pale.

"Don't worry. It's not yours," Nora said as she walked past him into the building.

She headed straight for his office as he followed along like a child who knew he was in trouble.

"Can I help you with something?" he asked as Nora barged into his office and he entered behind her.

"You can shut the door."

Steve did and then walked around to his chair behind his desk and sat down.

"To what do I owe this pleasure?"

"Steve, please just listen."

She paused and thought carefully before she spoke.

"I don't hate you," she finally said.

"OK. I don't hate you either."

"Up until this morning, I thought I did."

"Oh, I see," he said.

"It was easy for me to point to you after we did what we did and say you were the cause of this. You were my superior, and you knew that I was married, but that didn't stop you from making your intentions crystal clear."

Steve looked down at his desk, visibly uncomfortable, as Nora continued.

"If I were to stop the tape right there, then I would be justified in being angry with you; however, we both know what choice I made," she said.

Steve looked back up at her to see where she was going with this.

"*I* made the decision to walk into your office that day. *I* made the decision to have sex with you. *I* accepted that invitation. If there's anyone that I should be resentful toward, it's me. You're just a symbol . . . just a painful reminder of what I did wrong. Every time I saw you in person or in my head, it evoked this guilt in me that I quickly masked with rage toward you," she said as she fought the tears she felt welling up.

Steve stared blankly.

"I guess what I'm saying is that I drove up here today to tell you that I don't have any bad feelings toward you, Steve. I forgive you and accept you as you are. I know that I can't possibly forgive myself until I do that. That's it. That's all I have to say."

Steve nodded and seemed to be deeply considering what he had just heard. After a moment, he spoke.

"Jesus, Nora," he finally began. "I thought it was just sex."

She winced, cocking her head with a smile of disbelief.

"Goodbye, Steve," she said and walked out of his office.

CHAPTER 17

DANIEL SAT IN the basement with his beer and began reading the first page in Merle Blatty's journal, dated April 1973 . . .

I reckon I better get this written down and out of my head before I start to lose my marbles. My name is Merle Cliff Blatty, and I am fifty-three-years-old at the time of this confession. I suppose that's a good enough word for it. I was going to write journal entry, but confession feels more appropriate.

I'm not trying to tell you my entire life's story because there's no need. I'm nothing special. No one who finds this writing long after I've passed needs to know what my childhood was like or what baseball team I rooted for. I'll include only the necessary details of my life that helped form the larger picture of what's going on here. My only intention is to document my encounters with absolute evil.

My wife, Gertie, and I were married in our early twenties, and we moved to this farm and had a boy shortly after that. My son, Sam, God rest his soul, got bit by a copperhead when he was eight years old and passed. Needless to say, it was the worst experience of our lives. Gertie never got over it, and Sam's death eventually led to hers.

I know I wasn't there for her like I should've been. My reaction was to stay busy and keep my mind occupied. I built the fence around the farm, brought in some chickens, and dug a well in the basement. I know now that the devil doesn't just use idle hands to do his work.

She hit the booze hard and spent her days sobbing in random corners of the house. I'd come home from work and find her passed out in the early evenings. I told her something had to give, and she knew it before I said it. She agreed to go to church on Wednesdays and Sundays, and that's what we did. Gertie quit hitting the booze, but she became dependent on something else entirely.

She joined an all-women's prayer group that met before the Wednesday service. One of the ladies in that group listened to my wife's story of losing Sam. This woman—Rita was her name—told Gertie that she had heard of ways to communicate with spirits from the other side. She'd been studying books on the occult out of morbid curiosity I suppose, and she told Gertie she wanted to put it into practice. When Gertie came home and told me that, I about lost it. I thought, what kind of church group has ideas about talking to dead people? I told her that it seemed like witchcraft to me, and I wanted no part of it. Gertie was not happy with my reaction, but as far as I knew at the time, that was the end of it.

About a month went by and Gertie seemed her old self. She was off the booze, she was back to cooking and keeping the house in order, and she was even putting together quite the garden in the backyard. I no longer walked into rooms and found her crying. She even made some new friends she met through Rita from church. Everything appeared to be getting back to the way it was before Sam died. Looking back now, I realize that I probably only saw what I wanted to see.

I came home early from work one Friday and saw two cars parked in my driveway. I knew one of them was Rita's, but I didn't recognize the other one. I walked into the house, but no one was home. No one was upstairs, and *the living room and kitchen were empty. I thought maybe Gertie and her group of friends had gone on a stroll across the farm until I heard the chanting coming from the basement.*

I opened the door and crept down a few steps. I peeked from the top of the stairs and saw Gertie, Rita, and two other women sitting in a circle on the floor. They were in the dark with a bunch of lit candles in the middle of them. All of them had their eyes shut and were repeating the same phrase in a foreign language. I know now that it was Latin.

I sat there and watched until they stopped. It was quiet for a minute, and then Rita started talking first. She asked if Sam could hear her. I remember feeling like I was going to lose my lunch when I realized what they were doing. They were holding a séance, trying to talk to my dead boy. She asked if Sam was in the room with them. I didn't hear anything respond to her, but they all giggled in awe like they did. I saw my wife start to cry and then talk directly to Sam like he was right there in front of her face.

That was enough for me. I stormed down the steps, and they all shot up like a bunch of kids doing something they knew they shouldn't. I screamed and demanded to know what was going on in my house. I told those women to get the hell out. They ran up the steps hooting and hollering and out the front door. Then I saw a side of Gertie I had never seen before. She screamed at me for interrupting her connection to Sam. I told her she was crazy and that our boy was not in the basement with them, but she insisted that I didn't see because I didn't believe. She told me he was there—talking to her from inside the well—and I ruined it.

Over the weekend, anytime I walked into a room, Gertie walked out of it. She was more distant than ever, even more so than when she was boozing. I tried to talk to her a couple of times, but it just turned into a shouting match.

I went to bed alone and woke up in the middle of the night to find that she still wasn't there. I walked downstairs. She was nowhere to be seen, but I knew exactly where she was. The basement door was shut, and there was this glowing light coming from under it. I jerked it open and ran down the stairs.

The basement was hotter than blazes and smelled something awful. Gertie was lying in the middle of the floor on her back, arms and legs spread out like she was making a snow angel. She was staring up at the ceiling with a great big smile on her face. I noticed the little door was open, and there was light coming out of it like something in there was on fire. Before I could look inside, the glowing disappeared, and we were alone in complete darkness.

I grabbed Gertie and shook her, but she was unresponsive. I threw her over my shoulder and carried her up the stairs and laid her on the couch. I couldn't get her to break from the trance she was in. She just stared at something that I couldn't see and smiled in a way that she never had before. It was only when I said that I was going to phone Dr. Jones that she snapped right out of it. She was confused and irritable. I tried to comfort her and talk to her, but she just ran up to our bedroom.

Things only got worse after that. The few times that I could get her to speak, all she would talk about was contacting Sam or getting through to the other side of the barrier. She was losing what little weight she had, wasting away before my eyes.

I couldn't take it anymore and started finding any reason to not go home right after work. I finally started joining the boys at the bar after clock out, and pretty soon I was doing exactly what I had resented her for: getting drunk to dull the pain.

I know now that if I hadn't been so numb through those last few weeks of her life, then I would've seen the evil take hold . . . I maybe could've prevented the infestation.

Whatever she was talking to in the basement during the séance tricked her into thinking it was my boy. It lured her down there alone and afraid and it eventually took full control of her.

The night Gertie died I was passed out drunk in bed. I felt a warm hand squeeze my ankle and woke up to see her climbing a chair at the foot of our bed. It was my wife's body there in front of me, but it wasn't her inside. Her eyes had changed . . . teeth looked different . . . even the way she was smiling at me was like two hooks were stretching out either side of her mouth. It looked like steam was coming off her skin.

I had never felt such terror in my life. Maybe if I hadn't been paralyzed with fear, I could've jumped off the bed and saved her, but I couldn't find the strength to move. I saw that she had a rope around her neck that was tied to the ceiling fan. Those eyes glowed bright orange like a fire was burning in her mind. She laughed with a voice that wasn't hers, and then she jumped.

From that moment on, I knew my wife wasn't crazy. I knew her circle of friends weren't crazy. I knew they had opened some sort of gateway to the other side trying to find Sam, only something else found its way through instead. The thing is, people do seances all the time that don't work. Why did Gertie's? I knew, but I was too full of guilt to admit it. I dug that well and opened Hell's back door, and Gertie gave permission for the evil to come through.

After I laid Gertie to rest beside our boy, I bolted up the well in the little room and covered it with crosses. I latched the door shut, moved all of Gertie's belongings into the basement, and knew that I had a lot of studying and practicing to do before I could confront what was down there again.

From that day until this very moment that I'm putting this pen to paper, I have traveled all over this great country trying to find other people who have had experiences similar to mine. I started out reading magazine articles, old newspaper interviews—anything that would give me a lead on tracking down cases involving the supernatural. Most of them were dead ends . . . frauds, charlatans just looking to profit or get attention.

But, after a few years of legwork, I finally encountered a house in North Carolina that was dealing with paranormal events that I couldn't explain. Again, I felt overwhelmed and unprepared. I had spent so much time looking for anything that would help me understand what happened to Gertie that I failed to plan on what I would do if I actually found it.

Luckily for me, there was a priest called in to investigate the house. He was a man in his sixties named Father Stollings. The Church frowns on exorcisms these days, so very few priests are ever given that duty. Even fewer report findings of a legitimate possession.

I told Father Stollings my interest in the situation and what had led me there. I remember him smiling and nodding his head the whole time we talked like I was describing something that wasn't completely unbelievable. Father Stollings then filled me in on what he believed was going on in this house and how it was similar to my own story. He told me the house was under attack from demonic forces, and only the power of God could eradicate it. I watched Father Stollings cleanse the house using specific rituals and techniques. Sure enough, the paranormal events stopped.

I asked the priest if I could assist him on future situations such as this, and he obliged. He trained me and a young priest named Father Martin together. The three of us got along just fine. I could tell that Father Martin had a bright future ahead of him.

Father Stollings knew that I wasn't a man of the cloth, but he would frequently say that it was my belief that gave *me Power, not a smock or being on the church's payroll. I learned everything I know today from that man. When he passed in '65, I knew it was time for me to get some practice of my own under my belt.*

For the next several years, I continued my tour through America, searching for people who were looking for help but weren't getting any. I started going to hospitals, sanitariums, and psych wards looking for someone who had encountered evil yet everyone dismissed them as crazy. Sure enough, I ended up finding what I was looking for.

I assisted a few families during this time. I didn't perform any type of exorcism or cleansing ritual myself. I more or less served in a diagnostic role. If the subject's friends and family or even the Church had dismissed them, I stepped in to investigate. Most turned out to not be genuine, but there were a few I was able to document as being credible. I would then contact the local clergy and would have to fight just to convince them to come in and take a serious look.

Watching these men of the cloth perform the same rites and rituals that Father Stollings performed made me have the firm realization that I no longer wanted to be the middleman. If Father Stollings was right and my faith was what gave me the Power to combat evil, then I was going to put that to the test.

It is my intention that the remainder of this journal serve as documentation for my work as an unofficial exorcist. I am currently writing this while sitting on my front porch as the sun sets over God's country. Again, the year is 1973, I am fifty-three years old, and less than twenty-four hours ago, I completed my first exorcism.

Daniel looked up from the open notebook on his lap. "Jesus."

He thumbed to the next page titled: "Number 1: The

House on Sycamore Lane." He opened his fourth beer and started reading.

Nora pulled down Sunny Branch Way a little after 5 PM. The long drive back home after confronting Steve felt like five minutes. She had sung or hummed every song that came on the radio, even the ones she didn't usually enjoy. Part of a giant weight had been lifted off her shoulders. She knew that she wouldn't fully be set free from her guilt until she confessed to Daniel, but she also believed that doing that would only harm her family to alleviate her own burden and that was unacceptable. No, she would still keep her secret; she just would no longer hate herself for it.

Her euphoria was sucked away like water down a drain when her house came into view, and she saw Daniel home from work. She looked at the time on the dashboard and saw that he wasn't supposed to be home for at least another hour. He had specifically told her that he would be at work later than usual today to catch up after taking so much time off.

She didn't like how she was feeling. She didn't like having to make up lies to cover her tracks, especially after what she had just been through. She drove up the driveway and parked her car. Many possible reasons for why she had been gone all afternoon flooded her mind. She looked around her car and realized that she hadn't bought anything. She'd have to factor that into whatever lie she told.

The box in her trunk came to mind. She took her keys out of the ignition and walked around to the back of the car. She opened the trunk and grabbed the box of school supplies that she had been procrastinating removing from her car. It was packed full of writing utensils, office supplies, and notebook paper. She had just planned on leaving it there until she started her new job, but knew this would be a convenient excuse to bring it in the house.

The house was quiet when Nora walked through the door with the cumbersome box. She placed it on the kitchen table and yelled for Daniel, but he didn't respond. She walked upstairs and saw that their bedroom and Alice's were both empty. She went back downstairs looking for any sign of life. Daniel's briefcase was under his desk in the living room. She turned back toward the front door thinking maybe Daniel and Alice were in the yard somewhere when she saw the basement door out of the corner of her eye. She felt a flare of hesitation in her gut, but it passed as quickly as it had come. Not giving it a second thought, she approached the basement and opened the door, immediately noticing that the light was on.

"Daniel?" she asked as she walked down the steps.

She saw her husband sitting on the floor beside Merle's opened chest. He had a notebook open on his lap while the others were scattered around him with the VHS tapes. Several empty beer bottles stood against the stairs in a neat row. Nora approached her husband from behind, but he still didn't acknowledge her presence.

"Daniel?" she said as she poked his shoulder with her knee.

He jumped and spilled a little bit of his beer on the journal he was reading.

"Good God. You scared the shit out of me," he said as he patted the journal dry with his shirt.

"What are you doing down here?"

"Learning all about the former inhabitant. Wait until I tell you what's in here, Nora."

"Why are you home so early? I thought you had to work late?"

Daniel looked annoyed that she didn't share his enthusiasm.

"I moved appointments back another week."

"What? Why?"

Daniel looked at all the scattered documents around him.

"I had to know what was in here. I couldn't focus. I was doing my clients a disservice."

"You cancelled a week's worth of appointments so you could sit in our basement and get drunk while you read an old man's diary?"

"What's your fucking problem?"

She was at a complete loss for words, staring at him in disbelief.

"Don't talk to me like that."

She finally saw some remorse come over his face as he blinked and rubbed his eyes.

"I'm sorry. This is just important to me. I just need a week. OK?"

"OK, Daniel," she said with concern.

She backed away from her husband and walked up the stairs realizing that he didn't even ask her where she had been. She stopped before entering the kitchen.

"Where's Alice?" she asked.

"Went swimming with Luke a little bit ago."

"Luke," she whispered to herself as she remembered that she had wanted to speak with him earlier that day but couldn't remember why.

She thought about the night before, but it was a blur. There was something about being in the basement and thinking of Luke that made her start to panic, but she just couldn't see through the fog in her mind. All she knew was that Steve no longer had any power over her, and for that she was grateful.

CHAPTER 18

EARLIER THAT SAME EVENING, Alice had stood in the front yard watching Luke head her way. Her dad had just made her promise to be good on her swimming date with her new friend, and then he had gone inside. Her mom still hadn't made it back from whatever errands she had to run. Alice smiled as Luke was almost to her porch. Luke feigned a pathetic attempt at a smile in return.

"Are you worn out from work?" Alice asked as soon as he was in earshot.

"Not at all," Luke replied with a deep rasp in his voice. "I could work all day."

"I know my dad appreciates that."

"It's just so damn hot out here," he said as sweat poured down his face.

He looked into her eyes but seemed to be looking through her. His mouth hung slightly open as he breathed heavily. The sun was behind his head, and Alice had to shield her eyes to look at him. An orange flash brighter than the sun flamed across his eyes. Alice knew *her* eyes must be playing tricks on her.

"Are you ready to go swimming?" he asked. "I'm hotter than I've ever been in my life."

Alice reached down and grabbed her towel off of the porch swing and said, "Yep. Let's go."

"The four-wheeler is at my house. I didn't drive it over today."

"Why not?"

"I just wanted to walk. It feels like it's been decades since I've stretched my legs," he smiled.

"OK . . . "

Luke's normally tan complexion looked unusually pale with red blotches that Alice could swear were moving like some living ink blot test. His eyes had heavy dark circles under them, and his hair that he would usually keep tucked behind his ears hung in strands matted to his cheeks. Whenever the breeze would blow, Alice got faint whiffs of something rotten. He took a step closer and held out his hand.

"Want to walk to my house with me and get the four-wheeler?"

Alice held out her hand and smiled as he took it.

His palm was clammy and hot. His long fingers gripped her small hand firmly as they began walking down the driveway.

"You are burning up," she said. "Are you sure you're feeling OK?"

"Fine," he said with an agitated tone.

"How far away do you live again?"

"Less than a mile."

"You sound different. Are you getting sick?"

"I've been out in the sun all day. I just need a drink," he said, still looking down as they walked.

"I can run back in the house really quick and get you a water."

"That's OK. I'll get one at home."

The two of them walked down Sunny Branch Way. Alice had never been down this part of the road. She looked at the lush green trees that surrounded them in all directions. A little ditch ran parallel with the road. A small stream of water leftover from the storm the night before flowed in their direction.

Alice heard a loud engine coming around the bend in

159

the road. A large diesel pickup truck came speeding at them, fully on their side of the road. Alice jumped into the ditch, but Luke stood his ground as the truck jerked at the last second to avoid hitting him. The driver looked out his window at Luke who was staring back at him, unfazed.

"Sorry, Luke!" the middle-aged man said as he came to a stop. "Young lady, are you OK?"

Alice stepped out of the ditch. Her feet and sandals were soaked.

"Yes. Don't worry about it," she said.

"I musta rode that curve a little too hard. Luke, you OK?"

Luke still hadn't said anything as he continued to stare at the driver. Alice watched the driver's face go from concerned to shocked. She could only see the back of Luke's head.

"Just fine," he said.

The driver looked like he was going to be sick as he slowly looked away from Luke and put his truck in gear.

"You all take care," he forced out. He looked at Alice and then nervously back at Luke before driving away.

"What was that all about?" Alice asked.

Luke turned to face her.

"I don't know what you mean."

"Who was that?"

"Not sure."

"But he knew you."

"Come on. Let's go."

He grabbed her hand and practically dragged her down the road. His long-legged stride was almost a jog for her.

"Luke, can you slow down for the short girl?"

Luke decreased his speed, and they walked in silence for the remaining few minutes of their journey. Alice did her best to ignore the increasingly uncomfortable grip around her hand. They finished a straight stretch in the road and were approaching a rundown one-story house nestled in some trees ahead on the left.

"This is it," Luke said as he started to veer across the road pulling her with him.

Alice studied the house and could tell that it had been beautiful once, but the elements had gotten to it over the years. She saw Luke's four-wheeler parked on the far side of the yard. There was an old blue and white Ford truck parked in the gravel driveway.

"Is that your dad's truck?"

Somehow since they began their walk, Luke's appearance had gotten even worse. His skin was paler and the red blotches were brighter, almost glowing like a lava lamp. An orange flare flickered across his eyes as he looked down at her. Alice knew what she saw that time, and it was no trick of the light. Her eyes widened, and he smiled.

"Come on. I have to show you something."

Luke stepped into the front yard, dragging her with him. For the first time since they began their walk, she seriously considered yanking her hand from his and running away. Before she could give it a second thought, they were approaching the entrance to his house. He gave the flimsy door a hard shove, and it swung open.

"I can just wait out here," she said, but he jerked her inside.

She winced from the pain in her shoulder, realizing that he could yank her arm right out of its socket if he felt like it. He shut the door behind her. She was about to voice her concern when she noticed Luke's father in the living room sitting in his recliner with a beer. He was in his late forties and was short and stocky with a basketball-sized belly. Aside from the dark hair, Luke looked nothing like him.

"Hey, son," the man said with a buzzed inflection in his voice. "Who's your friend?"

Luke turned his back to his father and locked the front door.

"Luke, what are you doing?" Alice said low enough for only him to hear.

He put his face close to Alice's and grinned as his eyes glowed orange.

"Luke is burning in Hell," he whispered.

She pulled away in shock. The smell of rotten eggs permeated her nose. Heat radiated off him, making her feel like she was standing in front of an open oven. He watched her slide back against the wall close to the door, and he slid between her and the exit.

"Sit," he growled and threw her onto the couch.

"Hey, now what the hell do you think you're doing?" his father said, starting to get out of the recliner.

Luke took two strides toward his dad and punched him in the side of the face and cracked his jaw. Alice screamed from the couch as the intoxicated man's eyes rolled back as he fought to stay conscious. His dislocated jaw hung sideways.

She jumped up and ran for the door, but Luke grabbed her by the throat and lifted her off the ground. She clawed at his searing grip, fighting for air. Her flesh felt like it was burning under his grasp. He shoved her into the wall, and she fell down into a coughing fit.

"I'm burning up," Luke said as he jerked at the collar of his white shirt, annoyed.

He stumbled backward against the wall, disoriented. Alice watched with confusion from the floor. He covered his eyes with his hands, and she saw red boils forming all over his arms. One after another began to pop, sending little squirts of black discharge onto the already stained carpet. She tried to scream, but her throat was too sore.

"It's so goddamn hot!" he screamed, pressing against the wall so hard that he left a smear of bloody puss.

He gripped his hair in both hands, wailing as he peeled off two clumps of scalp like wet wallpaper and dropped them to the ground. Alice looked over at Luke's father who was wide-eyed in shock on the recliner. He made eye contact with Alice and pushed himself up. Luke didn't notice and ripped his shirt down the middle.

"I'm burning up, burning, burning . . . "

His voice was getting increasingly raspy and animalistic. More bubbles were popping all over his exposed chest like fleshy volcanos.

"Not yet!" he hissed.

He looked up just in time to see his father drop his shoulder and barrel into him, slamming him harder into the wall and splattering several boils on his back.

Wasting no time, Alice jumped off the floor. She ran deeper into the house, praying for a way out. The first room in the hallway was obviously Luke's. There was a window above his bed, and she sprinted to it. She grabbed both metal latches and lifted the heavy pane of glass. She stood on the bed and slid her left leg out, straddling the open windowsill. Her head bent forward, and her flattened torso barely cleared the opening. Her right foot still dangled in Luke's room as she held onto the window with her hand.

The ground was only five feet below her. She quickly swung her other leg out and dropped onto the warm grass. Luke's father screamed inside, but the sound was abruptly cut short. Alice turned toward the woods in front of her and began to run.

"Alice!" Luke screamed from the open window now twenty yards back.

She looked back and saw a melting, crimson face glaring at her as it slid its fleshless arm out along the exterior of the house. She felt like she was going to lose control of her bladder, but she turned back and kept running.

"Come with me, Alice," it cackled behind her.

She dodged trees and hopped treacherous roots as she fled. Her house was in the opposite direction of where she was heading, but she didn't care. Her first priority was to put as much distance between herself and that monster before finding her way back home.

"ALICE!" the thing inside Luke's body howled.

Her pace slowed as she reached an incline in the forest.

She hurried uphill with a desperation she didn't know she had in her.

"Join us, Alice!"

The voice was closer. Her adrenaline reserves kicked in, and her legs moved faster. She saw the peak of the incline just ahead of her. She knew that if she could reach it, she could easily change direction and lose her pursuer.

"There's nowhere to run, Alice," it teased from the base of the hill below her.

Alice dared not look back. She knew that if she got a good view of the entity, she would go into shock. Twigs and dry ground crunched behind her as the thing trailed her. She sprinted up and over the hill. She felt her stomach rise to her throat when she saw the steep drop in front of her. There was thinning vegetation on an unforgiving slope of jagged rocks.

Her instincts forced her straight down the decline. She fought to stay on her feet, but after three slippery steps, she landed on her tailbone and started to slide. She hit a hole and toppled over to her side, descending faster as her body rolled like a loose log. The creature was shrieking somewhere behind her, but she had lost all sense of direction.

She came to a hard stop as she crashed into a tree at the bottom. Her vision swirled around her like a whirlpool. She pushed herself up and leaned against the tree looking up at the blurry thing staring down at her from the hill. She saw it release something the size of a football from its hand. The object rolled down the hill, bouncing higher and higher as it picked up speed.

Alice closed her eyes as it took one final bounce before thwacking into her sore stomach. She looked down in her lap with still-fuzzy vision. She blinked and focused on two eyeballs staring back up at her, fixed in an expression of terror. Her sight cleared, and she realized she was staring at Luke's father's head. It was missing the bottom jaw, and its torn cheek skin dangled loosely like a trench coat. She screamed, unable to move, unable to process what was happening, hoping to wake up in the comforts of her bedroom back at home. Those dead eyes stared back at her, reflecting her horror.

Rocks and other debris slid down the hill. Alice knew it was too late to do anything. The creature reached the bottom of the hill and crawled over to her as she slumped against the tree. She closed her eyes and sobbed. Heat radiated off the thing that was right in front of her, but she dared not peek. Five long, claw-like fingers combed through her hair and then palmed her head like a basketball. It tightened its grip. The sharp nails pierced her scalp and began dragging her back up the hill, despite her kicking and screaming. It jerked her head up and slammed it against a rock, knocking all the fight out of her. The charred hand wrapped her long hair around it like a dog leash and proceeded to drag her limp body across the dirt.

CHAPTER 19

NORA DUMPED THE bowl of spaghetti into the strainer hanging onto the sink. The steam covered the window in front of her, obscuring her view of the sunset past the front yard. She scooped up globs of noodles, filled three plates, and then topped them with sauce and meatballs. Timed perfectly, the oven dinged letting her know that the garlic bread was ready. She sat two plates on the table and placed one in the microwave for Alice whom she thought should be getting home soon. She walked over and opened the basement door.

"Daniel," she said down the stairs.

No response. She heard Buck behind her walk from the living room to the kitchen as he curiously eyeballed the open basement door.

"Daniel!"

Still nothing.

Annoyed, she turned off the lights. There was finally some commotion down there.

"Hey! Turn the lights back on," Daniel said.

Nora flicked the switch up and heard her husband shuffling around

"You OK?" she asked as she walked down the stairs and caught sight of him.

Daniel was leaning against the wall and wincing.

"Yeah. My damn legs fell asleep," he replied and then looked at her. "What'd you want?"

"Dinner is ready. Take a break and come and eat."

Daniel anxiously looked at the open journal on the floor.

"Daniel," she said sternly. "Come. And. Eat."

He nodded, pushed himself off the wall, and followed her upstairs.

The two of them sat at the kitchen table eating their food. Daniel had taken another beer out of the refrigerator to have with his meal.

"How many of those have you had?"

"Just because you can't drink, pregnant lady, doesn't mean that I can't."

She squinted at him in disbelief.

"That's not at all what I meant. I just don't want you to pass out on the basement floor tonight."

"I definitely won't," he smirked. "What I'm reading is far too compelling."

"The ramblings of an old hillbilly?"

"It's so much more than that," he said glancing up from his plate with the look of a poker player holding a winning hand.

She leaned forward.

"Consider my interest piqued."

He smiled and took another bite, slowly chewing a mouthful of pasta and contemplating where to begin.

"OK," he said as he swallowed his food. "So, the former inhabitant, Merle, was most definitely an exorcist."

Nora shivered as she suddenly remembered being on the front porch with Luke. She remembered him saying those very words but couldn't recall any other part of the conversation.

"What do you mean?" she asked, trying to hide her bewilderment.

Daniel smiled like he had the scariest ghost story on deck and he was about to unleash it on an unsuspecting crowd of kids surrounding a campfire. He filled her in on everything he had read about Merle's tragic life. When he got to the part about Gertie's final moments, he slowed down and spoke quietly, aiming for a particularly spooky climax.

"One night he goes to sleep and wakes up with her standing at the foot of his bed. He says her eyes were burning orange and she had sharp teeth . . . " he began.

An image of Steve down in the basement with glowing orange eyes appeared in Nora's head, and her heart skipped a beat.

" . . . and before Merle's drunk ass could do anything, poor Gertie hanged herself from the ceiling fan. Right . . . up . . . there," Daniel said pointing to their bedroom.

Nora dropped her fork and stood up from the table. She ran over to the kitchen sink and vomited up everything that she had just eaten. Panic and confusion fogged her mind between scattered memories that she couldn't connect. Daniel stood up from the table and walked over to her and put his hand on her lower back.

"Shit, Nora. I'm sorry," he said. "Is this a pregnancy thing or are you really freaked out?"

She gripped the sides of the sink and dry heaved once more. She spit and then grabbed a dish towel and wiped her face. Daniel carefully reached around her and turned the faucet on to flush everything down. She looked around to face him.

"I didn't think you would react like that," he said.

Nora shook her head.

"It's not just your story, Daniel," she explained. "I keep having weird visions and remembering things that couldn't possibly have happened. I just feel like something isn't right here."

"You sure it's not the baby?"

"No, it's not the fucking baby, Daniel. Something is not right with this whole situation," she said as she walked out of the kitchen with the dish towel.

Daniel listened to her go upstairs and slam the door. Moments later the shower in their bedroom started running. He turned back to the kitchen table and picked up his beer. He took a final gulp and chucked it in the trash before opening the refrigerator to grab another. He sat back down and resumed his meal.

The front door slowly opened behind him. He heard someone step inside and then the screen door slammed shut. Daniel shoveled another fork full of food into his mouth without turning around.

"How was the swimming hole?" he asked, feeling the booze run through his system.

Behind him, something was dragging his daughter's body by the hair. Her limp limbs slid quietly across the floor. A disembodied voice that sounded enough like Alice's answered for her.

"Fine, Dad. I just need to go rinse off."

Daniel continued to eat as Alice was pulled up the stairs, thumping on every step.

"Stop stomping, please!"

He took a drink just as her door shut. He wiped the remaining bit of sauce on his plate with his final bite of garlic bread and stood up from the table. Between the beer and the dinner, he felt like he was going to burst. He rinsed his plate and grabbed another beer anyhow.

Nora stepped out of the shower, humming along to the Garth Brooks song on the radio. She had never been the biggest country music fan, but with this station having the strongest signal way out at the farm, it was starting to grow on her. She was drying herself off in their bathroom when Daniel entered the bedroom and shut the door behind him. She walked out with just a towel on her head and jumped when she saw him.

"Sorry," he said. "*Hey*, I like this look."

Nora grabbed her robe off the dresser and put it on.

"Was that Alice I heard?" she asked.

"Yeah. She's in her room drying off or getting dressed or something."

"Did you talk to Luke?"

"No. Should I have?"

She really didn't know why she had asked that. She knew that there was something she couldn't remember, and that Luke was the key.

"Just curious," she replied.

Alice's bedroom door quietly opened, but neither of them heard it over the music. Something stumbled into the hallway and walked down the stairs, propping itself up on the banister to keep from falling. It stepped onto the living room floor and fell down on all fours, desperately crawling into the kitchen.

The basement door opened and shut. Something slid down the stairs, pained and slow in its descent. The secret door unlatched and swung out like a hungry bird awaiting a feeding. The last of the creature's strength gave out and it was suddenly visible. The pathetic, charred-black demon used its claws to pull its frail body into the little room as the door swallowed it whole. It gripped the edge of the well and heaved itself up. At last, it looked down into the burning well and slid into the inferno.

Nora opened her bedroom door and walked down the hallway to Alice's room. She was about to barge in but stopped herself and knocked. There was no response.

"Alice?" she asked as she tapped her knuckle against the wood a few times. "Are you OK?"

Daniel strolled out into the hallway, barely gripping his beer between two fingers.

"Just go in," he said behind his wife.

Nora opened the door and stepped into the room. Alice was lying on her bed under the covers looking away from them. Nora walked over to her daughter's bed. She shook her several times.

"Alice. Alice. Wake up!"

Alice's eyes slowly fluttered open. She looked delirious and couldn't focus on anything in the room. They quickly fell shut again, and she rolled back over on her side.

"Alice!" Nora exclaimed as Daniel watched from the open doorway.

"Leave me alone," she slurred, concussed and half asleep.

Daniel walked across the bedroom and looked down at his sleeping daughter.

"Does she smell like alcohol?" he asked.

"I can't really tell with you being in here." Nora replied.

He reached over and caressed his daughter's cheek. She was sleeping peacefully. The welt on the other side of her head was concealed by her hair.

"I do believe our daughter has officially gotten drunk," he said.

Nora looked up at her husband.

"Great," she said. "We're that old now?"

"We're that old, and we're about to be back to warming up baby bottles."

"Baby bottles and beer bottles—those are our kids right now," she said as she stood up from the bed.

Daniel took a gulp of his own beer.

"Let her sleep it off," he began. "We'll deal with her in the morning."

Nora followed him out of the bedroom, turned off the lights, and shut her door quietly.

"I take it I have your permission to beat the shit out of Luke now?" Daniel asked.

"You do."

"Want to get some fresh air with me on the porch?"

"That would be nice."

The two of them sat together on the porch swing. Nora

rested her head on Daniel's shoulder as he moved them back and forth with his feet. The bright moon illuminated the farm as insects and tree frogs competed with one another to see who was louder.

"I'm sorry about earlier," Nora said.

"What do you mean?" Daniel asked, genuinely unsure of what she was referring to.

He was having trouble remembering how many beers he had had.

"Freaking out like that. Maybe my hormones are just going crazy right now," Nora answered as she looked out at the twinkling stars. "This place isn't that bad after all."

"No, it isn't."

They swung in peaceful silence for a moment as the breeze blew against their exposed skin.

"Hey, I never got to finish telling you about Merle's journals," he said.

"What about them?"

"Well," Daniel began as he leaned forward with excitement, "after Merle's wife offed herself, the man goes on a cross-country mission investigating different hauntings. He participates in legitimate, the-power-of-Christ-compels-you-type exorcisms with a couple of priests."

"No way."

"Yeah. I just finished reading about him performing his first two exorcisms. This stuff is wild, honey. The first one was in 1973. The owners of the house tried telling the police that they were seeing a woman covered in blood appear in their kids' bathroom mirror and then one night she reached through the mirror and grabbed their daughter by the throat," Daniel said as he excitedly shot his arm out like he was strangling someone.

"OK, that's enough," Nora said getting up from the swing.

"What?" Daniel laughed.

"I just don't like this stuff. I don't think it's funny. These were real people and, honestly, it creeps me out."

Daniel was visibly annoyed by his wife's apparent lack of interest.

"You know what?" Nora began with some genuine enthusiasm. "I bet you could take his journals to some sort of museum or even a newspaper writer. I'm sure locals would be . . . "

"Why the fuck would I do such a thing?" Daniel interrupted as he got up from the swing holding his beer. "That is seriously the dumbest thing I've ever heard you say, and that's saying something."

Nora smacked him in the face so hard that he saw stars.

"I can't do this anymore," she sobbed. She turned to go back inside, letting the screen door slam behind her.

Daniel stood in the same spot, drunk and only slightly perturbed by what had just transpired. He took another drink of beer and headed back down to the basement.

CHAPTER 20

NORA WAS THE first person to wake up the next morning. A sun ray beamed through the crack in the curtains just enough to disturb her. Her eyelids fluttered open. She stretched and yawned, quickly realizing that she was alone in their bed; Daniel's side had not been disturbed. His usual bottle of water on his nightstand was not there either. She let out a deep sigh and stood up.

The warm wood creaked under her feet as she walked into their bathroom to relieve herself and brush her teeth. It was quiet in the hallway. Nora figured that her daughter would probably be the last one to get up if she had gotten drunk for the first time in her life the night before, but then she remembered how intoxicated Daniel was when she left him on the porch. She went downstairs to make some breakfast, trying to wrap her mind around the fact that her teenage daughter and her husband were nursing dueling hangovers.

When she stepped off the stairs, she turned left to go into the living room, expecting to see Daniel passed out on the couch, but he was nowhere to be seen. She turned around and looked straight to the basement door in the kitchen. There was light coming from under the crack. He had been down there all night.

"Are you kidding me?" she said to herself as she headed in that direction.

She jerked the door open and descended the steps.

"Daniel?"

She stepped onto the basement floor and looked with disgust at her husband slumped over in the corner asleep. He was sitting on the floor, snoring deeply, with his back leaning against the wall and his chin resting on his chest. All of Merle's journals were piled beside him except one open on his lap. Judging by the page Daniel had passed out on, it looked like he was nearly finished reading that one as well.

Nora walked across the floor nudging beer bottles out of the way with her foot. She counted nine of them, and those were just the ones he drank down here. She didn't even know they had had that many beers in their refrigerator.

Daniel's face was colorless and moist. Both the sweat on his forehead and the dark crescent moons under his eyes were back. Nora looked at the closed little door beside her husband. A coldness trickled down her spine, but she didn't know why. It was déjà vu without the slightest clue as to what was familiar. Out of nowhere, she felt like she was being watched. She looked into the dark cracks surrounding the small door. There was something there that she couldn't quite see. It was a maroon round shape floating in the black void. The longer she stared the more she realized that it was a face. And then it blinked.

Daniel grabbed Nora's arm, and she launched up off the ground and shrieked.

"What are you doing down here?"

"Jesus, Daniel! You scared the life out of me," she yelled as she instinctively rubbed her belly and the baby within.

"Sorry," Daniel said, sitting up a little straighter.

He rubbed his groggy eyes.

Nora looked back at the door but saw nothing but darkness.

"I swear I just saw something. What did you say was in there?"

He opened his eyes and looked over at her to see what she was talking about.

"Huh?"

"What is in here?" Nora asked, pointing to the secret room.

"A bottomless well. Weird religious stuff. You know, the typical things you'd hope to find in an exorcist's basement."

She was not amused. The fact that Daniel had zero concern for her feelings made her that much angrier. She crouched down in front of him.

"Look at me," she said.

He did.

"I believe in science, OK?" she began. "You know that about me. I studied microbiology in college and teach everything from chemistry to physics. I believe in science."

"OK?" he said, just wanting her to stop talking so his headache would go away.

"I'm trying to tell you that I don't scare easily, Daniel. I don't believe in supernatural phenomena, Bigfoot, haunted houses, or little green fucking men from outer space. But this house, Daniel . . . *this house* . . . scares the shit out of me."

He took his wife seriously now. He saw the dread in her eyes. All he could do was nod his head as he searched for words.

"I feel like I'm losing track of time," she explained. "I keep forgetting things and then remembering little flashes of what actually happened. I've never felt this out of control before, and I know you feel it too."

Daniel shook his head as he got to his feet.

"No, no. I just drank too much last night. I am sorry about that."

"I'm not talking about last night, Daniel! I'm talking about you the other day completely convinced that you had only been in the basement for a few minutes when it had been an hour. I'm talking about how you looked white as a ghost and your eyes were all sunken in—much like they are right now by the way—and you just tried to play it off like it wasn't a big deal. I'm telling you that something is happening in this house that we can't comprehend because we keep forgetting what actually happened!"

Daniel looked down at his feet. He knew that his wife was right. The more she pointed out the confusion and chaos, the clearer everything became. Then he began to remember being down here just a few nights ago and something terrible happening. Before he could tell Nora that maybe she wasn't so crazy after all, his bare feet became engulfed in flames that shot up his legs and continued until they covered his face. He screamed as he finally remembered Merle standing in this very spot being cooked alive after he had warned Daniel of something. He remembered something sinister bursting out through the well and chasing him up the stairs. Nora wrapped her arms around her screaming husband and the fiery vision disappeared. He was hyperventilating and sweating, but he was not a charred corpse.

"Oh, my God," Daniel said as his dry mouth gulped. "Did you see it?"

"See what?" she cried.

"The flames. There were flames on me. My legs. My face . . . "

"I didn't see anything."

A voice—Luke's voice—echoed through her head: *It haunts their mind.*

Nora held her husband as his breathing returned to normal.

"Can we go upstairs now?" she asked.

"I think that would be wise."

He bent down and grabbed the last journal that he had been reading.

"Take this."

Nora held the journal in her hand and watched Daniel

pick up the stack of VHS tapes. She looked at him with confusion.

"Whatever we're dealing with here . . . Merle was the only authority on the subject," he said. "Everything I read last night—all the different hauntings and exorcisms that the man was involved in—they all happened somewhere else in the country. But I have a feeling that whatever is on these tapes may shed some light on our situation."

Nora nodded her head in agreement and turned to walk upstairs as Daniel followed. When they entered the kitchen, they saw Alice sitting at the kitchen table staring out the window in a daze. She was still wearing her bathing suit. All thoughts of what had just taken place in the basement left both of their minds when they saw their daughter.

"Honey, are you OK?" Nora asked.

Alice slowly looked at her parents emerging from the basement. Her eyelids hung low as she squinted

"Huh?"

Daniel seemed to sober up instantly when he noticed the poor shape his daughter was in. He walked around to the other side of her.

"What happened last night, Al?" he asked.

"My head hurts."

She looked down at her bathing suit.

"How did I get here?"

Daniel looked at Nora with concern.

"How did you get where, honey?" he asked.

Nora could tell that Daniel had shifted into psychologist mode.

"The last thing I remember is meeting Luke out front."

"That was yesterday," Daniel said as he watched the worry spread across his daughter's face.

"How much did you have to drink last night, Alice?" Nora asked, trying too hard to sound calm.

Alice looked up at her with bewilderment.

"What?"

"Did you take any drugs?" Nora questioned.

"She just said that she doesn't remember even going with Luke," Daniel said to his wife.

"No, I didn't take any drugs. I wouldn't drink either," she lied. She was completely open to the idea yesterday when she was preparing to go swimming with Luke, albeit a little intimidated.

"Bullshit," Nora said as she walked away from her daughter.

"Honey," Daniel said to Nora, trying to diffuse the situation.

His head hurt just as much as he imagined Alice's did. The last thing he wanted to deal with was a full-blown Hill family royal rumble.

"No," Nora flat out said. "The only way you come home in the shape she was in last night is by getting blackout drunk or high as a kite!"

Alice reflexively put her hands on the sides of her head to protect her splitting migraine from her mother's shouting. As soon as her left hand touched her temple, she winced.

"What is it?" Daniel asked as he looked closely at the purple welt hiding beneath her dark hair.

He gingerly brushed a few strands out of the way, and she recoiled in pain.

"Oh, sorry."

Nora immediately dropped her accusatory attitude and approached her injured daughter to see for herself.

"Alice, you don't remember how this happened?" she asked.

"Is it bad?" Alice replied.

"It looks painful," Nora said. "Your memory is completely blank?"

"I already said that the last thing I remember is seeing Luke in the front yard."

Daniel and Nora exchanged worried glances once more.

"We should take her to the hospital," Nora said to her husband.

"No!" Alice blurted out as she stood up. "I don't want to go to the hospital. Just give me some medicine and let me eat breakfast. It only hurts when I touch it anyway."

Daniel gripped the small stack of VHS tapes that he held against his hip.

"Let's give it a couple of hours," he calmly said. "Let her eat and see if it clears up a bit."

Nora was in disbelief.

"I can't believe we thought she was just drunk. She has memory loss and a significant wound on her head, Daniel! She needs a CT scan."

"Maybe," Daniel said, keeping his cool. "Maybe not. I think the first thing we need to do is to find out what exactly happened. I think we need to track down Luke and get his story."

Nora had forgotten about Luke. She knew that she needed to talk to him. Whatever lapses in memory she was having, Daniel was having, and now Alice was having, could all be answered by the kid that used to tend Merle Blatty's farm.

Daniel could see that Nora agreed with him just by the look of consideration on her face.

"Why don't we all just eat some breakfast and take it from there," he said as he opened a cabinet by the refrigerator and withdrew a bottle of ibuprofen.

He handed Alice two and swallowed two himself. Nora had calmed down but was not ready to concede entirely.

"After we eat, we're going to find Luke. If Alice is still in this shape in a few hours, then we're going to the hospital."

Daniel nodded his head.

"Fine," Alice said.

Nora turned on the coffee pot and grabbed the pancake mix as Daniel slid out of the kitchen and headed upstairs.

"Where are you going?" Nora asked.

"Just grabbing a quick shower."

"Good. You smell like a fucking brewery," Nora said to herself, forgetting that Alice was still in the kitchen.

She turned around to see if her daughter had heard her, but she was too busy examining the assortment of scrapes and bruises all over her body.

Nora was terrified but did her best to prevent her mind from obsessively panicking. She never imagined *hoping* that her teenage daughter had injured herself while being shitfaced drunk, but the alternatives were incomprehensible.

Alice looked down at the marks on the back of her hand. She rolled it over and examined her palm. There were four fingernail indentations. An image of Luke—or something that looked like Luke—displayed in her brain. His large hand gripped hers and pulled her across a yard. She saw the house as clear as day, and then the memory stopped.

"Mom," Alice said from the table.

Nora stopped mixing the pancake batter and turned around.

"Yes, honey?"

"I remember where Luke lives."

CHAPTER 21

"I THINK I'M going to just stay here, Mom," Alice said as she swayed back and forth on the porch swing.

Nora eyeballed her daughter from the front door for more of an explanation. The family had finished breakfast thirty minutes ago. Alice was now showered and dressed for the day. Once she rinsed all the dirt and debris off her, her injuries didn't look nearly as bad as they had initially.

"Don't you want to talk to Luke?"

Alice thought about it for a second and then shook her head.

"No. I'm embarrassed enough as it is."

They heard Daniel moving around inside the house. Nora looked back over her shoulder at her husband walking down the stairs. He had showered and thrown on some old gym shorts and a sleeveless T-shirt. Black and grey stubble sprouted from his unshaven neck and cheeks. He nodded at his wife and headed for the living room. She turned her attention back to her daughter.

"Why are you embarrassed?" she asked.

"It's not the coolest thing in the world to show up at a boy's house with your parents because you can't remember your date the night before," she said, partially lying.

The idea of seeing Luke without knowing if she had made a fool of herself scared her, but she was secretly feeling woozy. She knew that if she copped to it, then her parents would take her to the hospital. She just wanted to be left alone and relax. It would all come back to her.

"Honey," Nora began. "If I were to guess, I would say that you and Luke had a little too much to drink, you fell and bumped your head, and he helped you home. He was probably too scared to tell us, or maybe he didn't think it was that big of a deal."

Alice just swung and stared into the yard.

"Maybe you just slipped getting out of the water and took a tumble. Who knows?"

"You don't think it's odd that he hasn't been here this morning?" Alice responded.

Nora heard Daniel walking from the living room back upstairs. She looked back and saw him carrying the VCR that he had just unhooked.

"What are you doing?" she asked.

Daniel didn't slow down a second.

"I'm hooking this up to the TV in our room. You know why."

She didn't know why. Her mind was a blur. Before she could ask him to elaborate, she remembered Merle's tapes. She remembered Daniel holding them just a half hour ago. Panic ran through her system at the thought of how unreliable her own mind was right now.

"We're about to leave," she said to Daniel.

"I'm aware."

She listened to the commotion of him unplugging and rearranging things up there.

"Mom, are you going to answer me?" Alice said.

Nora turned to her daughter who was staring at her.

"I'm sorry, honey, what?"

"Nothing," Alice replied as she leaned back in the swing longways and stared off into the distance.

Daniel came back down the stairs. He grabbed his car keys off the entryway table.

"Ready to go?" he asked Nora, who was still visibly shaken.

"Yes," she replied, doing her best to mask her worry. "Alice, you said it's a half mile down the road? The small house on the left as soon as you come around the big curve?"

"Yeah."

Daniel leaned over and kissed Alice on the forehead. She reached down and picked up her can of Coke and took a sip.

"We'll be right back, Al," he said, motioning for Nora to follow him to his car.

A few minutes later Daniel and Nora were driving slowly toward Luke's house. They had only passed two houses since leaving the farm, neither of which were before a curve in the road or small. Daniel approached the abrupt turn and veered around the dangerous blind spot. He continued onward for less than a minute when they noticed the run-down house off the side of the road.

"There it is," he said.

They coasted down the sloping gravel driveway. There was an old truck parked on one side of the house and Luke's four-wheeler on the other. Daniel killed the engine, and they both got out at the same time and walked to the front door. He gave a swift three knocks and took a step back.

It was silent inside.

He looked over at Nora to gauge her reaction. She stomped toward the door and beat it with her balled-up fist so hard that it came ajar. She gave it a gentle shove with her fingertips.

"What are you doing?" Daniel whispered.

"Luke?" she yelled into the open entry and then turned back to Daniel. "This kid practically beats our door down at the ass crack of dawn every morning. I'm not worried about disturbing his hangover, OK?"

She turned her focus back to the door.

"Hey, Luke!" she yelled even louder as she crossed the threshold.

Daniel stepped in behind her.

"Anybody home?" he hollered. "Sorry to barge in, but this is kind of an emergency."

A foul, rotting stench hit them as soon as they were both inside the small front room. Nora scrunched up her face and shut the door behind them. She then got her first view of the living room and screamed at the top of her lungs. Daniel jumped at her shriek, having been looking the other way. He quickly stepped in front of her to see what she saw. He immediately felt his breakfast bubble up his esophagus.

On the floor before them was Luke's father's corpse. There was a stain on the front of his pants from where he had soiled himself upon expiration. A stagnant pool of dark blood was pasted to the carpet where most of his head used to be. Everything above his lower jaw had been ripped clean off. His tongue was still attached, but it had flopped backward and now lay in the crimson syrup like a dead fish.

Daniel instinctively reached back and felt for his wife. She was still screaming with her hands over her mouth. Tears poured down both cheeks. Daniel turned to face her. She was still staring at the carcass by the recliner.

"Nora," Daniel said, his face pale. "Nora!"

Nora met her husband's eyes. He put both of his hands on her shoulders and bent down so that he was all that she saw.

"Shh . . . focus on me," he said calmly. "We have to get out of here. There's only one person that I can think of who did this, and he could be heading to our house right now."

She nodded, but the abject terror in her eyes ceased to abate.

"You think Luke did this?" she asked.

"Alice came home with a head injury. Luke's nowhere to be seen. And now . . . this."

"Can't be . . . " she muttered.

She couldn't picture the young man (who she admittedly barely knew) committing a crime like this. She couldn't fathom Luke being a monster capable of hurting anyone, let alone Alice.

Daniel reached around her and grabbed the doorknob. Something gurgled over her husband's shoulder. Nora stood on her tiptoes and saw Luke's father sitting up. What was left of his head turned so that if he had eyes, he would've been looking straight at her. The arch of yellow teeth on his exposed bottom jaw held his contorted tongue in place. The corpse tried to breathe, but a geyser of black bile shot out of his open throat like a whale's blowhole.

Nora screamed even louder as she dug her fingernails into her husband's torso so hard, he bled. Daniel spun around to see what she was looking at, but there was nothing different than what he had saw moments ago.

"What?" he asked. "What is it, Nora?"

He continued to stare at the motionless cadaver staining the carpet. He looked back at his wife.

"Daniel! Daniel!" She was begging him to turn back around. "It's getting up. It's alive!" The corpse painfully started to get to its feet.

Daniel looked again at the dead man who was obviously not moving. He did his best to control his panic for the betterment of his wife.

"Honey," he said as he faced her again. "You're in shock. Let's just step outside and decompress."

The dead man plodded across the room expelling gas and excrement until it came to a stop directly behind Daniel. Nora was wide-eyed and immobile. The corpse carefully leaned forward and belched a hot squirt of bloody mucus atop Daniel's head and back. The dark goo oozed down Daniel's face like a cracked egg. Nora felt the urge to vomit as she watched it drip over his eyes and into the corners of his mouth.

"Everything's OK, honey," Daniel said, oblivious to the horror and the mess covering him. "I'm going to open the door now, and we're going to step outside."

The dead man's puffy maroon arm reached around Daniel toward Nora. She screamed and turned around, yanking the door open and fleeing into the bright sun. Daniel looked behind him one final time at the lifeless remains of Luke's father on the carpet and then stepped out onto the porch and closed the door.

Nora ran across the yard and opened the car door. Daniel hurriedly followed. She looked through the windshield at the partially headless man now standing on the front porch. It brought both of its hands up to its beer belly and started to caress it as if a child were inside. She couldn't avert her eyes from the spectacle.

It lifted its stained shirt, exposing its swollen abdomen. Nora had to blink. She couldn't believe what she was seeing. There was movement inside the monster's belly: small hands and feet desperately pushed the skin from the inside.

Daniel opened the car door and slid into the hot leather seat. He looked over at his wife who had tears rolling down her cheeks as she stared at the closed front door.

"Honey?"

She continued to watch the corpse rub its belly like a loving mother. Suddenly, it dug its fingernails through the taut flesh and ripped the skin open like a plastic bag. The abomination inside plopped onto the porch and rolled down the steps into the yard. Nora gasped at the sight of the dead baby covered in slimy membrane and dirt. Both the shell of Luke's father and the fetus were laughing in sync.

Nora covered her eyes as the voice of Luke said, "It haunts your mind."

"Just go, Daniel. Go," she cried.

Daniel started the engine and backed out of the driveway into the main road. Just as he was about to shift gears, he saw Luke standing in the middle of the road holding Alice's dead body in his arms. All of the blood left his face as he stared at his daughter's lifeless eyes frozen in a blank stare. He screamed something primal, something ferocious, reserved only for times of feral slaughter.

Nora jumped with a startle and looked over at her husband and then to the empty road in front of them. She realized that he was seeing something that she couldn't see, exactly like she had just been tricked.

"Daniel," she said as she placed her hand on his forearm.

His muscles were bulging as he gripped the steering wheel.

"Daniel, there's nothing there. What do you see?"

"That son of a bitch," Daniel cried. "He killed our baby, Nora. He killed our baby!"

Daniel jerked the car in gear and floored the pedal. The tires burned against the hot pavement, and then they squealed forward at full speed.

Daniel screamed as the car barreled toward its target. Nora tried to grab the wheel at the last second when she finally saw what Daniel was headed toward. He swatted her hand away and shouted, "Die, you motherfucker!" as he drove head-on into a tree on the side of the road.

CHAPTER 22

ALICE LET OUT a long sigh as she watched her parents drive off. She winced and rubbed her throbbing temples, careful not to put too much pressure on her head wound. The black BMW turned right onto the main road and disappeared among the trees. She wondered what Luke would tell them. There was a memory of her walking to Luke's house with him and then up on the front porch, but as soon as they stepped inside, the image froze like a movie reel stuck on a frame.

Something was moving down the hill, hidden by the trees to the right of the porch. She looked toward the commotion. There was movement and heavy panting, but she couldn't see through the thick vegetation. Finally, she recognized the bloodhound as Buck pranced home. As soon as his head popped through a bush and saw her on the swing, he came trotting toward her with his tongue flopping against his face.

"Buck," she said with a high pitch. "Where have you been, buddy?"

The dog ran up to her, and she rubbed his warm fur. His dangling tongue was like melted taffy jotting in and out of his mouth for hydration.

"Come on. Let's get you something to drink," she said as she eased out of the swing and walked to the screen door.

She stopped dead in her tracks when she saw Luke standing inside. Buck cocked his head sideways.

"Oh my God!" She took a step backward.

Luke retreated toward the stairs and into the shadows underneath.

"Please, don't scream," Luke said.

"What are you doing here? My parents just went to go look for you. Luke, what *happened* last night?"

She opened the door and entered the house.

"Alice, stay where you are. Don't look at me."

Confusion ruffled her face.

"Luke, what's wrong?"

"I don't have much time. Please, just listen. Close your eyes."

"What?"

"Alice, I'm begging you. Trust me. Close your eyes."

"OK . . . " Alice said, letting her eyelids shut.

She listened as Luke took two steps toward her. Unable to resist, she peeked through one eye. She gasped when she saw the walking cadaver before her. It was Luke but badly decomposed and sewn back together. He was still wearing the same tattered clothes from the day before. His once long, perfect hair was now split down the middle by a grisly scar that ran from the front of his scalp to the back. Alice covered her open mouth as she realized the scar and many others all over his body were being held together with stitches; his skin now nothing more than a fleshy quilt. She looked into his sunken, hollow eyes and saw him—the essence of him—trapped in this rotting temple.

"Don't scream. It's me. Underneath, it's me. *Remember*," he commanded and held out his decaying hand.

A force like a rogue ocean wave rushed through her being, and she closed her eyes. Hundreds of images from the day before flooded her mind. She saw Luke walk her into his house. She saw his father. She saw the demon emerge from Luke and attack the man. She saw herself flee, and she saw herself get captured. She felt the demon drag her for a mile across rocks and through wilderness and finally up to her bedroom.

And then she opened her eyes.

"Luke, oh my God!"

She was breathing heavily as she started to panic, unable to comprehend the information overload.

"You're dead, but you're . . . *here*?"

"Yes," he said gently. "And I'm running out of time, so you need to listen."

Alice thought about the thing that was inside Luke and wondered how this could be any different. She started to back up toward the front door.

"How do I know it's you?"

"If it wasn't me, your friend behind you would be tearing me to shreds right now."

She turned around and saw Buck standing on the porch looking in through the screen with his tongue darting in and out of his open mouth.

"Hey, Buck," Luke said.

Buck's ears perked up as he wagged his tail.

Alice relaxed and looked back to the shell of the boy she could've loved.

"There's an evil in your house," he began. "The well in your basement is how it gets from the other side to your world. It's the same passage I dug my way out of to talk to you right now. Your entire family is in danger. I have to show you something because you need to know. If they figure out that I crossed the barrier, then it's over."

She didn't know what to think, but she believed him.

"OK."

Luke extended his arms and placed his hands on her head.

"Relax and close your eyes."

She did.

And then Alice was falling down a tunnel of rushing water. She felt like she was on a supercharged water slide

191

at the park back in Ohio. Her heart rose up to her throat as she descended through space and time. She sunk through a warm jelly-like substance into a black abyss. The need to scream came on strongly, but Luke's omnipresent voice said, "Almost there."

The ground came out of nowhere and slammed against her bare feet. Everything in which she was just enveloped evaporated into the air of her new surroundings. She looked around and realized that she was standing in front of their farmhouse, but it looked different. The house she was staring at had a different second floor. She wondered if this was how it looked before the fire.

Someone gripped her hand. Luke stood beside her—the old Luke, before the demon possessed his body and then ate its way out of him. He smiled at her. Before she could ask what was going on, a boy and a girl around their age came running past them holding hands. She recognized the boy just from his frame and laugh, but his hair was a bit shorter.

"Is that . . . " Alice began.

"Yes," Luke answered. "That's me."

"Who's with you?"

"Amelia," he said as he watched the two lovers run toward the house. "This is the day she died."

Alice looked up at him and then back at the other him and Amelia. Luke looked at Alice.

"It's vital that you know what you're up against," he said. "Let's follow them."

Luke walked through the yard with Alice at his side. The other Luke and Amelia ran onto the porch and sat down beside each other on wicker rocking chairs. He was wearing a white tank top that was drenched in sweat from working on the farm. Amelia wore a yellow sun dress covered in flowers. He put his hand on top of hers.

"So, what was the surprise that you had me meet you here for?" she smiled.

"Well, you know how I told you I cut my hand on the

mower yesterday?" he said as he held up his left hand that was wrapped in a white bandage

"Yeah?"

"It's not a cut," he smiled.

The Luke on the porch started to unwrap the bandage as Luke and Alice watched from the front yard.

"What is it?" Amelia asked, confused but excited.

The bandage came off, revealing a spider web tattoo on the back of his hand.

"Is that a real tattoo?" she asked.

"Yeah."

"A spider web?"

"Yes," he began. "Do you remember when we were in the swimming hole, and we kissed for the first time?"

Amelia nodded her head.

"We were asking each other what all of our favorite things were," he said. "I asked you what your favorite book was, and you said . . . "

"*Charlotte's Web*," Amelia finished.

"*Charlotte's Web*," he echoed.

Amelia gently grabbed his forearm and pulled the artwork close to her face.

"You got this for me?" she asked with a smile.

"No, no. I got it for me."

She shot him a skeptical glare.

"I got it for me, so that every time I look at it, I can think of you," he said.

Amelia put her hand on the back of his head and pulled him closer for a kiss.

Alice and Luke continued to watch from the front yard. She thought that she would be jealous seeing Luke kiss another girl, but she felt nothing but joy and understanding.

"That was a smooth move," Alice said to her ghostly tour guide.

"I thought so," Luke said with a grin.

"Why are we here, Luke?"

He looked away from his old self and former love and down at Alice.

"You're about to see."

The Luke on the porch chair suddenly stood up.

"Oh, shoot," he said.

"What?" Amelia asked.

"I forgot Old Man Merle's toolbox up by the goat pen. He should be home soon. I need to run up there and grab it. Want to walk with me?"

Amelia began to rock herself in the squeaky chair. The sun's rays made her skin glow in the yellow dress.

"Can't I just wait for you here?" she said with a sultry smile.

"I'll be quick. When I get back, you gotta get outta here. I don't want the old man to think I've just been hangin' out with my girl all day when I'm supposed to be working," he said.

"You better hurry up because I'm not leavin' until you come back and kiss me," she replied.

Luke smiled and jumped off the porch. He jogged right past the other Luke and Alice.

"Stay, you dummy," Luke said to the memory of himself running through the yard.

After a moment, the other Luke had disappeared around the bend. Luke turned his attention back to Amelia on the chair. Alice watched as well. Amelia pressed her bare feet against the porch, rocking herself in the rickety chair.

Amelia got up from the chair and walked to the front door. She looked over her shoulder and saw that she was alone. She grinned, turned back to the house, and went inside.

"What's she doing?" Alice asked.

"She was always so curious about the old man. All the spooky rumors and stuff."

Luke and Alice followed her in.

The house was empty of course. Amelia checked her

surroundings like she was looking for something specific. After a moment, she saw the basement door through the kitchen.

Alice's pulse began to throb when she realized where they were headed. Even though she knew this was just a memory or a dream, the thought of watching something happen to Amelia terrified her. She looked up at Luke, but his face was fixated on the girl in front of him. Alice imagined having to watch the person that you love die in front of you and how hard that must be so she remained silent. She then realized that she and Luke both had that in common now.

Amelia jerked open the basement door and turned on the light switch. She excitedly crept down the stairs like a child on Christmas morning. Luke and Alice followed. Amelia walked around the piles of Merle's belongings, unimpressed. She had heard tales about the haunted basement but was very underwhelmed.

"At least I can say that I've been down here."

An orange glow flickered from beyond the little door, and she noticed immediately. She scrunched her brow in bewilderment. As she walked across the basement to the small door, Luke and Alice watched from the stairs. Amelia unlatched the door, pulled it open, and was immediately sucked inside. Alice screamed from the stairs as a puff of smoke blew out, and the door slammed shut.

Alice looked at Luke who was staring at the secret room with a burning rage. He exhaled deeply and shut his eyes.

"And here I come," he said as he glanced up at the kitchen.

The front door opened, and heavy footsteps crossed the floor above them.

"Amelia?" he called. "Are you in here?"

The basement door was pulled all the way open, and the old Luke stood at the top of the stairs, wide-eyed. He stormed down the steps, passing straight through the other Luke and Alice.

"You're too late," Alice's Luke said to his past self, who was frantically looking around the basement unaware of the spectators on the stairs.

"Amelia!" he screamed.

The glowing began again from behind the little door. Luke's eyes widened as he ran over to it and tried to jerk it open, but it wouldn't budge. A raspy voice cackled beyond it. The laughter amplified and sounded like it was crawling closer to the door. It was a sexless, hoarse taunting that made Luke's guts bubble.

It knocked three times on the door.

"Luke, it's me," Amelia's voice said from behind the glowing wood. "Won't you let me out?"

"You're not Amelia," Luke whispered more to himself than to the thing he couldn't see.

"Of course it's me, Luke," it said. "Your Amelia. I'm short and pretty and like cute, yellow dresses."

The thing giggled. Luke slowly started backing away from the door.

"You even know my favorite book. *Charlotte's Web*, remember?" it said in a voice that was sounding less and less like Amelia by the syllable. "That's why you got that ridiculous tattoo on your hand, huh?"

More laughter. Luke was almost to the stairs.

"But don't you remember what happened to Charlotte in the end, Luke?" it asked with a growl. "She fucking died!"

The little door swung open, and Amelia's body crawled out on all fours. He stared at her lifeless eyes just as one burst out of its socket and dangled by the optic nerve like a bobber on a fishing line. He watched in horror as the other shot out as well. A flaming orange light now burned in the empty sockets. Her lips tore as they stretched across sharp fangs. She crept sideways while continuing to face him. Just as she reached the wall, her right arm and leg lifted off the ground and began to climb. Luke stared in disbelief as all four limbs now adhered to the wall like a spider. Her smile widened.

He trembled at the bloody grin. Without warning, Amelia scurried across the wall towards him. He stumbled backward, and just as he was inches away from running through Alice again, Merle appeared at the top of the basement stairs holding a flashlight.

"Duck, boy," he said.

Luke quickly flattened himself against the stairs. Merle shined the beam of light on the demon. It hissed and smoked as it retreated down the wall back into the rear of the basement. The old man walked through Alice and her Luke, who were still watching the spectacle, and brushed past the terrified boy. He kept the light on the beast as it moved backward into the secret room and the door slammed shut. The flickering glow turned to darkness.

Merle turned to Luke who was now sitting on the stairs.

"That your girl?" Merle asked.

Luke nodded his head.

"Do everything I say, and we might be able to save her," Merle said. "We have to act now."

Alice felt her Luke squeeze her hand. She glanced up at him.

"We're out of time," he said.

Everything around her dissolved, and she was once again shooting through a gelatinous mass of time and space. She was confused and disoriented, but she didn't care. Anything was better than the horror she had just witnessed. She felt like she was flying at rocket speed and was going to vomit.

And then it stopped.

Alice opened her eyes and realized that she was still screaming. She was back in her house standing by the front door. Luke was nowhere to be seen. She looked in all directions and even shouted his name, but she was alone.

Footsteps were coming from outside. Alice peered through the screen door at her parents walking as quickly as they could up the long driveway. She could tell that they were hurt. Buck galloped across the yard to them. Her dad had what looked like blood on his forehead, and her mom was limping.

Unable to fully comprehend what had just happened or what she had just experienced, Alice opened the door and ran to them with tears running down her face. She just needed her mom and dad.

Daniel wrapped his arms around his daughter and then Nora joined in. The three of them held each other and sobbed as Buck rubbed against their legs.

CHAPTER 23

T HE SUN COOKED the moisture out of the dirt across the farm, causing a thick wave of humidity to hang over the land. There were no clouds in the blue sky, and the wind had ceased to blow.

Having just returned from the hospital to get themselves checked out and to make sure the baby was fine, Daniel, Nora, and Alice were now sitting in a circle on the front lawn beside the hot rocks composing the driveway. Nora's vehicle was still clicking as all the interior elements wound down.

Buck was now observing them from the shaded comfort of the porch. Daniel had a white bandage covering the laceration on his forehead, and Nora had her bruised leg stretched out as she carefully rubbed it. They knew that for such a nasty car accident, they were lucky to have sustained such minor injuries, especially the baby. The three of them were all emotion as they collectively tried to wrap their minds around what was happening. The one thing they could agree on was that they were in no hurry to step foot in the house.

"I saw Luke clear as day," Alice began. "I watched you leave and then saw him standing in our house. He looked like something from a scary movie. His skin was all stitched together in patches . . . "

Her parents looked on as she told her story.

"I get it now . . . why he looked like that, I mean," Alice

continued. "The last time I saw him alive was at his house when I thought he was taking me to swim. It wasn't him though. There was something inside him that ripped its way out. It kept saying that it was burning and then it just peeled Luke's skin off. I think that's why he was sewn back together like that."

Alice sobbed as she turned to look at the front porch where she had last seen him.

"What did he say?" Nora asked.

"He told me not to be scared and then he showed me the day that his girlfriend, Amelia, died."

"How did he do that?" Nora wondered.

"I don't know. I was standing inside one second and then I was out front with Luke watching the old Luke and Amelia. We watched them go in the basement. Something from the well *possessed* Amelia. She was chasing Luke, until the old man showed up with a flashlight and backed her down into the secret room."

Nora suddenly recalled Luke's flashlight. Her mind then went to Luke on the porch telling her about how demons from the well haunt your mind or possess you entirely.

Daniel now remembered the demonic creature that had chased him out of the basement the night he saw Merle's apparition. One memory triggered the next as the three of them collectively felt the fog in their minds dissipate.

"And then," Alice continued, "the old man told Luke that he would try to help him save Amelia. Before I could see what happened next, everything disappeared, and I was back in our house. That's when you guys showed up."

They all sat in silence, trying to fight off the perpetual doubt that kept returning and telling each of them that none of this was possible. When they started talking again—when they dragged the dark truth out into the light—everything became clearer.

"Well," Daniel began. "We saw what happened to Luke's father."

Alice closed her eyes and shed more tears as she vividly recalled witnessing the murder. Nora put her hand on Alice's leg.

"Your father and I saw terrible things just now, too. I saw one thing, and he saw something completely different, but we couldn't see what the other saw. I can't explain it, but Luke could."

Alice looked at her mother for clarification, and so did Daniel when he realized what she had just said.

"What do you mean?" he asked. "Luke told you something about this?"

"Yes. I woke up one night and went to the basement. I felt like I was hypnotized or something. I saw a terrible creature down there . . . " Nora said but then stopped.

She wanted to be careful not to reveal anything about seeing a demonic version of Steve. "I know that it was trying to kill me, but then Luke showed up and got me out of there."

"Luke came in our house in the middle of the night?" Daniel asked with shock.

Alice apparently shared her father's sentiments judging by the look on her face.

"Yes," Nora replied, finally with full clarity of mind. "He scared away whatever was in the basement and took me out on the front porch. He told me this house wasn't safe and that he'd been keeping an eye on us since we moved in. He didn't want the same thing that happened to Amelia to happen to us, I guess. He also told me about Merle Blatty being an exorcist and how the evil in the basement killed his girlfriend. He even said it came after him at his own house, but he fought it away. He said that if you get exposed to whatever is down there, it possesses you or drives you crazy."

"Is that why we're all seeing things?" Alice inferred, as Daniel thought carefully about what he had just heard. "Yes," Nora said excitedly. "It also explains why we are losing track of time and can't remember things."

They let that sink in, all feeling like they had just figured out some evil magician's trick.

"It also means that we can't just pack up and leave this house," Daniel stated. "Wherever we go, we'll take our tainted minds with us."

Nora nodded as Alice looked at the ground and closed her eyes.

"I've seen something down there, too," Daniel said, trying to keep the truth flowing. "I saw Merle appear. He was quite the sight. Still partially melted from the fire. He was trying to help me, though. Much like what Luke was doing when he appeared to you just now, Alice. He wanted me to go through his belongings to understand what is happening here."

"What belongings?" Alice asked.

"Years' worth of journals and documentation detailing his exploits as some sort of paranormal researcher and then progression to being a full-blown backwoods exorcist."

"This is unreal," Alice shook her head.

"I read the journals," Daniel continued. "Obviously, he wasn't crazy. Plus, we haven't even watched his homemade movies yet."

Nora felt her heart skip a beat at the thought of watching whatever was on those tapes, but she knew that it must be done.

"Dad, what do you think is on the tapes?"

"Each one is labeled with a different person's name and year," he replied.

"What was the most recent tape?" Alice questioned, even though she already knew the answer.

"Amelia," he answered.

"We have to watch the tapes," Nora said to her family.

He nodded in agreement.

"There's a reason why Merle wanted me to find his chest, and it wasn't to preserve his twisted legacy."

"He wanted to help us," Alice began. "He wanted to help

us just like Luke did. Luke mentioned something about crossing a barrier to show me that vision of Amelia. The old man must've done the same thing with you, Dad. There's a reason why they're coming back from the dead to communicate with us."

"They know how to beat it," Nora concluded.

Again, Daniel nodded.

"Something tells me that the video of Amelia is going to pick up right where your vision left off," Daniel said to his daughter.

"So what are we waiting for?" Alice replied.

Daniel smiled. She was his daughter indeed.

There was nothing overtly sinister or maniacal about the inside of their house. It was just as they'd left it. The sun was shining through the open windows giving their living room a rustic beauty. The smell of lemon furniture polish even hung in the air. Daniel was nearly overcome by how perfect it felt, until he realized that no one had dusted anything recently. He knew then that he had underestimated how insidious the thing in the basement really was. It was trying to coax him into letting down his guard.

The three of them wasted no time walking upstairs to the TV and VCR set-up Daniel had arranged earlier. Nora shut the bedroom door behind them as Alice sat on the bed and Daniel picked up the VHS tapes. He looked at the names on the tape labels again.

"Should we watch all of these or . . . " he began.

"Just put in Amelia's tape," Alice said.

Nora sat down on the bed beside her daughter.

"I agree," she said.

Daniel placed the other tapes back on the floor and held the one that said "Amelia '92." He turned on the TV and

VCR and then looked back at his family. Nora nodded at him. He inserted the tape. The VCR swallowed the cassette, and the little gears inside whirred to life, rotating the plastic dials and rolling film. The TV remained on a solid blue screen as the family stared with anticipation.

A dark image flashed on the TV but immediately cut back to blue. It did this several times until the VCR tracking finally leveled out with the homemade movie. Merle's recording began to play.

The video camera was resting on something to produce a static shot of a dark, empty room. It looked like it was at the right height to have been mounted on a tripod, but Daniel didn't recall finding one of those when he had rummaged through Merle's belongings.

"That's the basement," Daniel said pointing to the image on the screen. "You see right there in the corner? That's the door to that hellhole."

A figure stepped into the frame with his back to the camera.

"That's Luke," Alice said, recognizing his build immediately.

"Amelia?" Luke spoke to the secret room. "Are you in there?"

Almost instantly, an orange flickering glow came from behind the small door. The light grew in intensity until the entire basement was visible.

"Luke?" Amelia's voice said. "Is that you?"

"It's me. Please, come out."

The latch on the outside of the door slowly turned upward, and the door creaked open. Amelia's head peeked around the doorframe. She saw that Luke was alone, and she carefully crawled out onto the basement floor. There was fear in her eyes. She scampered over to the nearest corner and sat there holding her legs against her chest.

"She didn't look like that in my vision," Alice said to her parents as they watched the tape. "Her eyes were fire, and her teeth were sharp. She just looks scared now."

Luke took a step closer to the girl cowering against the wall.

"Is that really you?" he asked.

Amelia looked up from her folded arms.

"It's me," she began. "But I don't know where that thing went. I'm so scared, Luke. Can you please just hold me?"

Luke instinctively took a small step forward but then hesitated to go any further. Amelia noticed.

"Luke?" she said softly.

"How do I . . . how do I know it's really you?" he asked timidly.

Amelia smiled subtly.

"It would be a leap of faith," she started. "Kind of like jumping off a waterfall into a swimming hole that you don't know is deep enough."

"It is you," Luke said as he ran over to her.

He knelt down and wrapped his arms around her. With her eyes closed, she held him back.

"It's definitely not her," Alice said to her parents.

On the screen, Amelia opened her eyes, and they were a burning orange.

"Holy shit!" Daniel blurted.

Nora and Alice jumped at his exclamation.

"Look at her eyes!"

Amelia's mouth opened wide revealing a row of sharp fangs. She moved toward Luke, about to sink her teeth into his exposed neck.

"Now, Luke. Now!" Merle screamed from somewhere out of frame.

Luke immediately gripped Amelia with all of his strength and lifted her up. Amelia hissed and twisted trying break free, but he had her wrapped too tightly. Merle came running into the shot with a massive metal chain draped over his shoulder.

"Lay her down, boy!" Merle commanded.

Luke pinned Amelia's back to the floor easily, showing

off his high school wrestling expertise. Merle ran around to Luke's side and carefully draped the chain across Amelia's chest and legs.

Nora thought that the chain looked familiar and then it clicked.

"Daniel, that's the same chain hanging under the stairs in the basement."

"It sure is," he replied, as he stared intently at the TV.

Luke was reluctant to release his hold on Amelia.

"That isn't heavy enough to hold her unless we tie her down," he said.

"It's strong enough, boy. It's been coated in holy water."

Amelia was in a blind rage, spitting and screaming in an inhuman tongue as she fought to writhe free.

"Calm yourself, demon," Merle said to the girl on the floor.

She shot him a glare of pure repulsion.

"Fuck you, old man!" the demon sneered in its true voice.

Luke turned his face from its mouth and held his breath, visibly trying not to gag. He quickly stood up once he saw that the chain wouldn't allow her to go anywhere. He took a step back and waved away the air by his face. A dog started to bark off camera.

"That must be Buck," Daniel said as he watched the events unfold on the TV.

The demon's facial featuress disfigured Amelia's angelic face. Her skin grew bumpy and grey. Her cheekbones bulged out, causing her glowing eyes to sink further into their dark sockets. Her jaw hung low and jutted forward exposing the sharp teeth. Saliva and blood leaked out of the ripped corners of her mouth. When she breathed, gurgling mucus was audible on the tape.

"Luke, stand back now," Merle said.

Luke obeyed.

He leaned against the wall as the old man stepped forward.

"Look at me, demon."

One of the demon's eyes shifted its focus to Merle while the other remained fixed on Luke. The demon smiled ear to ear.

"To what do I owe this pleasure?" it said.

"I should ask you the same thing," Merle replied.

"Oh, I couldn't resist the chance to take a fresh breath of the air up here." It grinned.

"How did you get here?" Merle asked.

"You know this already," it answered.

"Through the well?"

"Naturally."

Merle laughed now.

"There's nothing natural about you. You're an abomination," he said.

"You're too kind," the demon said, winking at Luke, before turning its attention to Merle. "I'm assuming you want me to elaborate?"

"If you don't mind."

Buck snarled off camera. The demon's elongated brow furrowed.

"If that wretched creature makes another sound, I'll command it to chew out lover boy's entrails," it sneered.

"Heel, old Buck," Merle ordered. "Please, what is it about my well? What kind of power is in there?"

"It's a gateway. Nothing more."

"A gateway to where?"

"You know where: Hell. And more importantly, a gateway *from* Hell."

"Did my wife create this gateway?"

The demon's eyes rolled back to the whites as it laughed uproariously.

"The hubris of Man never ceases to amaze us," it said. "Poor, sweet Gertie can't create a gateway to Hell. Only the Master can do that. The gateway has been here since the Fall. Your wretched whore wife only invited us through."

Merle looked away from the creature. One corner of his mouth turned upward in a small smile. He once again faced the demon.

"You're saying that there are portals to Hell that have been here since Lucifer was cast out of Heaven, and humans can somehow open them?"

The demon only grinned.

"Your poet, Milton, was not entirely inaccurate in his depiction," it said.

"Milton? As in *Paradise Lost*?" Merle asked.

"You're not as stupid as you appear."

"I'm familiar enough with the tale," Merle began. "Lucifer and his army were defeated during the war in Heaven and sent to Hell. Lucifer escaped Hell through a tunnel that led to the Garden of Eden. His goal was to bring chaos and sin to God's creation. One could argue that he succeeded."

The demon hooted with laughter as it rocked back and forth under the chain.

"We're not finished yet, exorcist," it taunted.

Smoke started to rise up in small swirls from various parts of Amelia's body. The demon's eyes widened.

"What's happening to you?" Merle asked.

"Fuck you and your god! He created the heavens but couldn't even make a body worthy of hosting *our* divine essence."

It spit bloody mucus across his face.

"That's why your pathetic Gertie ended her life. I wish she hadn't. It was *so* delicious being inside her. She still hangs in Hell by the way," it cackled as the smoke intensified.

"Then why do you come to our world? Why do you come if you burn or kill the possessed?" Merle demanded as the demon squirmed.

"You humans will never appreciate a stroll through the Garden until you've felt the flames of Hell." It winced a grin. "Blissful Pandemonium."

The demon switched back to Amelia in the blink of an eye.

"Luke, help me," she said.

Luke looked at Merle.

"It's not her, boy. Don't be fooled."

"It is me, Luke," Amelia began. "That thing left me. It's scared."

Small flames started to flicker all over Amelia's body as her skin reddened and blistered. She screamed.

"Get the chains off her! She's dying!" Luke pleaded.

Merle grabbed Luke by the shirt with both hands and pulled him close.

"Our only hope is to exorcise this demon before her body gives out," Merle yelled in his face. "If she dies, the demon goes back to Hell victorious. We're sending this creature up to meet its true Master. Now, grab the crucifix and holy water and prepare to repeat after me."

Merle released Luke and withdrew a rosary from a pocket in his overalls. He wrapped it around his fist several times until the cross was in his palm. He held his hand open and pointed it toward Amelia. Amelia looked at Luke and pleaded.

"Luke, take the chain off, please. It's burning me alive!" she cried as more flames flickered through her flesh.

"Ignore her and focus. We don't have much time!"

"She's dying!" Luke screamed as he bent down and yanked the chain off her.

"No!"

Amelia grabbed her reddening face with both hands and ripped it apart at the nose. The blood-covered, demonic face beneath inhaled deeply and moaned with pleasure. It continued to split Amelia's flesh as it sat up and exited its cocoon.

Buck barked off camera.

Luke stumbled back against the basement wall. Merle ran over to the secret room door with the cross and stood tall like a soldier at attention.

"Luke," he pleaded. "We have to exorcise this demon right now. Grab your . . . "

"Silence!" the demon hissed as it backhanded Merle.

The old man just wiped his face and held his position.

"Demon, I command you, in the name of the Father, the Son . . . " Merle continued as the demon turned its attention to Luke who was motionless and wide-eyed.

"Amelia was the sweetest blossom I've ever tasted. I can see why you mourn her," the demon taunted.

Merle continued the exorcism while looking down at the demon from behind it. The demon sneered. Luke clenched his fists and charged the creature, tackling it to the ground. It laughed as Luke repeatedly hammered its face with his fists.

"Luke, stop!" Merle yelled. "That's what it wants you to do. It wants to go back to Hell! We have to exorcise it!"

Luke delivered blow after blow until the demon stopped moving, and its head was nothing more than a mushy crater. The demon's remains charred and turned to ash. Luke stood up and then looked to Merle by the little door.

"We failed," Merle said, letting his head drop.

Luke took two fast steps toward the old man and punched him in the face. Merle fell off camera, and there was a loud thud. Buck ran into the camera frame and bit Luke on the leg. Luke pulled back and screamed a primal wail at everything that had just happened. Buck charged him again. Luke fled the frame with the dog hot on his tail.

Merle stumbled back into frame. He took quick breaths as he walked over to the open room with his rosary still wrapped around his hand. His eyes were moist, and his posture slumped.

"You know what?" he said into the dark opening. "If you want me . . . come get me."

He turned his back on the open door, walked over to the video camera, and shut it off.

CHAPTER 24

THE HILL FAMILY continued to stare at their reflections in the blank TV screen moments after Merle cut the tape. Daniel slowly turned his head to his wife and daughter. They were still staring in shock at having just watched Amelia's death via a botched exorcism. He tried desperately to think of something to say but could not. Instead, he just looked back at the TV. The thought came to him to try and think of something to lighten the mood and offer them hope. Just when he took a breath to speak, the black screen cut to another image.

"It's not over," Daniel said.

The video was a close-up shot of Merle's overalls as he stood in front of the camera. He backed up and came into full view. The old man was standing on his front porch at what looked like evening time. He sat down in the wicker rocking chair and stared at the camera but looked away. His eyes had sunk deeper into his withered face. He looked like he had lost some weight.

After sitting quietly for ten seconds, he put his elbows on his knees and leaned forward to stare at the ground in defeat. He kept looking around like he was expecting to find someone spying on him. The man looked tortured and paranoid. Finally, he took a deep breath and looked straight into the camera lens.

Daniel felt Merle staring directly at him through the screen.

"I don't know why I'm filmin' this right now," Merle said.

He had a deep rasp in his voice like he was sick. He coughed a little and spat in front of his feet.

"I guess my hope is that when I'm gone, someone might find this tape and figure out somethin' that I'm missin'."

He looked back down at his feet again.

"It's been months since the demon killed Luke's lady friend, Amelia . . . poor girl. I saw Luke for the first time a few days ago. The boy showed up at my house sayin' that whatever was in the basement had poisoned his mind. I made him a cross flashlight which is just tape on the front of a regular flashlight that makes a beam in the shape of a cross. I told him to point it at the son of a bitch next time it appeared to him. He came back the next day and told me the demon came to him in the middle of the night, but he blasted it away. That boy must have more faith than he admits to. The religious stuff only works if you believe."

Nora immediately thought of Luke saving her with that same flashlight. She felt a great sadness for the poor boy and his short life.

On the screen, Merle leaned back in his chair and slowly rocked. The old man looked like he was at death's door and was well aware of it. He gave half of a smile.

"I think Luke's gonna be all right," he said. "If it came after him and he fought it off . . . I think he's going to be OK."

Alice felt tears welling up in her eyes at the death of the boy she had only just started to know—the boy who came back to help her. She felt a sudden flush of anger at how unfair and cruel life could be. Luke was supposed to be the man of her dreams—showing up on her farm, taking her on a tour of the countryside. He was supposed to be hers. Then, she remembered seeing how happy he was with Amelia and how he had even gotten the tattoo for her. She felt selfish and stupid. He wasn't ever going to be hers. He was always going to belong to Amelia.

"Yes, Luke will be just fine, thank God," Merle continued. "I have no idea what's in store for me though. I've accepted the fact that I'm going to die. I'm not scared of death. It's been too long since I've seen my wife and my boy, and I know I'll go with them and the good Lord after I take my last breath here. That's not what scares me.

"The worst part about all this is the not knowin' when it's gonna come. There's lots of sounds on a farm. Any one of them could be the demons in the basement finally decidin' that it's time to take another stroll up above," he said as he put his hands on his head and rubbed his eyes.

Buck barked off camera, and Merle jumped. After a moment, he looked back at the camera.

"Just an animal scamperin' around the woods," he said as he calmed down. "I haven't slept for shit and can't bring myself to eat more than a few bites of anything. This mornin' I was fixin' a cup of coffee in the kitchen. I heard somethin' . . . no, I felt somethin' standin' on the other side of the basement door. It was just there, listenin' to me, probably smilin' in the dark at how mad it's driven me lately. I think it was a warning."

Merle took a deep breath.

"I feel like it's comin' for me tonight. Must be it. And you know what? I'm ready for it. I'm ready for it to get it over with."

He looked off camera, presumably at the front door, judging from where he was sitting on the porch.

"You hear me? I'm ready for you!"

Merle coughed and spat again. He emitted a sigh.

"Well, if this is it for me, then I guess I better start gettin' right with the man above. I'm gonna grab the old Gospel, get my pipe and dog, and head to my favorite rock to relax before the night comes. May God have mercy on my soul."

Merle stood up from his chair and turned off the camera.

Again, the Hill family sat in disbelief as they saw themselves sitting on the bed in the blank TV screen. The three of them shared a somber mood that was palpable.

"I think that's it," Daniel said, breaking the silence.

"Yeah," Nora said.

Alice continued to stare at the screen and think of Luke. All she wanted was to see his face once more.

Daniel stood up and walked over to the VCR. He raised his finger to press the eject button.

"Wait!" Alice shouted from the bed, causing Daniel to jump. "There's something else." He backed away as another image came into focus.

Luke positioned the camera on a tree stump in the woods where he would later go on to make his camp. He stepped back and sat on a log near the future location of his tent. He tucked his hair behind his ears and began to address the camera.

"Hello," he said and then stopped. He shook his head and finally said, "I, uh, I don't know who I am speakin' to, but I guess I should try to continue what Merle started with this tape. If you're watching this, then you're either the new owner of the old man's house or the police. Either way, I think I should give a bit of an update."

The tape started to get fuzzy with static as the image bounced around inside the screen.

"Damn it," Daniel said as he stood up and smacked the side of the VCR.

The tape unfroze as Luke continued to talk.

"It's been months since Amelia died. They still haven't officially declared her dead. She's still just a missing person. Lyin' about not knowin' where she is has been the hardest thing I've ever had to do. Especially seein' how upset her parents are and all. The police questioned me pretty good, but Dad is good friends with the sheriff, and they know that I would never have hurt her.

"I haven't been the same since it happened. Yeah, I did

see some things like Merle just said on this tape, but it hasn't come back. I watched the beginning of this tape and saw the exorcism. Watching it on tape and knowin' what was going to happen was harder than being there in person.

"I heard Merle's part about feeling like it was his time to die. He was right. Part of his house burned down that night with him in it. I still can't believe the old man couldn't fight it off. Maybe he wanted to go. I don't know. I just hope that maybe whatever was in that basement went away once it finally got Merle. This shit is so crazy . . .

"Anyway, I got word that someone bought the house. I was drivin' home and saw that the FOR SALE sign had a big SOLD sticker on it. A few days later there was a construction crew at the house repairing the burnt parts. That's when I started hangin' around in the woods watching them work. I just had to be sure that the thing was gone for good.

"I'm not positive, but I'm pretty sure one of the guys went down into the basement. If he did and stays OK, then it means that the demon thing is gone. If something happens to him, then I'll know that his mind was poisoned, and we're still not safe.

"As I'm recordin' this right now, nothing bad has happened since the old man died. The contractors finished the house today, and I broke in to take a look around myself. I had to find the tape that Merle made of Amelia's exorcism because I'm in it obviously. I took my flashlight and went down into the basement. There was nothin' weird about it. Nothin' came out of the little room. There was no fire or burnin' smells. It was just quiet. It was dead.

"I found the old man's chest with all of his journals and recordings and the camera. I found Amelia's tape—the one that you're watching right now—and watched it myself. I'm adding my part to this tape to let you know that it's all true. What you just watched isn't some Hollywood special effects. It all happened. I don't care what you do with this tape now. If it's meant to get turned in to the police, then so be it. Livin' with a lie is no fun at all.

"So, now all I gotta do is pack this tape and camera back up in Merle's box and seal it away in the little room. I'm going back there right now. If you're watching this, then you already know all the precautions I've taken with hangin' the rosary over the well and sealing the lid with the old man's cross.

"After I close down that little room, I'm gonna nail that damn basement door shut. I might even do it in the shape of a cross, just to be safe. I know Merle would appreciate that. He always said that the religious stuff only worked if you believe. I was never much of a believer until I saw what I saw. I guess it's true what they say about seein' is believin'.

"Anyway, it's time for me to sign off here. Whoever is watchin' this . . . I hope that nothing strange has happened to you since moving into the house. I hope that you're not too pissed at me for nailin' a cross in your basement door. If you've found this tape, I hope that how I sealed the well shut is the only creepy thing that you've seen.

"I plan on keepin' an eye on whoever moves in here just to be sure nothin' happens. Maybe we're friends, and you're watchin' this right now and you're freaked out and think I'm a liar. Maybe no one will ever watch this because the new owners just chucked out everything that belonged to the old man. Whatever happens . . . is meant to happen."

Luke stood up from the log. He looked around the woods before walking over to the camera. He picked it up and looked into the lens.

"Goodbye."

The tape was finally over.

CHAPTER 25

NORA AND ALICE sat on the porch swing watching Daniel direct a tow truck down their long driveway. His black beamer was on the back of the rig that was churning gravel as it made its way toward them. For the first time, Alice saw the damage to her father's totaled car. The front was smashed like an aluminum can. The windshield looked like a glass jigsaw puzzle. Mud and grass were caked on what was left of the bumper and hood.

"Oh my God," she said.

She looked over at her mom sitting beside her.

"How did you all survive that?"

Nora was nervously rubbing her pregnant belly. She felt the baby kick and smiled.

"I'm not sure," she replied.

The wreck had happened in slow motion. Daniel hit the tree head-on. The front of the car folded around the thick trunk as a loud metal crunch shook their world. The windshield splintered immediately but didn't completely break. Daniel's head lunged forward and smacked the steering wheel. Nora had time to brace for impact because she was not wrapped up in Daniel's delusion. She knew they were headed straight for a tree, and she planted her feet on the floorboard and cradled her belly. Their seatbelts kept them both from ejecting through the glass.

The tow truck carefully placed Daniel's car in the driveway beside the house, made a sweeping turn in their front yard, and left after Daniel paid the bill. Daniel walked up to his family on the porch as the sun began to head for the hills behind him.

"Well, we're down to one car for now," he said.

"It could've been a lot worse," Nora said.

"Oh, I know. Believe me, a car is the least of my worries right now."

He stepped onto the porch and began to pace its length back and forth.

"What are you thinking about, Dad?"

Daniel stopped and looked up, oblivious to the contemplative nature of his frantic stroll.

"I'm trying to wrap my mind around all this and formulate a plan," he said, a bit annoyed by having his train of thought derailed.

"Let's start with what we know," Nora began. "We all agree that it would make no sense for us to just leave, right?"

Daniel gave an obvious nod.

"Yeah, because all of our minds are fucked," Alice blurted out.

Nora shot her daughter a look, but Alice didn't care.

"That's an accurate summation," Daniel said, unfazed by his daughter's language.

"Luke wanted us to know what happened," Alice said. "Dad, you said the guy who lived here before appeared to you and told you to read his journals and watch his tapes, right?"

"That's right."

"If they both crossed over to make us see what happened to Amelia, then it seems like there must be something pretty important there," Alice said.

Nora looked from her daughter to her husband, who was nervously rubbing his beard stubble as he thought about what Alice said.

"Daniel, what's on your mind?"

"Well . . . if we're accepting everything that we've heard

as fact—even the testimony of a possessed person—then Merle's wife activated some kind of dormant doorway to Hell with her séances she was hosting to communicate with her deceased son. She gets possessed and kills herself. The demon on that tape said the possessed person will die one way or another, right?"

Nora and Alice simultaneously nodded their heads as Daniel paced and pontificated.

"So, we know that much of what the demon said is true. Merle seals off the basement and turns his life over to demonology, for lack of a better term. Flash forward a few decades and Amelia somehow awakens the doorway and gets possessed. We know what happened next."

"What are we supposed to do, Daniel? How do we get out of this nightmare?"

She rubbed her temples. The three of them all looked like they had been through a war.

"I . . . don't know. What are we supposed to do—perform exorcisms on ourselves? Are we possessed? I mean, seriously? I'm one more episode of crazy away from marching downstairs and taking a piss into that fucking well! Maybe that will put out the Hellfire."

Nora rolled her eyes at her husband's outburst, but Alice thought of something.

"Wait. That's it."

Daniel waited for more information.

"It's the well. You said it yourself, Dad. Gertie activated the portal, so we just have to figure out a way to close it," Alice said.

"Great. I guess we just need to find someone who specializes in closing haunted wells," Daniel said as he walked to the other end of the porch.

Nora felt like Alice was on to something.

"Daniel, there wasn't *anything* that you read in those journals that said something about how to deal with a situation like this?"

Daniel thought and thought. He closed his eyes and tried to focus. He scanned the pages in his mind—each anecdote, each description. Nora had often told him that he had the best memory she'd ever seen and that's why he was such a good psychologist: he listened and remembered. The events of Merle's life as described in the journals played at full-speed in his brain.

One detail stood out, and his eyes shot open.

"Merle was trained by someone," he said and then walked into the house.

"I think he's onto something," Nora said as she smiled at Alice.

There was some commotion inside. Daniel burst onto the porch clutching one of Merle's journals. He held it out in front of him as he caught his breath.

"Father Stollings!" Daniel said, winded. "Father Stollings is the priest that trained Merle."

Nora looked confused.

"Wouldn't he be long dead?"

"He is. Died in . . . " Daniel trailed off as he flipped to the page that provided the details he needed. "1965. He died in 1965. But, he also mentions a protégé by the name of Father Martin."

"How does that help us?" Alice asked.

"Well, if he trained Merle, I would imagine that he did the same for this Father Martin guy. I'm going to find out what parish in North Carolina Father Stollings served and then get this Father Martin to come up here and seal this well."

Nora and Alice took in what he said and realized this was the best possible course of action.

"In the meantime," Daniel began, "let's order some takeout or something. I'm starving."

Father Martin was finishing his sandwich on a bench in Chapel Hill, North Carolina. The short, dark-haired man was in his mid-fifties and looked as contented as a bullfrog on a lily pad. He watched the few university students who were there for the summer walk across the scenic campus. He imagined the conversations they were having, the lives they were planning, the dreams toward which they were aspiring. He smiled, and his cheeks nudged his glasses.

The tall tree that stood over him kept him shaded from the harsh sun. He took the last bite of his late lunch and wiped the corners of his mouth with a napkin. His watch read 3:57 PM. About thirty minutes ago, he was in the office of a professor in Religious Studies. He frequently consulted with scholars. Once anyone in academia began researching modern day exorcisms, his name eventually came up.

The professor was a nice enough fellow, Father Martin thought. He was very respectful and welcoming. Father Martin always heard how professors hated religion and preached their own atheistic agenda. He supposed some of that was true; however, most of his experience had shown that the truly successful philosophers became so by having an open mind. This professor—Dr. Something or Other wanted to invite him to be a guest lecturer this semester. He gladly accepted his offer and then strolled across campus to enjoy his lunch.

The priest was no stranger to this field, having spoken in numerous lecture halls about his life in demonology. His presentation hadn't changed much in the ten or so years he'd been doing it. He would show up with an overhead projector and a stack of images to display. He always started off by describing how he came to believe in God and joined the Catholic Church, while showing pictures of himself as a younger man of the cloth. He would throw in a few jokes about the smock and the irony that it was a chick magnet. The classes always laughed at this.

Next, he would ask them questions to gauge their prior

knowledge of the Catholic Rites of Exorcism. This always stirred a lively debate with the engaged crowd. Many students would reference the movies they'd seen depicting demonic possession. He would always smile and chuckle to himself and remind them that what they'd seen was typical Hollywood theatrics. The real thing was much less of a spectacle. The skeptics would take this opportunity to assert their dominance. He would always hear them out and respond politely.

The next chunk of the presentation would be his case files. He would talk about the numerous possessed persons he had encountered, detail their common symptoms, and show actual pictures of exorcisms to the students. This was his favorite part: hearing the gasps and other uncomfortable sounds as they nervously shifted in their seats, some averting their eyes. No matter how they reacted, he had them in the palm of his hand.

He always left the final ten minutes open for questions. There were always questions. The skeptics were silent by this point. No matter what anyone believed, the images of the possessed or, afflicted, as some of the professors called them, had a firm impact. Normally, he would receive a standing ovation and an open invitation to return the following semester.

Birds cawed above him. He looked up as a crow swooped down and snapped at his hair. He dodged the aggressive animal and shooed it away with his hands. The bird cawed again as it flew away. Father Martin stared in bewilderment until the bird disappeared on the horizon. He had been attacked by a crow once before in his life: the day his mentor, Father Stollings, passed away.

The priest walked at a leisurely pace toward the lot where he had parked his car. He tried to enjoy the beautifully manicured landscape but could not stop thinking about the bird. It was best to always heed the warnings of the universe, he believed.

He stepped off the grass and onto the concrete. The lot was empty when he arrived, but now his car was one of two. The other, a station wagon idling in a corner spot under a weeping willow tree, caused him no regard. The ravenous crow had his full attention. He opened his car door as the driver of the other vehicle stepped out of his.

"Excuse me," a man said from the other end of the lot.

Father Martin looked up at the young man approaching him. The sun was behind the stranger, and the priest had to squint to look at him.

"Yes?"

"Are you Father Martin?"

"I am. And who are you, son?"

The priest examined the disheveled man closely. He didn't look good. His skin was pale, and he had heavy dark bags under his eyes. He looked like he hadn't changed his clothes or had a shower in a couple of days.

"My name is Daniel Hill. I just drove here from West Virginia. The people at your church told me I could find you here. It's urgent that I speak with you."

Father Martin saw the worry in Daniel's face. He had seen that look several times before on the faces of the loved ones of the possessed.

"Sure, Daniel," he said. "Please, follow me back to my office."

CHAPTER 26

FATHER MARTIN'S OFFICE in the rectory barely fit his desk and the two chairs in front of it. There was an overflowing bookshelf running the length of one of the walls. Pictures, academic achievements, and religious décor adorned the opposite wall. A large window overlooking a courtyard was behind the desk. Merle's journals were scattered across the desk.

Daniel sat in one of the uncomfortable wooden chairs in front of the priest's desk, but it was turned around so that he and the priest were both looking in the same direction. A TV and VCR on a rolling cart had been wheeled into the office, and they both watched the end of Merle's final tape. Father Martin's heart broke as he witnessed Amelia die. In all his time in the field, he had never witnessed anything so violent as that young lady being ripped apart. Merle addressed the camera, then Luke, and then it was over. Daniel turned around to gauge the priest's reaction.

Father Martin was still staring at the blank screen. His eyes had saddened in the time he had watched the tape. Gone was the untouchable serenity that radiated through the holy man, and a look of grim despair had replaced it.

"What do you think, Father?"

The priest snapped out of whatever thought he was trapped in.

"Well, Mr. Hill," he began.

"Daniel."

"Daniel, after reading through these journals with you and watching this tape, I'd be lying if I said I wasn't deeply disturbed."

"Disturbed? I thought this would be a typical Wednesday for someone in your field."

That made the priest grin ever so slightly.

"Far from it," Father Martin began. "Most of what I encounter on a daily basis is not demonic possession. Ninety-nine percent of my cases are nothing more than misdiagnosed mental illness."

"Do you refer them to a psychologist?"

"Mental health professionals were the first stop for many of them already. Why would I kick them back down a rung?"

"You said that . . . "

"I know what I said," Father Martin interrupted. "Nearly all of them were mentally ill. The problem was that they *believed* that they were possessed by demons, or the devil in some cases. I know that I don't have to tell a psychologist like you how strong the power of belief can be."

Daniel nodded his head in agreement. The priest elaborated.

"Their belief is so strong that it creates physiological manifestations: they lose weight; their skin pigment pales; they get sick. This sudden change in physical appearance can even convince other family members that they're dealing with demonic possession. We then get into shared hysteria and all the paranoia that comes with that. If the afflicted party believes that they're possessed, then they believe that an exorcism can cure their ailment. I perform the exorcism and suddenly they're cured. They snap right out of it. They recover, and their lives go on. I've seen it happen time and time again, Daniel."

"I believe you," Daniel said. "But that's not the case for all of them, right? What about the others?"

Father Martin took a deep breath. He looked up to the

225

crucifix on the wall, at Christ looking down at him in anguish.

"There are a few cases where the afflicted individual knew or performed acts that were supernatural. You've no doubt seen exaggerations of this in popular culture: levitation, speaking in foreign languages, superhuman strength, knowing things which that person couldn't possibly know."

"Popular culture?" Daniel chuckled. "I've been seeing crazier shit in my *house*, Father. Excuse my language."

The priest smiled and leaned back in his chair. He interlocked his fingers across his belly and began to nervously twiddle his thumbs.

"I suppose I should explain my name being mentioned in Merle Blatty's journal and my connection to Father Stollings and all this."

Daniel leaned forward, all ears.

"Merle was a bit older than me. I first met him when he was already working with Father Stollings. Merle would accompany Father Stollings on investigations. He was not a man of the cloth but a fervent believer in God nonetheless. Father Stollings always said that it was faith that gave one strength over the darkness, not a cassock.

"Anyway, I only investigated one case with the two of them. A young boy—eight or nine years old—was displaying strange behavior. The family was not religious by any means. The boy began having spells where he would lose track of time and see things that weren't there. The parents took him to every type of doctor imaginable, but they couldn't find anything wrong. The parents heard him causing a commotion in his room one night. They entered the room and found that he had written the entire Book of Revelation. The words were upside down and in Aramaic. Eventually, they contacted the Church . . . *our* Church.

"We were given the green light to investigate. The boy, by this time, was bedridden. He was very unhealthy—refusing to eat; prone to angry, profane outbursts. The family even said his voice had changed. When we arrived at the house, the demonic presence was overwhelming. The atmosphere was thick and humid. The smell of sulfur hung in the air . . .

"We spoke with the mother and father before going up to see the child. After talking with them for no more than ten minutes, we could tell that something was not right with them as well. They had gaps in their stories. They both looked sick as well. They even admitted to seeing things that couldn't possibly be real. Whatever was going on in that house was hitting the child the hardest, but inflicting chaos on all those around him as well."

"That sounds familiar," Daniel said. "But, no one in my house is possessed. Luke was, but he died."

Father Martin's right eye twitched slightly, but he continued on with his story.

"After we talked with the family, we went to the boy's room to investigate. Keep in mind that we were not there that day to perform an exorcism. We were just collecting as much concrete evidence as we could to get permission to perform one. But, once we entered that bedroom, we knew that we had no time to waste on bureaucratic red tape.

"The boy was in the fetal position under the bed. He was acting like a scared animal. He kept his face buried in his hands and kept bleating like a sheep. Father Stollings got on the ground to speak with him, but the boy wouldn't make eye contact. It wasn't until Father Stollings asked if either of us had any holy water that the boy broke out of his trance. He scurried out from under that bed on all fours. I remember jumping back and seeing Merle startle, but Father Stollings didn't flinch.

"The demon crawled up the wall, completely ignoring the laws of gravity. Its eyes were open holes to the fire burning inside his skull. He looked at all of us at the same time, like one of those paintings, you know?"

Daniel nodded as he listened.

"Father Stollings ordered me to bless some water and bring it and his Bible to him at once. I did, and he proceeded to perform the Catholic Rites of Exorcism. We aided in recitation of our parts of the prayers. As we neared the end of the ritual, the boy's skin began to rise and fall in different places all over his poor body. Father Stollings pressed forward, knowing what was coming if he didn't conclude. The boy leapt from the wall and just stopped, suspended in midair like someone had hit the pause button.

"Father Stollings cast the demon out, and the boy dropped straight into my arms like a marionette whose strings were just cut. I saw the boy come back to life right there before me. I watched as he looked around like he hadn't seen his own home in months. And just like that, we had succeeded."

"And that's what Merle had failed to do? Because he didn't have enough time?" Daniel asked.

"Apparently so. But, ultimately, we did not succeed."

"How do you mean?"

"I got word less than a month later that the entire family had died."

Daniel raised both eyebrows. The priest was pained by the recollection and did not want to say more.

"What happened?"

"The neighbors reported a disturbance. The police showed up and found the father and the child deceased in the basement. Their bodies were nailed to the wall upside down as if they were crucified in an obvious display of blasphemy. They had also been disemboweled. The mother's fingerprints were all over the murder scene."

"Where was the mother?"

"They never found a body. But, if I were to guess, I would say that she was possessed just the same as her child had been. Only, we weren't there to stop her from burning alive. Her ashes are probably still down in that basement."

Fearful thoughts flooded Daniel's mind.

"Not a day later, Father Stollings, passed away. I'll never

forget how I heard the news. I was walking to the rectory on my way back from town when a giant crow flew down and attacked me. It was the oddest thing I'd ever seen a bird do. I swatted it away, but I just felt like something terrible was about to happen. As soon as I got back home, they told me Father Stollings had died in his sleep.

"I don't know why I did what I did next, but I had to go back to that little boy's house. I was there during the exorcism. I saw that it worked. Why in the name of God did this family get targeted *twice* by demonic forces? There had to be something there. I took Father Stollings's exorcism bag from his room. I waited until nightfall and went back to the house. I snuck under the yellow caution tape and pried open the back door with a crowbar. I went down into the basement with my flashlight.

"I remember closing my eyes in that gloomy dungeon and praying that God use me as a beacon of His light. I opened my eyes, and my flashlight was pointing to a small well in the corner of the room. I walked over to it and shined my light down into the bottomless pit.

"I must've triggered something because the abyss started to glow and then a hot wave that smelled of rotten eggs belched out of it. It was the same smell that I encountered during the exorcism. I opened Father Stollings's bag right there and took out the holy water and the Rites of Exorcism. I didn't know why I was doing it—there wasn't a possessed person there—but something about this well was unholy.

"I began the rites and then sprinkled some drops of holy water into the well. The fire below immediately raged to the top. I had awakened whatever was down there, and it was not shy. I grasped my rosary and closed my eyes and continued with the exorcism. I heard creatures crawling around me . . . snapping and snarling into my ear—all tactics of intimidation. I knew that as long as I kept moving forward, I was protected. I knew that I was walking on water like Peter in the Gospels.

"The enemy was trying to trick me. It was trying to cloud my mind with chaos and confusion . . . with fear. As I neared the end of the ritual, I realized that I did not have it all memorized. I would have to open my eyes to consult the book in my hand. For the briefest moment, I felt panic. But, as I neared the end of my sentence, the next line appeared in my mind's eye as clearly as if it were on a page. I concluded the ritual and cast the evil out.

"Everything—the sounds, the glowing lights, the flaming smells—all of it disappeared down the well, and there was nothing but darkness beyond my closed eyelids. I opened my eyes and stared at the empty basement. I looked into the open well and saw the watery bottom just a few yards down. I had sealed the gateway."

The priest had a faint smile of satisfaction, but then became concerned.

"What is it, Father?"

"In Merle's journals and in the videotape that we just watched, there is a well in the basement that was described as being a gateway to Hell," Father Martin said.

Daniel nodded in agreement.

"It appears that you are dealing with the same malevolent forces, Daniel."

"Yes, and it also appears that you are the man to help me combat them, Father."

The priest slowly stood up from his chair and looked out of his window into the courtyard.

"Will you help me?" Daniel asked.

"I knew what I had to do when another crow attacked me just before I met you in the parking lot," Father Martin said. "That was Father Stollings telling me once again to get my ass to work."

The priest turned back to face Daniel.

"We must leave right now. Until we seal the gateway, your entire family is in grave danger."

CHAPTER 27

A SUDDEN GUST OF wind slammed the outside shutters causing Nora to jump and drop her bottle of water. Alice came running into the kitchen from the living room.

"What was that?" Alice asked.

Nora bent over and picked up her drink.

"Just the stupid wind," she laughed.

They had all been on edge since yesterday when they watched the tape together. Their nervousness increased when Daniel left for North Carolina early that morning to seek out the priest. He pulled out of their driveway around 8 AM, and they hadn't heard from him since. Nora looked at the kitchen clock and saw that it was almost 5 PM.

It had been a quiet night. They had all slept together in Daniel and Nora's room. Daniel volunteered to sleep on the air mattress at the foot of the bed beside Buck so that the two ladies could have the bed. Nothing happened. Even Buck got a full night's rest. Despite this, they somehow all woke up even more exhausted than they had been the day before.

"Have you heard from Dad?" Alice asked, even though she knew the answer was no. The two of them hadn't separated except to go to the restroom or the kitchen. They had agreed before Daniel left that it was safer to stick together in case they started having delusions.

"No," Nora replied one second before the phone rang. She jumped and dropped her water again.

231

"Oh, for shit's sake!" she yelled.

Alice covered her mouth to hold in her laughter. Nora picked up the plastic bottle and pretended to throw it at Alice when she saw her laughing. Alice flinched, and Nora answered the house phone hanging on the wall beside the refrigerator.

"Hello?"

"Hey, honey," Daniel said on the other end of the line.

"Daniel, how are you? Are you OK? Did you find him?"

"Yes, yes. Everything is good. I made it here just fine. I didn't see anything weird. Everything is fine."

"Where are you now?"

"I'm calling from Father Martin's office. We're gathering up the box of Merle's stuff and hitting the road right now. I'll be home in five hours."

"OK, thank God."

"Is everything OK with you guys?"

"Yes, we're just a little jumpy I suppose," she chuckled as she turned around to share a laugh with Alice, but Alice was gone. Nora walked toward the living room, untying the tangled phone cord as she made her way.

"OK then," Daniel said. "I'll see you all in a little bit. I love you."

"Love you, too."

She stopped in front of the stairs and looked up at Alice's open bedroom door. The light was on.

"Alice?"

There was no response. She dropped the phone and stormed up the stairs, careful not to go too fast and risk hurting her unborn child.

"Alice?"

Silence.

She ran into the open bedroom and saw that it was empty. She knew that Alice must've just come up here. The door had been shut, and the light had been off. Her palms started to dampen as her heart rate increased.

232

"Alice?" she cried. She ran into their bedroom and flicked on the lights. Aside from the air mattress still on the floor, there was nothing out of the ordinary. She ran into their bathroom, but it was empty as well.

"Alice, where are you?" she yelled as she ran back out of their room and past Alice's room. She was just about to take a step down the stairs when she froze and turned back around.

Inside Alice's bedroom, a window stood wide open.

She hurried over to it and looked into their backyard. Alice was slowly walking across the overgrown lawn with her right hand held out as if she was holding someone's hand, but there was no one there. She looked at the invisible presence beside her and smiled a lover's smile.

Nora felt terror welling up inside her.

"Alice!"

The young girl just kept walking toward the woods, led by something Nora couldn't see. She quickly turned around and ran down the steps. She burst through the front door, which woke Buck up from his nap on the porch, and took off sprinting around the side of the house. The old dog clumsily got up and followed the frantic woman. As soon as Nora ran into the backyard, she saw Alice nearing the rows of dense trees.

"Alice!" she screamed. "Alice, no!"

Buck's ears shot up as he was now at full attention. Nora looked down at the dog.

"What are you doing? Go help her!" Nora commanded, but Buck just looked toward the trees and cocked his head in confusion. "Help Alice!"

She looked back up toward her daughter, but no one was there.

"She's . . . she was right there . . . "

Nora stared in confusion at the empty yard. Even if Alice had reached the woods, she would still be visible.

"Where did she go?"

Buck apparently detected no threat, or else he would've been in full pursuit. Nora just stood there and put her hands on her hips as she caught her breath. She was way too pregnant to be moving that fast.

"What is going on?"

"Mom?" Alice said from behind her.

Nora spun around to see Alice standing in her bedroom window looking down at her and Buck in the backyard.

"What are you doing?" Alice asked.

Nora was beyond perplexed.

"I just . . . I just saw you walking toward the woods holding someone's hand."

She turned back to the woods and pointed.

"You were going that way."

Icy fear flooded her veins as she realized that she had just been tricked. She turned back to her daughter. A red, grinning face peeked over Alice's shoulder. Buck began to bark violently. Nora's eyes widened, and her voice locked up. She wanted to scream but could only point. Alice saw the terror in her mother's eyes and spun around to see what was behind her. Nora watched as two clawed hands grabbed Alice and pulled her away from the window.

"No!" Nora screamed as she took off running to the other side of the house.

Buck bolted ahead of her and ran up to the closed screen door, scratching and begging to be let in. Nora jerked the door open, and Buck leapt up the stairs in two bounds. He sniffed and barked his way around the empty bedroom. Nora ran up behind him and saw that her daughter was nowhere to be seen. Buck placed his front paws on the open window and sniffed out into the air. He looked back at Nora unable to provide an explanation.

"Mom!" Alice screamed from downstairs.

Nora whipped around and started running back down the stairs. Buck hurried past her and caught her right leg just as she lifted it up. She lost her balance and tumbled forward, landing on her side and rolling down the second half of the stairs before colliding into the opposing wall at the bottom and banging the back of her head.

Her consciousness began to fade. She had landed so that she was looking through the kitchen at the open basement door. She watched helplessly as a snake-like arm dragged her daughter by the hair down into the darkness. Buck barked and snarled as he galloped toward them, but the basement door slammed shut just as the dog smashed into it. He winced and shook his snout and sneezed. The last image Nora saw before she passed out was Buck barking and scratching with futility at the closed door. Her heavy eyelids fell as the smell of sulfur flooded her senses.

A few hours passed, and darkness descended on the farm.

Buck repeatedly licked Nora's face and rubbed his wet snout into her cheek. She was in dreamless state of unconsciousness. Buck's tongue lapped one of her eyelids open, and she began to blink as she came to. She looked around the room, confused and delirious. Memories of what had happened earlier came together in her mind like puzzle pieces. She quickly sat up with her back against the wall.

The baby kicked inside her. The fall she just took definitely could've hurt her child. She looked down at her belly and rubbed it with relief.

"Thank God."

Aside from a sore back and already injured leg, she was relatively OK.

Alice, she thought.

Nora pushed herself up to her feet and nearly fell back down from dizziness. She bent over and put her hands on her knees to regain her composure. The fall must've taken more out of her than she initially thought. The image of her daughter being dragged into that dark basement flashed through her mind, and she stood straight up—willing herself to be OK for Alice's sake.

Buck ran to the basement door. He whined, pacing back and forth briefly, and then jumped to his hind legs and rested his front paws against the wood. Nora looked outside and saw that it was nighttime. She stumbled into the kitchen and looked at the clock: 9:33 PM. Daniel and Father Martin shouldn't be too far away by now.

She approached the closed door, and Buck made room for her. She looked down at the deep claw marks the old dog had made in the wood. The good boy had probably been trying to get in for several hours. She reached down and patted his head.

Smoke that looked like vaporized mucus seeped out from under the crack in the basement door. Nora thought it looked more like a smoke bomb or the artificial fog machines used in theatrical productions rather than any natural byproduct of something burning. For a split second she imagined that her basement was on fire, but the thought quickly abated. This was just another trick on her mind by the demonic presence in the well. It wasn't real. It couldn't be. She extended her hand and grabbed the doorknob.

"Ouch! Shit!" she exclaimed, recoiling, while cradling her burned palm.

Panic rushed through her system as she realized that maybe her basement actually was on fire and that her daughter was down there. Wasting no more time, she pulled up the bottom of her shirt to cover her hand. She grabbed the hot metal knob and jerked it open.

A river of foul mist covered the dark basement floor and crawled up the stairs. She had never seen anything like it. The kinetic fog seemed to have a mind of its own. It slithered up and over each step as it oozed into the kitchen. She shuddered at the thought of its source.

The basement was shrouded in shadows as a glowing

amber light burned from somewhere below. Nora didn't have to guess where it was coming from. Every instinct in the fiber of her being shouted for her not to go down there—just wait for Daniel and Father Martin to arrive and then they'd be better equipped to handle the situation.

But then she thought about the tape of Amelia burning alive from the inside out as the demon ripped its way through her. She knew she couldn't risk waiting. Who knew how much time Alice had before the same thing (or worse) happened to her? Nora took a deep breath, wiped her teary eyes, and began to descend the stairs.

The steps creaked under her weight. Buck started to follow her, but the door slammed shut behind her. She screamed as she spun around to see that she was clearly going nowhere. Buck barked furiously on the other side. She watched as his snout sniffed through the bottom crack. She prayed for strength and then continued forward.

The unseen area of the basement came into view the further down she walked. The secret door was open, and the fog rolled out of it. A flickering light glowed in the well as if a fire burned at its bottom. Nora scanned the rest of the basement but could not see her daughter.

"Alice?" she said timidly and then coughed. Her throat was coated with the thick, humid moisture in the atmosphere. She gagged as her tongue tasted the sour sheen on the roof of her mouth. "Alice, where are you, baby?"

She stepped onto the basement floor. Carefully, she crept over to the open door to the secret room. She bent down and peered inside. The small room was empty too. The well was uncovered as smoke and sulfurous heat bellowed from the top like a volcano. She dared not crawl in there to get a closer look.

Something giggled from under the stairs behind her.

Nora spun around and saw a version of Alice lounging in the chain attached to the wall like it was a hammock. Her heart froze when she saw her daughter's mangled face.

Nothing of Alice's features remained. Her forehead was elongated, creating a skeletal bone structure atop deep black eye sockets where small orange embers burned. The sides of her small mouth ripped through her cheeks nearly up to her ears, and sharp, silver teeth gleamed behind her chapped lips. Her tattered clothes hung from her withered limbs which were covered in bloody sores and scratches.

"I quite like this flesh," the demon whispered. "I think I'll keep it."

The creature grinned and let its head fall back in thunderous laughter and then leaped off the wall and crab-walked toward her—limbs popping and dislocating from their sockets.

Nora had nowhere to go except back. She lunged into the open room and pulled the little door shut. She listened as claws caressed the outside of the wood. The shape of the figure moved behind the exposed cracks, watching Nora with curiosity.

The glowing flames behind her slowly disappeared down into the well. She turned toward the darkening gateway. She crawled across the ground and carefully peered into the hole in the floor. The demon inside Alice giggled from the other part of the basement. Nora inched closer to the well just as flames burst up through the darkness. Two fiery arms enveloped her in a warm embrace and pulled her down.

CHAPTER 28

DANIEL HAD DRIVEN at least fifteen miles per hour over the speed limit the entire drive back home. They had stopped one time to use the restroom and get gas. Father Martin took the opportunity to tell Daniel about his experiences as an official exorcist. After ten minutes, it became a regurgitation of his collegiate lecture. Nonetheless, Daniel hung on every word.

Just a little after 10 PM, they turned onto Sunny Branch Way. Father Martin regarded Daniel's busted BMW.

"Such a shame," he said. "Glorious machines, they are."

Daniel grinned in the darkness.

"Nora bought that for me as a gift. That's what hurts the most."

"Your wife bought that for you? That's enough to make a priest break his vows and settle down."

Daniel chuckled slightly. He knew the priest could sense how on edge he was, and he appreciated the man bringing levity to the situation.

Daniel drove to the end of the gravel driveway until they came to a stop closer to the porch. He hit the brake when he was as close to the house as he could possibly get. He shut off the engine and looked at Father Martin. The priest unbuckled his seatbelt.

"Are you ready, son?" Father Martin asked.

"I suppose. Are you?"

"We don't get ready. We *stay* ready."

Daniel liked the assurance in the holy man's voice.

"How do you do that?" he asked with a grin.

The priest did not return Daniel's lightheartedness. He was all business.

"Prayer," he said. "Every day, prayer. Constant contact with God. It is imperative to keep that channel open."

Daniel just nodded his head. He then found it concerning that his wife and daughter hadn't rushed out of the house to see him yet. In the stillness of the night, he heard a faint sound coming from inside.

"Do you hear that?" Daniel asked as he opened his car door and stepped out.

Buck was barking by the front door. Several lights were on, but Daniel saw no one inside the house and began to panic. He leaned his head back into the car.

"We have to get in there. Something's not right."

Daniel sprinted up onto the porch and burst through the front door. Father Martin grabbed his bag and tried his best to keep up. As soon as Daniel stepped foot in the house, Buck was there whining and wagging his tail.

"Nora? Alice?" Daniel shouted into his apparently empty home.

He first looked into the kitchen and saw that the basement door was shut. That was a good sign. He glanced up the stairs Alice's door was open and the light was on. He started to run up the stairs when he heard a small voice behind him.

"Daniel?" Nora said from the floor to the right of the front door.

He stopped in his tracks and spun around to see his wife slowly coming to. Father Martin stepped into the house and immediately crouched down beside Nora, who was delirious.

"Nora!" Daniel exclaimed as he ran to his wife.

He held her face and examined her for injuries. Other than a small knot on the back of her head, she appeared to be fine. "Honey, what happened?"

She blinked several times, trying to steady her blurry vision. She was beyond baffled. Slowly, she began to remember.

"Alice . . . I saw something trying to take Alice into the woods . . . " she trailed off as she tried to recall the events.

"Nora, where is Alice?" Daniel asked.

"I . . . I don't know."

The image of the demon standing behind Alice inside her bedroom popped into her head.

"Oh, my God. It wasn't real, though. I was tricked into going outside so that devil could get Alice."

Daniel's heart rate increased.

"Nora, where is our daughter?"

"I ran back up to her room, but it was too late. That thing dragged her to the basement. I tried to follow, but Buck made me fall down the stairs."

Daniel immediately thought about the baby. He looked down at her belly, which Nora was already cradling.

"The baby is OK, Daniel," Nora said preemptively. "I just felt her kick again."

She looked up at her husband and then to Father Martin.

"My daughter is in that basement."

Tears started to stream down her face.

"Please, go get her back."

All of the power in the house suddenly cut off, and the three of them were in total darkness. Their eyes slowly began to adjust to seeing only by the moonlight. Daniel heard Father Martin unzipping his bag and looked over to see him withdraw a flashlight and then click it on.

"You do stay ready, huh?" Daniel said.

The priest shined the light upstairs and then into the living room before turning around and settling on the kitchen.

Daniel held his wife and kissed her head.

"Let me help you up," he said as she wrapped her arm around his shoulder.

He lifted her to her feet and opened the screen door.

"Where are we going?" she asked.

"I want you to rest on the porch. There's no reason for you and the baby to be in here for this."

Nora allowed Daniel to escort her outside. They walked over to the porch swing with Buck following closely behind. Daniel gently eased her into the swing and propped her feet up. Buck laid underneath her with a look on his face that dared anything to come near her.

Father Martin remained inside the dark house with the flashlight fixed on the basement door in the kitchen. He saw the glowing light shining through the crack under the door and the sulfurous smoke tauntingly swirling out. There was raw evil down there—an ancient force more powerful than any man. One false move, one shadow of doubt, would be their doom. He knew what he had to do, but he couldn't do it alone. He walked onto the porch with his bag.

"Time is of the essence, friends," Father Martin said. "Daniel, it is imperative that we get down there, but there is one thing I must warn you of first."

Daniel stood beside his wife, waiting on the priest to finish his explanation. Father Martin talked as he began removing items from his bag.

"What we are dealing with down there is pure evil. It exists only to cause chaos, disorder, and pandemonium in God's creation. Lucifer is the father of lies. I'm not suggesting that the devil himself is in your basement, but his legions certainly are. They succeed in deception by combining the truth with lies. Whatever is down there . . . if it speaks, don't listen. Whatever it says . . . don't believe it. It will use your deepest fears and your darkest secrets against you. Anything that you think is tucked securely away in the recesses of your mind will be exposed. Keep your focus on the mission. I know it is easier said than done, but keep the faith and don't get distracted. Are you religious by chance?"

Daniel and Nora exchanged worried glances.

"No judgement here," Father Martin assured them. "Do either of you believe in God?"

"We're definitely not opposed to the idea that there is a God, Father," Daniel began. "We're just not crazy about organized religion. Catholicism in particular. No offense."

"None taken," he replied with a smirk. "We've certainly earned our reputation, I'm sorry to say. Let me ask you this: do you believe that what I'm about to do could successfully save your daughter and seal this barrier in your basement?"

"It's like you said about the power of belief . . . " Daniel started. "If whatever is down there *believes* that you have the ability to exorcise it, then *I* believe that you will be successful."

"Fantastic," Father Martin said. "Remember that. Remember, when it gets really nasty down there, to have faith in me. Leave the faith in God to me, if you wish. Do everything that I say and don't get distracted, and we all just may walk out of this unscathed."

"I will," Daniel replied.

The whole time the priest was speaking he had been withdrawing items one by one from his black satchel. He put a small leather-bound book in his right pocket. Daniel saw that the title was something written in Latin. He withdrew a black rosary and wrapped it several times around his left hand so that the cross was in his palm. He carefully placed two vials of holy water in his left pocket. The final item was a decorative article of clothing that Daniel didn't recognize. It was a piece of purple velvet that wrapped around the back of the priest's neck and hung down over his chest in two flaps like graduation regalia. Bright golden crosses were emblazoned on the material.

Midway through Father Martin's speech, Nora began feeling the weight of her past mistakes. She imagined Daniel going down into the heart of darkness with the priest and hearing the demon recant the details of her infidelity. He would surely lose his focus and the entire mission would be in jeopardy. Her secret sin could result in losing her daughter and her husband.

"Good," the priest responded. "Then we must be on our way."

Father Martin handed Daniel a vial of holy water. He looked at it like it was a piece of alien technology.

"It's holy water, son," the priest said. "When I tell you to use it . . . use it."

"OK," Daniel said as he nervously rolled the glass container between his thumb and index finger.

He turned around to face his wife. He bent down and kissed her on the lips.

"I love you. I'll bring Alice back."

"I love you, too."

Tears formed in her eyes as her nervousness intensified. She felt like she was going to explode if she didn't say something immediately. Father Martin opened the screen door as Daniel followed.

"Daniel, wait," Nora cried.

He looked back.

"I had an affair. Earlier this year . . . I had sex with another man."

Daniel stared at her with no detectible reaction. Father Martin's eyes widened as he looked from Nora to the back of Daniel's head and then back to Nora. Daniel inhaled deeply and glanced into the yard.

"I'm so sorry, honey," Nora said as she started to get up. "It was once, and it was a mistake. I've hated myself ever since. It meant nothing."

"I know," Daniel finally said.

Nora froze before she was fully sitting up in the swing. Daniel walked over to her.

"Don't get up. Just relax."

Nora stared at him with confusion.

"You *knew*?"

He raised his eyebrows and nodded his head.

"Of course, I did. I'd be a lousy psychologist if I couldn't read people, wouldn't I?"

"Why didn't you ever say anything?"

"What's the point? I knew you were beating yourself up worse than anything I could ever do. I knew that you knew you screwed up. I also know that I wasn't there for you when you needed me. I was so wrapped up in my work that I shut you and Alice out. It was only a matter of time before you found someone to fill the void, so to speak."

Nora shed tears of shame.

"Obviously, if it was more than a one-time mistake, then I would've addressed it, but I had a feeling that the truth would come out when it was time. Besides, the risk of losing my wife was just the wake-up call I needed at the time, I guess."

Nora started to speak, but Daniel just leaned over and kissed her and then pulled back.

"I don't know who it was, and I don't care. It doesn't matter. It's over. We're stronger than ever, and that's what matters, right?"

She nodded as she wiped her moist eyes.

"I love you, Daniel Hill."

"And I love you."

Father Martin cleared his throat from the doorway to hurry the moment along.

"I'll be back," Daniel said as he stood up and turned to the priest. "Let's go kick the holy shit out of this thing."

Father Martin held the door for Daniel as he entered the house and then let it slam shut behind them. Nora closed her eyes and rubbed her belly as Buck held his ground beneath her. For the first time since she was a child, she prayed like someone was actually listening.

CHAPTER 29

DANIEL FOLLOWED CLOSELY behind Father Martin as the two of them crept through the kitchen toward the basement which had a glowing light coming from under the door. The priest was quietly reciting the Lord's Prayer to himself. Watching him from the rear, Daniel could tell that he was using his right hand to make the sign of the cross as he prayed. They stopped at the closed door.

Daniel stared at the glowing orange light shining through the crack. A mustard-colored smoke seeped out from the bottom. He winced at the putrid odor. Something down in the depths laughed, and Daniel nervously adjusted his weight from one foot to the other.

Father Martin was undeterred. He reached out and grabbed the doorknob. There was a searing sound, like a steak dropped on a hot skillet, and he jerked his hand back in agony. Red blisters lined the inside of his burnt palm. Laughter erupted from the basement.

"Are you OK?" Daniel whispered.

The priest shook his hand, doing his best to block out the pain.

"I'm fine," he replied. "I'm just a little bit more motivated now. That's a mistake on that thing's part."

Daniel smirked as he grabbed a dishtowel from the oven handle. He handed it to Father Martin.

"Use this."

The priest wrapped the towel around the doorknob and opened it. Daniel gasped when he saw the otherworldly atmosphere that was his basement. Blankets of rotten smoke crawled up the stairs, the walls, and the ceiling and began to fill the kitchen. The only light source was an eerie glow—an odd shade of orange and yellow that Daniel had never seen before. The lighting moved like a flickering flame along the wall, but its source was currently out of their view.

"Let us proceed," Father Martin said calmly as he took a step down.

Their footsteps echoed in the darkness. Daniel listened as something breathed heavily in the depths; each exhale was a gurgle of mucus and phlegm. As soon as they were halfway down, Daniel looked to his right at the empty basement. The flowing river of smoke coated every surface and continued to move like dry ice. The breathing was coming from inside the open secret room where shadows moved about.

They stepped onto the basement floor. Father Martin gave a quick look around the room to make sure they were alone in the main area. Daniel instinctively looked behind him to see if anything was hiding under the stairs, but it was empty except for the chain hanging on the wall. Whatever was down there with them was inside the secret room.

Father Martin turned to Daniel.

"Do you have the vial?" he whispered.

Daniel nodded without taking his eyes away from the open door.

"Go ahead and take off the lid," he instructed. "Be prepared to do exactly as I say."

Daniel again only nodded as he stared at the source of the light, trying to get a glimpse of what was inside. His hand with the vial didn't budge. Father Martin snapped his fingers in front of Daniel's eyes.

"Pay attention!" the priest scolded.

Daniel blinked several times and then looked at him.

"That's not your daughter in there," he said.

"I know."

"Do you?"

Daniel looked him in the eyes.

"He is the father of lies. Remember that."

The priest did not look away until he saw that his words registered with Daniel.

"I got it," he said.

Something moved in the secret room.

"Daddy?" Alice's voice called weakly.

Daniel's eyes shot toward the sound of his daughter. Father Martin didn't even bother to turn around. He reached forward and grabbed Daniel by the jaw. Daniel looked with shock back at the priest.

"Not. Your. Daughter," Father Martin repeated. "Give me the vial." He snatched the holy water out of Daniel's hand.

Daniel's eyes were tearing up, but he finally understood. Father Martin nodded and then spun around to face the evil.

"Demon," he said firmly. "I command you in the name of the Father to come forth out of that pit."

Four extended fingers wrapped around the small doorframe. An arm bent backward at the elbow slapped the smoky basement floor. The grinning demon in Alice's body slowly pulled itself out and rested on all fours.

Daniel struggled to keep his composure at the sight of his daughter. Her translucent skin stretched across elongated limbs covered in bruised flesh. She was still wearing tattered fragments of her clothes, but they were adorned with holes and tears where the demon had scratched through to the skin. Her hairline had receded several inches above her deformed face. Clumps of thin, matted strands stuck to the side of her head. Her eyes were hollow diamond shapes—black holes housing a burning orange hellfire. As she smiled, her sliced cheeks opened up to each ear, revealing serrated teeth.

Daniel felt his stomach knot and realized that he had never known true horror until this moment. Even if they successfully performed this exorcism, he wondered how his daughter would even physically recover from this. He stared in terror as the demon cocked its head sideways and slowly stood upright. It looked at Father Martin and then at Daniel and then back at the priest.

"Your forgotten savior has no power over me," it said in a voice several octaves lower.

Father Martin smiled.

"And yet, here you stand," he said.

The demon's eyes flared with a subtle rage that Daniel picked up on, but it kept the hideous grin on its face.

"How perceptive," it said as it took a step toward them.

Father Martin made a quick slashing movement with his right hand that held the open vial of holy water. A blade of droplets cut through the air and sliced across the demon's face. It hissed and shielded its burning flesh.

"Silence, demon!" the priest commanded. "*That* was for the doorknob."

It slowly looked back at Father Martin with pure hatred.

"A burn for a burn," the priest said casually as he stormed toward the demon and placed his open palm on its forehead.

There was a searing sound, and the demon bellowed in agony. Daniel saw smoke rise from under the priest's hand. It was the hand with the rosary wrapped around it. The demon dropped to its knees before the holy man. Father Martin removed his hand to reveal the cross branded into its flesh. It stared at the ceiling in a vacant daze. Father Martin looked back to Daniel.

"Daniel, come quickly."

The priest dabbed holy water on his index finger and then handed the vial back to Daniel.

"I need you to make a circle on the floor with the holy water," Father Martin said.

"OK."

He mimicked how the priest was putting the water on his finger, and then he used his wet fingertip to begin painting a circle around the stunned demon. He watched as Father Martin used his finger to draw a wet cross in the middle of its forehead.

"Our Father, Who art in Heaven, hallowed be Thy name," the priest began as he traced the holy water cross several times. "Thy Kingdom come; Thy will be done on Earth as it is in Heaven."

The demon slowly started to lean back, contorting its spine into an arch until its head rested on the floor. Daniel stared at his daughter's withered torso, translucent and barely containing the ribs trying to break through.

"Give us this day, our daily bread, and forgive us our trespasses as we forgive those who trespass against us. And lead us not into temptation, but deliver us from evil," Father Martin said as he put the lid back on the vial and placed it in his pocket.

Daniel finished the circle around the catatonic creature and stood beside the priest.

"What now?" he whispered.

The basement floor began to tremble. Daniel nearly lost his balance, but Father Martin stood steadfast. Alice's arched body slowly lifted off the ground and continued to rise until it floated at eye level. Daniel stared in disbelief at his daughter suspended in midair.

"Silence this chaos!" the priest commanded and the tremors stopped.

Alice's body started to rotate in midair, but she stayed within the confines of the circle drawn on the ground. Its face was frozen in a ghoulish snarl. The smoke on the floor began to swirl like a funnel cloud as it moved along with the demon. The priest held up his hand, and the demon stopped spinning.

"Hail Mary, full of grace, the Lord is with thee," Father

Martin began. "Blessed art thou among women, and blessed is the fruit of thy womb, Jesus. Holy Mary, Mother of God, pray for us sinners now, and at the hour of death."

The demon's arch began to flatten out until Alice's body planked in the air. Father Martin continued as Daniel watched with astonishment.

"Glory be to the Father and to the Son and to the Holy Spirit. As it was in the beginning, is now, and ever shall be, world without end."

The basement was silent. Daniel could hear his heart beating inside his chest.

"In the name of the Father, I command you to face me."

The demon rotated until its legs rose upward and the bottoms of its feet were touching the ceiling. Its arms stretched outward forming the shape of an inverted cross. Its closed eyes shot open, revealing a fiery glow burning behind its eyeballs. Father Martin placed his injured hand on the demon's cheek in a gentle caress. He brought his face inches away from the creature.

"Depart, then, transgressor," he began in an almost somber tone. "Depart, seducer, full of lies and cunning, foe of virtue . . . "

What was left of Alice's body began to spasm.

" . . . persecutor of the innocent. Give place, abominable creature, give way, you monster, give way to Christ, in whom you found none of your works."

Daniel watched wide-eyed as the demon shook and retched and began to transform itself back from its horrid condition.

"For He had already stripped you of your powers and laid waste your Kingdom, bound you prisoner and plundered your weapons. He has cast you forth into the outer darkness, where everlasting ruin awaits you and your abettors."

The demon was shaking so fast that its movements were a frenzied blur.

"In the name of God the Father, I cast you out!" Father Martin screamed as he gripped the frenzied demon's cheeks. It paused mid-spasm as soon as the priest's hands made contact. The priest pulled the motionless creature's burnt forehead to his lips.

There was an explosion of light and sound that momentarily blinded and deafened the mortals in the room. The girl's body descended to the floor like a feather. Daniel hurried to his daughter's side. Her face was scratched and bruised, but it was hers again. He grasped her frail arm, examining it, and then the rest of her body. Her disfigured form had miraculously returned to normal. Tears of joy ran down his cheeks as he watched Alice open her confused eyes. He knew that she was in shock. He hugged her and held her as tightly as he had when she was just a baby.

"Thank God," he said over and over.

"Amen," Father Martin replied with a sigh of exhaustion.

"Dad?" Alice said with a hoarse voice.

"Shh, shh," Daniel said. "Don't speak, honey. Just rest."

He kissed his daughter as he rocked her back and forth on the floor.

"It's over, Al. It's over."

"We still have the matter of sealing the well, Daniel."

Daniel looked up at him, embarrassed that he had forgotten entirely about that task.

"No one is free until we do that," the priest reminded him. Daniel jumped with fright as the chain under the stairs flew across the room and wrapped itself around the priest's throat like an anaconda. Father Martin's eyes bulged. He started to speak, but the chain tightened and crushed his trachea. His face swelled purple, and the blood vessels in his eyes burst. The other end of the chain slithered into the open well. Something down there gave a swift jerk that snapped the priest's neck and pulled his lifeless corpse into the flaming pit as Daniel and Alice screamed from the floor.

CHAPTER 30

BUCK GROWLED AND REMAINED on edge from the moment Daniel and Father Martin went into the house. Every sound piqued his interest. Nora did her best to remain calm. She swung on her back with her hand dangling down on the dog's fur. She held her breath when the basement door closed and the voices of the two men disappeared.

It was only moments after that she heard the demon downstairs conversing with another male voice. The conversation was muffled and unintelligible, but she assumed it was Father Martin speaking. There were loud shrieks and growls. After about ten minutes of unbearable anxiety, the ground below her started to tremble.

Buck lost all assertion of dominance when this began. The dog's tail tucked between his legs as he hid under the swing. His whining was beginning to irritate Nora, but she took the time to soothe him and stroke his back. Settling the dog down was a welcome distraction from whatever was unfolding in the basement.

It had been several minutes since she had heard the demon's voice. The only one speaking now was the priest. Even though she couldn't decipher exactly what he was saying, how he was saying it gave her much assurance. Father Martin's tone was stern, his inflection assertive. Judging by the fact that the creature he was speaking to was silent, she assumed the exorcism was working.

Nora noticed the mustard-colored smoke start to flow out of the front door and across the porch. She smelled the sulfur before the smoke had even made its way to her. Buck growled at the swirling mist as it innocuously pooled around them. He settled back down when he saw that it was no more a threat than any other unpleasant odor.

Nora thought about the events that had happened that evening. The vision of her daughter running toward the woods to lure her out of the house; the haggard demon standing in the window behind Alice with that cutting grin on its face; Alice being dragged down into the basement as she was knocked down the stairs by Buck.

And then it all went dark.

Still, she felt like there was something missing. Her memory didn't sit right. It was like she was staring at an unfinished painting in her mind. Chaos: that's what the demons want to inflict. Puncturing holes in her memory and making her question her own sanity was a surefire way to do so.

A sound like thunder exploded from inside the house. Nora was jolted so hard from the shock that she kicked the end of the swing. The wood splintered, causing her foot to land on Buck's tail. He yelped and hopped to his feet.

Nora quickly got up and looked at the front door. The house was still dark. It was dead quiet. The battle was over, and she knew that one of the opposing forces down there had won. Buck followed behind her as she inched her way closer to the door. She peeked through one of the kitchen windows. The glowing light under the basement door was gone, and the smoke appeared to have been cut off at the source. She heard Father Martin speak, and her soul filled with hope.

Before she could vocalize her euphoria, there was a sound like something had just been ripped off of the wall. She heard a clanging like metal scraping metal and then a thud. Panic tensed her body as she slowly backed away from the window. Buck started to get aggressive again. He didn't like something down there.

Daniel screamed from the basement. It sounded like he said, "No!" Nora looked back at Buck who was revealing his teeth. The dog was her security system, and right now he was going off. Nora felt the baby kick inside her as if it was reading her mind. She desperately wanted to run down there, but she had her baby to worry about. She stood motionless on the porch, unsure of what to do.

Out of the corner of her eye, she saw a black object poking out from under the little table in front of the swing. It was the corner of something that she had forgotten all about. She walked over to it and picked up Luke's flashlight with the cross marked on the lens. She flicked it on and shone it on the ground, and the smoke that she pointed it at recoiled from the image.

"It works . . . "

She marched across the porch and jerked the door open.

In the basement, Daniel was still in denial over what he had just witnessed. They had saved his daughter, but Father Martin was dead. His body had been dragged into the flaming pit, food for God knows what. Daniel sat on the ground with Alice lying between his legs. He wrapped his arms around her.

"We have to get out of here," he said.

Alice was still woozy and shaken. She was physically weak and mentally drained. Daniel didn't even know if she could walk.

"Daddy, what's going on?"

He started to get up when the flames in the well were instantly put out by a geyser of black bile that shot straight up into the secret room. There was an orgasmic sigh as the slime floated up and out of the steaming hole. The hot liquid oozed out across the floor and into the main part of the basement like an oil spill.

Then, all at once, the eruption ceased. The flames inside

the well flickered back to life and lit up the room once more. The hot liquid dripped from every surface and onto both of them in the basement. They stared at the motion in the secret room. There was a shadow moving about in there, but Daniel couldn't see what it was.

"Oh, how divine: the succulent smells of Earth," a crooning voice said from inside the secret room.

Alice started to breathe heavily as she became more aware of what was going on around her. Daniel stood up and bent over to pick up his daughter. He didn't want any part of whatever had just spoken in there.

As soon as he started helping Alice to her feet, the puffy corpse of Father Martin crept out of the secret room and stood up. His flesh was bloated and purple. His neck was swollen and black from the strangulation. His eyes burned a deep blood red that was different than any of the possessed that had emerged before. The crosses on the priest's garb were now all inverted in mockery.

Daniel grabbed his daughter and maneuvered her around to his back, shielding her from the threat. The unholy thing looked at Daniel and smiled. This one was somehow different than what possessed Alice. It wasn't a grotesque mutilation of a human face; it was simply Father Martin's normal, reassuring smile. Whatever stood before Daniel now wasn't trying to overcompensate with sheer terror. It stood there in the priest's body, but its posture was more erect—more confident.

"Who are you?" Daniel finally said.

The unholy priest smiled as he let his eyes wander around the room, checking out his surroundings with supreme curiosity.

"Identity, names . . . What is a name, anyway?"

Daniel was unsure of how to respond. The priest put his hands in his pockets.

"Aren't names nothing more than labels? Another one of man's frail attempts to categorize everything around him? Names . . . they're nothing more than tools of control by inferior beings living in a world of chaos. Pointless, one might say, no?"

Daniel wanted to flee. He wanted desperately to yell for his daughter to run up the stairs and join her mother and for the two of them to drive off while he fought this thing, giving them just enough time to escape. But he knew their minds were all damned. He had no game plan now that the priest was gone—no more cards to play.

"Judging by that shocking display of pretension, I'd say you fashion yourself as someone important," Daniel said.

The piercing red eyes met Daniel's own. He felt their burning gaze sear the core of his being. He felt a surge of fear that quickly paralyzed his smugness. The priest smiled with satisfaction. This time there were two rows of pointy teeth behind the coiled lips.

"It never fails. Every time I set foot in this lost paradise, I am simply made ravenous—ravenous for the supple flesh of the living . . . the tenderest flesh of all: the unborn."

Daniel's protective instincts kicked in, and he clenched his fists and gritted his teeth. The devilish intruder noticed the aggressive stance and chuckled. In one blink, the dead priest transformed into an eight-foot-tall demonic behemoth. Wings of flames shot out from its back. Its gory mouth stretched open wide enough to swallow a human head. Rows of fangs the size of Daniel's fingers busted through bloody gums. Its eyes burned red and focused on Alice. It took three long strides towards her. Daniel desperately shoved his daughter toward the stairs just as the creature rushed him.

Just as Daniel and Alice were covered in the liquid eruption from the well, Nora was quietly creeping across the kitchen floor. She stopped just shy of the basement door and pressed her ear to the warm wood to listen. As soon as she heard the struggle, she yanked open the basement door and ran down the stairs with the cross flashlight beam bouncing off the wall. The demon paid the woman no mind and snapped at Daniel's head. He dodged just in time to save his skull but sacrificed his collarbone. He screamed in agony as the monster lifted him off his feet by its mouth. Blood gushed down his body as he squirmed to break free.

Alice, sobbing, ran to her mother. Nora lifted the flashlight toward the creature, but her arm froze before she could point the beam directly at it. The beast's red eyes peered at her from over her husband's bloody shoulder. Even though it had a mouthful of meat in its fangs, she knew that it was smiling at her. She felt the oddest sensation of recognition; she had seen those eyes before inside the well.

"Stay behind me," Nora said to her daughter.

Alice ran behind her mother and crouched down in fear. Nora used every ounce of energy to close her eyes and not be distracted by her husband's pleas.

"God, please be with us. Please, help my family. Help us be rid of this evil," she prayed.

And just like that, a cool hand gripped Nora's wrist. She opened her eyes and looked to her right. Luke was standing beside her staring at the evil with pure hatred. His body radiated light. He took the flashlight from her hand.

"I'll take this," he said.

The demon's red eyes widened when it saw Luke raise the intense beam of light. It released Daniel from its jowls and roared with a bloody fury that shook the ceiling above them. Daniel landed on the floor and rolled over on his side, gripping his pulsating wound.

The flashlight-cross hit the beast in the face. Smoke instantly fumed out of its melting flesh as it hissed. Luke marched forward, backing the creature away from the family. The smoldering demon used its arms to shield itself from the cross, but they just burned away as well. It barked and shrieked in equal measures of rage and pain.

Daniel watched from the floor as the spirit of Luke cornered the creature. He was so wrapped up in the spectacle that he almost didn't see Merle materialize in the other corner of the basement. He looked at the spirit of the old man, and Merle gave him a slight nod and then whistled.

"Here, Buck!"

The dog came bounding down the steps. Merle pointed to the snarling abomination in the corner. The dog ran across the basement floor and lunged at the cowering demon on the floor. He snapped violently, trying to get a good bite in, as Luke held the creature captive with the cross-light. The hound's teeth finally burrowed deep into its neck and pinned it down. Luke grabbed Father Martin's rosary and held it in front of the recoiling creature and said, "In the name of God, the Father, I command you out, you demonic piece of shit."

The fire in its eyes turned to ash that twirled up as if caught by a tiny tornado and spread across the length of the ceiling until it was stretched completely out of existence. Luke exhaled a deep breath of satisfied relief, imagining the fleeing smoke floating up through the house and all the way to the heavens. He looked down at Buck, who was still holding his bite on the lifeless body.

"Go ahead. I know you've been waitin' to do it," Merle said.

Buck gave one violent jerk and hollowed out the demon's throat. Strands of tendons and sinew dangled from the dog's mouth before he swallowed the mouthful in one gulp.

Daniel's face was frozen in an expression of bewilderment. He watched as the old man smiled at his dog's handiwork and then walked over to the little door. He crouched down to step inside. Daniel pulled himself across the floor toward his family. Nora was released from whatever hold the demon had over her, and she bent down to cradle her injured husband. Alice sat beside them, and then they all scooted closer to the secret room to watch what was about to happen next.

Merle was standing above the well with a cross in one hand and a bottle of what must be holy water in the other. The old man made the sign of the cross over his body, said some things in Latin, and then poured the holy water into the well.

The rest of the demon's body cooked under the beam of Luke's flashlight. An even greater explosion of light filled the room. The Hills all shielded their eyes from the overwhelming brightness. The light dimmed as it sucked every last vapor of sulfurous smoke back into the well. The ashes of the burnt creature floated in the air and vanished. Daniel opened his eyes just in time to see the top of the well shake and then collapse in on itself. The cosmic earthquake abruptly stopped, and everything was quiet.

The Hills all looked at each other knowing that the nightmare was over. Daniel hugged his wife and daughter in a mixture of cries of relief and laughter.

"I think these folks are gonna be just fine," Merle said to Luke.

Daniel broke the embrace with his family to look up at the old farmer who was now standing in front of him with Luke at his side. The two apparitions both smiled warmly at the family.

"Thank you," Daniel said. "Thank you both."

He tried to get to his feet, but putting weight on his injured side made him wince.

"Take it easy there, partner," Merle cautioned.

"You might want to put some ice on that, Mr. Hill," Luke teased.

"Luke, I don't know how many times I have to tell you to call me Daniel."

Nora wrapped her arm around Alice's shoulder.

"Thank you for saving my family," she cried.

Merle nodded to the woman.

"Ma'am," he began. "It is I who wants to thank you all for saving my family."

Nora didn't know what he meant.

"Because of your help in ending this . . . we can finally be at peace," he explained. "*You* can be at peace unless you just like livin' in an old exorcist's house." Merle grinned.

Alice looked at Luke.

"I'd be lying if I said I wouldn't miss you," she said. "I really wish we could've been friends."

Luke smiled back in that way that made Alice's heart flutter.

"We'll always be friends. I'm grateful for the little bit of time we had."

"The gateway has been sealed," Merle explained. "You all are safe now. You can move on, if you wish."

He looked at Luke.

"*We* can move on."

"I think we better," Luke said.

"I think so too, young man. We better not keep our ladies waitin'."

"Goodbye," Daniel said. "And thanks again."

The Hills held each other as Merle and Luke slowly vanished, smiling until the very end.

CHAPTER 31

Late May 1995, Southern Ohio

THE FINAL BELL for the school year rang, and the kids paraded through the halls toward their summer vacation. Nora sat on the corner of her desk smiling and telling her eleventh graders that she'd see them next year. The kids laughed, waved, high-fived, and the entire student body seemed to breathe a collective sigh of relief.

After a quick ten minutes, the building was a ghost town. Nora stood up and rubbed the back of her neck with her right hand . . . another year under her belt. She walked over to the chalkboard and erased where she had written "HAVE A NICE SUMMER!!!" She threw away the May lunch menu and poked her head into the hall. Aside from a few scattered papers, it was empty. She kicked out the door stop and let the hefty wooden door close by itself.

The principal's voice came over the intercom to congratulate all the teachers on making it through another year and to thank them for their hard work. Nora smiled as she walked back to her desk and collapsed into her rolling chair. At the end of a long school day, she always took a few minutes to catch her breath and regain her composure.

This past year had been an unusual one to say the least. After they had sealed the well on that last night they had spent at the farm in July nearly eleven months ago, they had booked a suite at a hotel back in Ohio and left without a second thought. They put the farm up for sale in August and accepted the first offer less than two weeks later. They took a financial loss but still considered it a win.

Nora had gotten her old job back even though she would be beginning the first few months of the school year on maternity leave. She didn't think twice about having to work with Steve. She had nothing to hide and refused to be ashamed or to live in fear. It wasn't until after she had accepted the job that she learned that Steve had taken a principal position in a different county.

Bringing a newborn baby "home" to a hotel room was not what they had originally had in mind, but that's what happened at the beginning of September. The delivery went as smoothly as one can. Daniel and Nora loved their new baby girl who had remained nameless until the night before she was born. Daniel had thrown out every girl name he could think of, but they were all shot down. Just as they were about to go to sleep, Nora whispered something. Daniel asked her what she had said, and she replied, "Maren. Her name will be Maren."

The next day Daniel cut the umbilical cord, and Nora held her second child for the first time. They knew how blessed they were to be alive themselves, let alone welcoming a new life into this world. Their hearts melted when they watched Alice hold her new little sister in the hospital room and rock her with a big smile on her face. Life was going to be different for them with a new addition to their family, but they welcomed the change.

By early October and while Nora was still home with Maren, they had bought a house that was out of their price range, but Daniel didn't care. He knew she loved it, and they could make it work. She assumed it was his way of apologizing for buying the farm in the first place.

The school year flew by. Alice was excited to be able to continue her education at the same school she had attended before moving to the farm. She picked up right back where she had left off with her friends and had even started dating

263

a nice boy in her grade. At first, she thought it was going to be super awkward dating someone where her mom worked, but Nora intentionally kept her nose out of her daughter's business. She wanted her to have her own high school experience without feeling like she was being watched nonstop just because her mother worked in the same building.

Daniel got back to work as soon as they were through with the farm. He even extended his hours to increase their income. He was nervous at first about being back in the chair, but after a few weeks of practice, it was like he hadn't missed a day. The events on the farm had taken their toll on him, completely changing his perspective on the world and what lies beyond it. It wasn't until his first patient, Sarah, sat down in front of him in his office that he realized how much he had actually improved at his job. When she talked, he listened, analyzed, and offered his feedback. It was the same method of cognitive behavioral therapy that he had previously employed, but what had changed was how *spiritually* connected he was to whomever sat across from him. He had always cared about his patients' wellbeing, but now he took the time to appreciate their humanity: every issue they had—their successes, their failures—he found beautiful now that he had gotten a glimpse at the darker side of existence that he knew he would never have to see again.

They all still wrestled with trauma in varying degrees. As soon as any of them were left to their own thoughts, their minds would sometimes jump back to the farm and what they had experienced. Of course they thought about the evil—the horrible sights that plagued their nightmares—but they also reflected on the beauty and love that had ultimately prevailed in the end. Like most things in life, these got better with time. The good was magnified, and the bad, if not forgotten entirely, was accepted.

At least, that's how it went for Daniel and Alice.

Nora sat in her chair staring at the clock above the door but not really looking at it. Her mind had gone to the place that it always went when she was alone and undistracted. It went back to that day when she had been lured out into their backyard at the farm. She spun around to see the demon behind her daughter. She ran back inside and up to her room only to be tripped by Buck and go tumbling down the stairs. She watched helplessly as the demon dragged Alice into the basement, and then she passed out.

But she knew now that that's not everything that had happened. She knew there was a missing piece to the puzzle that she only remembered subconsciously. This piece would replay so much in her dreams that she was just now starting to be able to recall it while awake. At last, it was becoming a memory and not a figment of her imagination.

She remembered getting up and going into the basement after her fall, but before Daniel and Father Martin made it back from North Carolina. She remembered seeing her daughter possessed and deformed before being pulled down, herself, into the well.

And, finally, she remembered falling through a hot, endless void, screaming and crying until that face with the red eyes appeared before her. She remembered seeing it smile in that confident way, paralyzing her as it extended its hand toward her pregnant belly. She remembered how it touched the taut skin under her belly button and then slid its fingers down. She remembered the vile creature grinning, and the burning mixture of pain and pleasure she felt inside her womb.

And then it was over.

She woke up when Daniel and Father Martin made it home, and she was back to lying on the floor by the front door. The memory of what had happened in the well had been purposefully erased from her mind by some agent of chaos, and she was left none the wiser.

Now, sitting alone in her classroom, she thought about

her baby girl. She wondered if what she remembered inside the well was real or just some insidious implanted memory that was buried in her mind just to drive her insane. Either way, she judged every move her infant child made. She watched with a worried eye thinking that maybe, just maybe, the evil that was in that well had latched on to Maren. She knew that the people who were possessed didn't survive long; the demon itself had said that they either burn up their hosts or kill them. Her baby was alive and well, though. But then she wondered, what would happen if a demon possessed an unborn child? What would happen to a demon that was born *into* this world?

The classroom door swung open, and Daniel and Alice walked in. They were both smiling. Alice carried her backpack, while Daniel held a bouquet of flowers. It was his custom to bring his wife roses on the last day of school.

"Congratulations," he said as he walked over to Nora.

"We made it, Mom," Alice said with a smile.

Nora stood up and shelved her worries for a later time.

"We did, indeed," she said, hugging Alice.

She gave Daniel a kiss.

"And thank you. These are beautiful."

"Can I take my lovely ladies out for an early dinner?"

"Sure," Alice said.

"What are we going to do about your other lovely lady?" Nora asked, referring to their baby.

Daniel looked at his watch.

"Daycare doesn't close for another two hours. Let's take advantage of what little free time we have."

"OK, then," Nora smiled.

She did her best to push the horrible memories down and focus on the good that was in front of her, but she secretly envied her family. Daniel and Alice appeared to be going on with their lives as if nothing had ever happened. She was infected by a plaguing fear that grew each day like a cancerous tumor. Something had to give. The thought of living like this reminded her of living with the secret of her affair, and that lifestyle was anathema to her.

CHAPTER 32

AFTER THEIR EARLY dinner, the Hills drove across town to the daycare with thirty minutes to spare before the 5:30 PM mandatory pick-up time. Each minute after that added ten dollars to the bill, which Daniel found out the hard way once and never again.

They came to a stop sign at a four-way intersection. Daniel reached over and turned the volume knob down on the radio, not wanting to pull up to the Christian daycare bumping the new Nine Inch Nails song (It had been Alice's turn to select the music.). He hit his blinker, turned right, drove about half a block, and then veered left into the church's parking lot.

Nora was the first one to see the red lights flashing against the side of the white building.

"Daniel, there's a fire truck and an ambulance," she said.

He looked toward the church and saw the idling vehicles.

"Hopefully it's just a drill," he said.

He pulled the car into an open space in the nearly empty lot. Alice poked her head between the two front seats to get a better look at what her parents were talking about. The fire truck was empty, but there was medic and a young EMT removing their bags, a backboard, and a cot from the back of the ambulance. They hurried inside the daycare entrance before Daniel could even shut his car off.

"It's not a drill," Nora said as her pulse quickened.

She threw open her door and sprinted across the pavement; a sense of dread grew with each passing step.

"Honey, wait," Daniel said as he yanked off his seatbelt and jumped out of the car.

Alice rolled down her window.

"Dad, why is mom panicking?"

He turned back to his daughter and threw up his hands as if to say this was just another one of Nora's overreactions. "Just stay here, honey. We'll be right back."

Alice fell back against her seat and bit her lip as she stared at the hypnotically flashing lights atop the emergency vehicles.

Nora opened the church's daycare entrance door and immediately noticed that the program director was not sitting at her usual spot at the check-in/check-out table. A woman screamed from the nursery at the end of the hallway. Nora's heart beat faster. Daniel pulled the door open just as it was about to shut and stepped in behind her. A male voice inside the nursery said, "Just remain calm. Police are on the way." Nora looked back at her husband. He saw a fear in her eyes that he thought he'd never see again, and then she rushed toward the sounds.

As soon as she reached the open doorway, she saw the fireman with his back to her. He was consoling someone in the corner. The medic and the EMT were on the ground with their gear. Nora covered her mouth with her hand and gasped, stumbling backward into Daniel. He put his hands on her shoulders and then looked at the scene unfolding inside the nursery.

One of the two daycare teachers was on the floor face down. The medic was crouched beside her head, obscuring Daniel's view, while the EMT was at her side. Daniel looked up at the middle-aged daycare worker, Maggie, with her back against the wall opposite him. A mixture of tears and mascara was streaming down her face like ink. The fireman was doing his best to make his voice louder than the screaming babies. All the infant cribs were along the left side of the room, but still not far enough from the chaos on the floor before them. There were at least three babies still yet to be picked up for the day, and their shrill cries were deafening in the small room with the cinderblock walls.

The medic turned to the fireman and said, "You wanna give us a hand with the roll?"

The fireman gave a nod and dropped to his knees beside the woman on the ground. The EMT was on her other side, and the medic was at her head calling the shots.

"All right, here we go," the medic began. "One, two, *three.*"

The two men on her sides rolled her over, while the medic steadied her neck. Once she was on her back, the medic did another countdown, and they lifted her onto the backboard and placed the backboard on the gurney. In between motions, Daniel was able to see her face. It was the young girl who worked in the nursery, Emma, who didn't look a day over eighteen. There was fresh blood smeared on her cheeks, and her eyes were looking in Daniel's direction but not seeing anything. The rusty odor of blood permeated the air. The medics were talking back and forth—different orders and directions and confirmations—but nothing Daniel could clearly hear over the wailing babies.

Maggie finally saw Daniel and Nora standing in the open doorway across the room from her. She shook her head back and forth in disbelief. The fireman said something over his shoulder to her about the babies, and she shuffled along the wall toward the cribs.

"It's OK, dearies. It's OK," Maggie said between sobs, but the babies weren't buying it. She did her best to avoid interfering with the two men on the floor. The fireman turned around and noticed the Hills. He carefully stepped around the other side of the room towards the spectators.

"You all don't need to be here," he said.

"Our baby is in there," Daniel said.

The fireman looked over his shoulder at Maggie doing her best to calm the infants. He turned back to Daniel and said, "Just take a step back until these guys clear out. Please." The fireman returned to facing the medic and EMT and stood in the corner out of the way.

Daniel nodded and did as he was told but made sure that he still had a full view of the scene.

"We need to stabilize this. Hand me the gauze and tape," the older medic said.

"We're gonna leave those in her neck?" the younger EMT asked.

"Yes. Her airway is patent. If we remove it, she could bleed out. We leave it in place."

The medic giving the orders stood up, and for the first time the Hills saw the full extent of the carnage on the floor. Emma was still and pale, breathing quick, shallow breaths with scissors protruding from her neck. The color left Daniel's face. He looked away and tried to think about anything else to prevent him from vomiting up the fifty-dollar filet he just ate. Nora screamed, drawing the attention of the medic and EMT.

"Ma'am, please clear out of here," the medic said. He was a tall bald man with a linebacker's build. "Just move to that end of the hallway while we transport her."

"My baby's in there," Nora muttered, pointing to the row of cribs.

The fireman stepped out of the corner and looked at Nora.

"They'll be done in a second. Give them some room."

Daniel gently tugged Nora back away from the door.

"Let's get her to the rig," the older medic said.

The fireman lead the way, motioning for the Hill's to get even further out of the way.

Daniel and Nora flattened themselves against the hallway wall as the fireman and the three men wheeled the young girl down the hall and then outside. Nora continued to stare at the empty hallway, oblivious to the screaming babies in the nursery. She knew *her* child wasn't screaming. She knew that it was the other two who were upset . . . not Maren. Daniel stepped around his wife and hurried into the room. Maggie was still sobbing as she rocked one of the crying infants.

"What happened?" Daniel asked.

"She must've fallen," Maggie stammered between sobs. "She fell. She must've been carrying the scissors, and she just *fell!*"

"Jesus Christ." Daniel took a step closer and placed his hand on Maggie's shoulder as his trauma training kicked in. "It's going to be OK. Everyone will get through this."

Nora was still in the hallway, staring at the door where the first responders had just exited, listening as the ambulance sirens faded away in the distance. She knew it was not "going to be OK."

Maggie continued to rock one of the babies.

"We had just given Gracie and Henry their bottles and laid them down. Emma was rocking Maren. I went to the kitchen to get her bottle, but then I heard them all start screaming again. I came back in here, and Maren was sleeping in her bed, but the other two were crying, and Emma . . . Emma was on the floor with the scissors in her neck!"

"Dear Lord." Daniel shook his head.

"I don't even know what she was doing with scissors," Maggie said. "We don't keep scissors in the nursery, Mr. Hill. We wouldn't want the little ones to hurt themselves."

"Don't you worry about that right now," he said in his most comforting tone.

Nora listened from the hallway.

There is no reason, she remembered. *Evil is just chaos.*

Daniel walked over to the row of cribs. The baby on the far end was still crying, but Maren, in the middle, was still sound asleep. He picked up his daughter and held her close to his chest.

"You feel warm, baby girl."

Maggie managed to quiet one baby enough to put her down, and then she went to work on the other one.

"How did you sleep through that, huh?" Daniel asked, gently swaying her.

Nora finally approached the open doorway. She looked at the mess on the floor, the crying woman, the screaming baby, and then to her husband, rocking their daughter while standing in a puddle of blood.

Pandemonium, she thought.

Daniel looked up at her, but she did not meet his gaze. She could only stare at her sleeping child—her perfect, beautiful, sleeping child—and do her best not to think about how a certain fallen angel was also once called "perfect" and "beautiful" in the beginning.

"Nora," Daniel said.

She looked up at a hanging corpse behind Daniel. It was her, about a decade older, but there was no doubt that Nora was looking at herself. Her corpse's eyes began to glow orange and bulge and contort until they exploded from the force of the growing flames within. The room reeked of sulfur, and the air grew thick as smoke oozed in from the vents. Her dead mouth curved up into a grin, and her body burst into flames.

"Nora!" Daniel said for the second time.

She broke from her trance and was again looking at her husband and her child and the sobbing daycare worker.

"It's all right, honey," he said. "She's OK. Maren's OK."

She wished she could believe him.

ACKNOWLEDGEMENTS

This book would not have been possible without the support of my mom, Jane Kessell, and my aunt, Becky Goodwin. Your loving encouragement is enough to keep an aspiring author going.

THE END?

Not if you want to dive into more of Crystal Lake Publishing's Tales from the Darkest Depths!

Check out our amazing website and online store.
https://www.crystallakepub.com

We always have great new projects and content on the website to dive into, as well as a newsletter, behind the scenes options, social media platforms, our own dark fiction shared-world series and our very own webstore. If you use the IGotMyCLPBook! coupon code in the store (at the checkout), you'll get a one-time-only 50% discount on your first eBook purchase!

Our webstore even has categories specifically for KU books, non-fiction, anthologies, and of course more novels and novellas.

ABOUT THE AUTHOR

Nick Roberts is a resident of St. Albans, West Virginia and a graduate of Marshall University. He is an active member of the Horror Writers Association and the Horror Authors Guild. His short works have been published in *The Blue Mountain Review, Stonecrop Magazine, The Fiction Pool, Haunted MTL, The Indiana Horror Review*, and anthologies by publishers, such as J. Ellington Ashton Press and Sinister Smile Press. His novel, *Anathema*, won Debut Novel of the Year at the 2020-2021 Horror Authors Guild Awards. His second novel, *The Exorcist's House,* will be released in 2022 by Crystal Lake Publishing. Follow him at www.nickrobertsauthor.com, www.facebook.com/spookywv, www.twitter.com/nroberts9859, and www.instagram.com/spookywv.

Readers . . .

Thank you for reading *The Exorcist's House*. We hope you enjoyed this novel.

If you have a moment, please review *The Exorcist's House* at the store where you bought it.

Help other readers by telling them why you enjoyed this book. No need to write an in-depth discussion. Even a single sentence will be greatly appreciated. Reviews go a long way to helping a book sell, and is great for an author's career. It'll also help us to continue publishing quality books. You can also share a photo of yourself holding this book with the hashtag #IGotMyCLPBook!

Thank you again for taking the time to journey with Crystal Lake Publishing.

Visit our Linktree page for a list of our social media platforms. https://linktr.ee/CrystalLakePublishing

Our Mission Statement:

Since its founding in August 2012, Crystal Lake Publishing has quickly become one of the world's leading publishers of Dark Fiction and Horror books in print, eBook, and audio formats.

While we strive to present only the highest quality fiction and entertainment, we also endeavour to support authors along their writing journey. We offer our time and experience in non-fiction projects, as well as author mentoring and services, at competitive prices.

With several Bram Stoker Award wins and many other wins and nominations (including the HWA's Specialty Press Award), Crystal Lake Publishing puts integrity, honor, and respect at the forefront of our publishing operations.

We strive for each book and outreach program we spearhead to not only entertain and touch or comment on issues that affect our readers, but also to strengthen and support the Dark Fiction field and its authors.

Not only do we find and publish authors we believe are destined for greatness, but we strive to work with men and woman who endeavour to be decent human beings who care more for others than themselves, while still being hard working, driven, and passionate artists and storytellers.

Crystal Lake Publishing is and will always be a beacon of what passion and dedication, combined with overwhelming teamwork and respect, can accomplish. We endeavour to know each and every one of our readers, while building personal relationships with our authors, reviewers, bloggers, podcasters, bookstores, and libraries.

We will be as trustworthy, forthright, and transparent as any business can be, while also keeping most of the headaches away from our authors, since it's our job to solve the problems so they can stay in a creative mind. Which of course also means paying our authors.

We do not just publish books, we present to you worlds within your world, doors within your mind, from talented authors who sacrifice so much for a moment of your time.

There are some amazing small presses out there, and through collaboration and open forums we will continue to support other presses in the goal of helping authors and showing the world what quality small presses are capable of accomplishing. No one wins when a small press goes down, so we will always be there to support hardworking, legitimate presses and their authors. We don't see Crystal Lake as the best press out there, but we will always strive to be the best, strive to be the most interactive and grateful, and even blessed press around. No matter what happens over time, we will also take our mission very seriously while appreciating where we are and enjoying the journey.

What do we offer our authors that they can't do for themselves through self-publishing?

We are big supporters of self-publishing (especially hybrid publishing), if done with care, patience, and planning. However, not every author has the time or inclination to do market research, advertise, and set up book launch strategies. Although a lot of authors are successful in doing it all, strong small presses will always be there for the authors who just want to do what they do best: write.

What we offer is experience, industry knowledge, contacts and trust built up over years. And due to our strong brand and trusting fanbase, every Crystal Lake Publishing book comes with weight of respect. In time our fans begin to trust our judgment and will try a new author purely based on our support of said author.

With each launch we strive to fine-tune our approach, learn from our mistakes, and increase our reach. We continue to assure our authors that we're here for them and that we'll carry the weight of the launch and dealing with third parties while they focus on their strengths—be it writing, interviews, blogs, signings, etc.

We also offer several mentoring packages to authors that include knowledge and skills they can use in both traditional and self-publishing endeavours.

We look forward to launching many new careers.

This is what we believe in. What we stand for. This will be our legacy.

**Welcome to Crystal Lake Publishing—
Tales from the Darkest Depths.**

Made in the USA
Monee, IL
19 April 2023